OTHER WORKS BY MAY MCGOLDRICK, NIK JAMES & JAN COFFEY

NOVELS BY MAY McGOLDRICK

A Midsummer Wedding

The Thistle and the Rose

Angel of Skye (Macpherson Trilogy Book 1)

Heart of Gold (Book 2)

Beauty of the Mist (Book 3)

Macpherson Trilogy (Box Set)

The Intended

Flame

Tess and the Highlander

The Dreamer (Highland Treasure Trilogy Book 1)

The Enchantress (Book 2)

The Firebrand (Book 3)

Highland Treasure Trilogy Box Set

Much Ado About Highlanders (Scottish Relic Trilogy Book 1)

Taming the Highlander (Book 2)

Tempest in the Highlands (Book 3)

Scottish Relic Trilogy Box Set

Love and Mayhem (also published as Arse━   ⸻   rmor)

The Prom⸻

C⸻ ⸺ ⸏ ⸜ ꞁ ⸏ ⸜ok 2)

Dreams of Destiny (Book 3)

Scottish Dream Trilogy Box Set

Romancing the Scot

It Happened in the Highlands

Sweet Home Highland Christmas

Sleepless in Scotland

Dearest Millie

How to Ditch a Duke

A Prince in the Pantry

Highland Crown (Royal Highlander Series Book 1)

Highland Jewel (Book 2)

Highland Sword (Book 3)

Ghost of the Thames

Thanksgiving in Connecticut

Made in Heaven

Marriage of Minds: Collaborative Writing

Step Write Up: Writing Exercises for 21st Century

NOVELS BY NIK JAMES

Caleb Marlowe Westerns

High Country Justice

The Winter Road

Bullets and Silver

Silver Trail Christmas

NOVELS BY JAN COFFEY

Trust Me Once

Twice Burned

Triple Threat

Fourth Victim

Five in a Row

Silent Waters

Cross Wired

The Janus Effect

The Puppet Master

Blind Eye

Road Kill

Mercy

When the Mirror Cracks

Tropical Kiss

Aquarian

LOVE AND MAYHEM

MAY MCGOLDRICK

MM BOOKS

Cover Art by Dar Albert. www.WickedSmartDesigns.com

Dedicated to the memory of

May Cody McGoldrick

With thanks for giving us your name...
and your spirit

1

Borders of Scotland, September 1513

THE ENGLISH WERE COMING.

It was up to them now. The survivors. The battle at Flodden Field was lost. So many men had died. The king and most of his nobles were gone. Now it was left to the few remaining warriors to take the painful news to the families. It was left to them to warn everyone that the English were coming. Each family and clan would need to fend for itself.

Limping through the Border hills toward Blackthorn Hall, the surviving remnant of the Armstrong men had spread the news along the way. Now they were almost home. Sir Iain Armstrong reined his horse to a stop at the split of the road. The two-dozen wounded and weary warriors behind him halted, as well.

The road to the right led to Blackthorn, Iain's own keep. He was bearing tragic news for his own family...for his own mother. The laird was dead. But there was no time for Iain to grieve his father's death. The villagers needed to be moved into the castle and every one of them armed. The gates needed to be barred. They would not surrender their ancestral hall to the enemy without a fight. He would not allow his people to be hurt and his land pillaged by the English.

Iain glanced at the road to the left. It led to Fleet Tower and to Marion, his betrothed. John McCall, the Earl of Fleet, had been another casualty of the devastation at Flodden, and Iain was now the protector of all that lay on this side of the hills, as well. He motioned for Alan, his trusted and seasoned warrior, to approach. On their journey north, they had begun to speak about what needed to be done. Pointing at the road home, Iain gave his man his final orders.

"Bring my mother the news. Begin the preparations. And as soon as you arrive at Blackthorn, send half a dozen men with fresh horses to Fleet Tower."

"The English cannon wiped out the McCalls, m'lord. They'll have no men of their own returning."

"I know that."

"We cannot defend both places against the enemy," Alan warned.

"I don't intend to try," Iain assured him. "Everyone at Fleet Tower will be taken back to Blackthorn Hall...for their own safety. Everyone, that is, but Lady Marion. She'll be sent north, to an abbey on the Isle of Skye."

"You know her temperament, m'lord. Marion will refuse as sure as we're standing here. She'll demand to stay with her uncle and those two aunts of hers."

"She'll go north," Iain said firmly. "Her father is dead, and keeping her safe has been left to me. Marion has no choice but to obey me."

Brother Luke eyed the array of dishes on the table with amazement and appreciation.

He knew he shouldn't have been surprised. The two women always prepared the most sumptuous meals imaginable for his visits. Still, Lady Judith and Lady Margaret, whom he'd known since his childhood across the valley at Blackthorn Hall, had outdone themselves this day... and it was not yet noon. Trays of mutton and capons. A plump, delectable fish nestled in greens. Bowls of fruits and sauces. Pitchers of cider and ale. He blessed himself and prayed that the Lord—and his brethren and his sisters over at Cracketford Abbey—would forgive his indulging himself. After all, he thought, he couldn't be discourteous to his hostesses.

The two middle-aged spinsters looked at him expectantly and he smiled broadly at them. Judith and Margaret beamed, and on the wall behind them, on the fine French tapestry he'd always admired, the lady who sat among the flowers with her delicate hand on the neck of the unicorn smiled back at him, as well.

"Doesn't Lady Marion care to join us this morning?" he asked as he drew a trencher filled with steaming mutton and broth toward him.

"I think not," Margaret answered.

"No, indeed," Judith repeated.

"When I saw her last," the first woman continued, "she was up on the parapet, keeping watch for her father's return."

"We *should* be hearing from them soon," Brother Luke commented, smiling at Judith as she filled his cup with ale.

"We *should* be hearing soon," Judith responded as she sat down again.

"Very soon, indeed, I should think." Margaret shifted in her seat, shooting an uncomfortable look at her sister. "Our dear brother William will not be joining us this morning, either."

Brother Luke tried not to look too pleased with the news. Certain oddities in the Earl of Fleet's younger brother had always made Luke feel a wee bit awkward. Sir William McCall had somehow come to believe he was the Wallace himself. Very odd. Lucky for William, his generous and kindhearted family thought nothing of it.

"Perfectly understandable. Monday morning cannot be the most convenient time to receive company."

"But it is," Judith replied.

"It is, indeed," Margaret added. She cast a hesitant glance in the direction of the steps and lowered her voice. "There has been a slight problem in William's routine this morning."

"A slight problem," Judith whispered.

Luke cast a wistful look at the scrumptious food before him. It would be unmannerly to start while the two women were speaking. "Pray, continue."

"Today is Monday," the older sister explained.

"Indeed, Monday," Judith agreed, looking at the clergyman as if that explained everything.

"What of it?" Brother Luke asked.

"Why, Monday is a solemn day," Margaret whispered.

Her sister nodded. "Very solemn."

"And why solemn?" The mutton was making his mouth begin to water. There were dainty white mushrooms peeking at him from the broth, and tiny onions floated along the edges. And the smell was absolutely heavenly.

Margaret looked around at the arched doorway leading to the stairwell and Judith followed her gaze.

"Because of the English," the older sister said.

"The English," Judith repeated, nodding.

Brother Luke forced an air of confidence into his tone. "Nothing to fear, my ladies. Our good King Jamie and his brave armies went south to solve that once and for—"

"William is preparing," Margaret interrupted.

"Indeed, preparing," Judith agreed.

"Preparing?" Luke asked, perplexed.

"As of late, he always paints his face on Mondays."

"Always on Mondays."

Brother Luke's recent visits must not have fallen on Mondays, as he didn't recall this ritual. "Do you mean—"

"Indeed we do."

"We do," Judith echoed.

Margaret leaned closer. "William has gotten it into his head that the Wallace painted his face on Mondays."

"Sir William Wallace," Judith added.

"William always paints his face on Monday."

"Paints his face." Judith gestured as if she were painting her wrinkled visage, just to make certain he understood what her sister had meant.

Actually, Brother Luke found himself at a loss for words. Though he couldn't understand it, these two lovely ladies were perfectly comfortable with William's peculiarities. He looked into both of their sweet faces. They simply accepted their aging brother as he was, with all of his...well, eccentricities. Luke nodded weakly.

"But this morning," the older sister continued, "as the poor dear went to mix his pigments, as he always does before he readies himself for battle."

"For battle."

"It appears he found that one of the new chamber lads had moved his pigments from his window ledge."

"From the ledge." Judith motioned to an invisible window ledge beside the table.

"And that was enough to throw poor William completely off balance." Margaret leaned back in the chair and shook her head solemnly. "Our brother has been in a dither all morning."

"Indeed, a dither."

"What do you mean?" Luke asked, suddenly concerned.

"He's been under his pallet all morning, and we cannot get him to come out."

The sisters looked at each other apprehensively. Luke stared at them, wondering what he should do. These two women were the kindliest and most generous souls of all the people whom he knew and visited. It pained him to see them in such distress over the absurd antics of a half-wit brother.

"The last time this happened," Margaret continued, "it was three days before we saw him."

"Three days," the younger sister agreed with a sigh.

Before the monk could answer, shouts could be heard from the courtyard. The sound of horses arriving. The two sisters immediately jumped to their feet and rushed to one of the windows facing out on the yard. Two of the windows had cushioned window seats, and the sisters knelt on one as they peered from the window. While they did, Brother Luke threw a longing glance at the food before him and reluctantly pushed away from the table.

"Oh my, Brother Luke," Margaret tittered excitedly. "It's your nephew...Iain Armstrong."

"Your nephew," Judith echoed.

Margaret pushed open the wooden shutters all the way and called out an enthusiastic greeting. Judith's short, round body covered the distance to the stairwell with surprising speed and she called up the stairs to her niece, announcing Iain's arrival.

In spite of their excitement, an uncomfortable feeling settled in the pit of Brother Luke's stomach when he saw that Iain was accompanied by only one other rider. His nephew had left Blackthorn Hall in the company of his father and the Earl of Fleet and at least a hundred armed warriors. His appetite suddenly gone, Luke went to greet the young man as he came into the great hall.

Iain Armstrong's blue eyes registered relief at the sight of his uncle, and he embraced the monk warmly. It was clear from the mail shirt he still wore that the young man had come directly from the battle. Indeed, Iain's clothes and boots were covered with mud, mixing with dark stains that were surely the blood of men. The young man's face was pale, and a deep gash cutting across his forehead disappeared into the brow above his left eye. Tall and powerful with the rawboned strength of a man still a year or two away from his prime, Iain stood back and looked at the two middle-aged women.

"How delightful!" Margaret clapped in joy, causing Iain to glance with surprise at his uncle. "You've arrived just in time to join us for this meal."

"Indeed," Judith whispered with glee. "Just in time!"

"I fear I cannot," the young man replied quickly. "We haven't much time, ladies. We need to move all of you to Blackthorn Hall."

The two sisters looked at each other in confusion. Brother Luke asked what he knew had to be the inevitable. "What happened?"

"We lost, Uncle," Iain said thickly.

"Will my brother John be coming back today, as well?" Margaret asked in her high-pitched voice.

Iain cleared his throat before answering. "No, m'lady. He isn't coming back today. I have much to explain, but time is running short. We must move you all first. I'll explain all when we are safe at Blackthorn."

"But the dinner is ready." Margaret motioned toward the feast spread on the table.

"Indeed." Judith nodded enthusiastically. "It's all ready."

Iain looked desperately at his uncle.

"Tell them all of it," Brother Luke advised. "Briefly, if you must, but tell them."

The young man's weary face turned to the older sister. "We lost, Lady Margaret. We were slaughtered in the battle. The king is dead. So is my father, and so is your brother, the good Earl of Fleet. But we have no time to mourn now, my ladies...for the English are surely coming."

At the sound of the gasp, all eyes were drawn to the arched doorway leading to the kitchens and a circular stairwell. The hem of Marion's dress could be seen disappearing up the stairs.

Judith put her hand on Iain's arm. "Then will the English be staying for dinner?"

Brother Luke shook off his own grief and motioned for Iain to go after his betrothed.

"Go to her, lad. I'll try to explain this to my good friends here."

Marion raced all the way up the winding stairs to the top of the great square tower house. Bursting into the fresh air and sunshine, she ran along the stone parapet and out onto one of the corner bartizans. Her breaths were short and the quiet sobs escaping her were lost in the whistling wind. She leaned out between the blocks of stone and looked down at the earth far below. Beneath her, yellow leaves were swirling in the air, carried by the breeze. Tears dropped from her cheeks, disappearing before they reached the ground.

Her father couldn't be dead. He couldn't be gone. He'd promised her he would come back.

"Marion."

Iain's sharp call snapped like a whip in the morning air. She didn't look at him.

"Marion, step back away from that ledge."

She leaned farther out; she would not be ordered around. She was in no danger of falling the four stories. His powerful hands were around her waist in an instant, though, and he lifted her bodily away from the edge. She stood with her back against the opposite wall, the flash of anger disappearing as thoughts of her father returned.

"You heard what I told your aunts," he said in calmer voice.

She stared at the tops of the trees in the distance and nodded. Her chin quivered, but she fought back the tears.

"I'm sorry, Marion. I'm sorry to be the bearer of such sad news."

It was the gentleness in his voice that choked her up again. She slid her back down the wall and wrapped her arms around her knees, burying her face against them.

"We have no time for grieving now." He crouched before her. "I told your aunts the same thing. The English are surely coming, and I need to move everyone here to Blackthorn Hall. I told your father I would see to his people's safety."

"Will we be safer at Blackthorn?"

Iain frowned. "I cannot say for certain. It's more defensible than your father's tower house. But you will be safe, anyway."

"What do you mean?"

"You're going north."

Her gaze locked on his face. "Where are you sending me?"

"To the Isle of Skye. There is an abbey there...with a convent. It will be perfect for you. And safe."

"I shan't go," she argued. "I want to stay with my family."

Iain shook his head firmly. "It's not your decision. It was your father's wish that if anything were to happen to him, you would be cared for properly. I gave him my word."

"I *am* cared for properly, by my family. I shan't—"

"Do not argue with me," he snapped, his tone harsh. "With any luck, you will not need to stay there too long, and I—"

"One day is too long. Aunt Judith and Aunt Margaret have been mothers to me for all these years. Uncle William has been like a father...whenever my own has been away." Marion preferred to not beg, but she would if she thought it would have any effect on this cold-hearted man. "And they need me, too."

"It's out of the question," he said, standing up. "Your own father, their brother, did not wish to leave you in their charge. He knew they're not able to care for you, and I think even less of them."

"You're vile and mean-spirited," she said furiously. "How could you say these things after all the times you have been a guest at their table?"

"You are my responsibility," he replied, his voice low. "I'll do as I must. And right now I'm telling you that you need to prepare to travel north."

She could not go. She had just lost her father, and now she was to be taken from the rest of her family. An idea occurred to her, and she looked up at him towering over her. "I am your betrothed, Iain. If you don't trust the care of my aunts, then move me to Blackthorn Hall."

"I cannot be certain of your safety there. Besides, it would not be right to move you there until we are wed."

"Then marry me now. It's not as if I have any options about choosing a husband. I have been stuck with you since the age of three."

Iain crouched down again, his head sinking into his hand. Marion looked at the bloodstained hand as his fingers dug into his long brown hair. She felt she might have a chance. For the first time, she noticed the nasty gash on his brow, but she fought back the urge to reach out and touch it.

"Marry me," she pressed. "Do it now and be done with it. Then let me live my life."

His blue eyes were actually filled with amusement when they looked up into hers.

"I cannot, Marion. And even if I could, I would not. You're going to Skye."

"But why?" she said, her anger returning. "Why can you not marry me?"

"Because, lass, you're only six years old."

2

Twelve years later, Isle of Skye

THE WALLS of the Convent of Newabbey rose up in the distance. A huddle of huts formed a neat village at its gates, and the smoke of the morning fires hung like a low cloud about the thatched roofs. A scruffy black dog spotted the man and ran out from a pen beside the closest cottage. His ferocious barking blended with the rhythmic hammering of the smith already hard at work in the forge.

From the top of his horse, at the head of a group of Armstrong men, Iain growled back at the dog.

"An excellent way to rid yourself of your disagreeable mood," Brother Luke advised, spurring his horse up beside his nephew's. "In fact, why don't you dismount and wrestle the beast to the ground?"

His comment drew only a narrow stare. The laird pushed ahead, and the group dutifully fell in step.

The smell of roasting mutton reached Brother Luke, and the stirring in his belly reminded him that he hadn't anything to eat today. Their group had risen early. The laird had been impatient to be on the road. Twice, Marion had failed to show up where she'd been directed to be. The messengers had been sent over a month ago. She was to meet the laird at Eilean Donan Castle, accompanied by half a dozen escorts that Iain had arranged for.

When Iain and the rest of his men had arrived there two days ago, an Armstrong warrior was waiting alone, but there was no sign of Lady Marion. She'd sent a message that she'd made a habit of not traveling on Mondays.

Iain had proceeded to their second meeting place. An inn at the crossing to the mainland at Kyle of Lochalsh. Again, there'd been no Marion. Only the message that she had the custom of fasting on Tuesdays. That made it difficult for travel. Even the dogs had known better than to step in the path of the Armstrong laird that day. He was not pleased. Brother Luke suggested that it was really the weather that was keeping her. It had rained incessantly for the entire week they had been on the road.

Brother Luke nodded pleasantly at the folk of the village as the laird dismounted from his horse. Everyone else did the same, and they walked along the lane that led to the gates of the priory.

Nuns were known for occasionally developing peculiar habits, especially when it came to reclusiveness. Brother Luke thought it natural that after Marion's twelve years of living with them, she could have developed similar tendencies. His nephew, though, didn't share his thinking. He was laird and a very busy man. Brother Luke knew Iain to be a fair leader, a man who was respected and obeyed. When he made a command, he expected nothing less than total compliance from his people and from his intended. A marriage was going to take place. The English king and the Scottish regent were both sending representatives to Blackthorn Hall within the fortnight to witness it, as the final union of McCall heir and Armstrong laird was a further guarantee to consolidate power after decades of uprisings and clan conflict in the region.

In short, it was time for Lady Marion to return home.

The gates that led through the high wall surrounding the buildings and the church comprising the priory were open, and when the group entered, an old porter rushed over.

"I was told ye might arrive last night. Maybe it was two nights ago, I cannot remember. But we knew ye were coming, m'lord." He motioned for the stable hands to rush over. "The prioress is waiting for ye at the chapter house."

Brother Luke looked around at the orderly plan of the priory grounds, at the church directly ahead, and at the stables and guest quarters to the left, with a small orchard rising behind. To the right sat the chapter house, with its business offices and school and what he assumed to be the nun's quarters beyond. He could see the smoke rising from what must be a kitchen building behind the living quarters, and he guessed there was probably a well-tended garden behind that. Between the nuns' quarters and the church, paths of white crushed shells crisscrossed a small quadrangle of greensward, cultivated herbs, and flowers. Neat, efficient, and pleasant, Brother Luke thought approvingly. This had been a good place for the wee Marion to grow up.

"Where do I find Lady Marion?" Iain asked, handing his horse to one of the stable hands. The rest of the horses were taken away, too.

"She might be in her cell. But I'm not certain, m'lord. Would today be Wednesday, perchance?"

"What difference does it make what day it is?" Iain asked, his patience obviously wearing thin.

The porter took his hat off and scratched his balding head. "I'm getting too old to remember everything I'm told, or keep track of what day it is, either. One thing I do know was that the lass told me if ye were to come on a Wednesday, that I was to tell ye that's her day of...of seclusion. Yer lordship cannot know where she is."

Seeing the laird's temper about to boil over, Brother Luke immediately stepped forward and placed a hand on his nephew's forearm.

"He's just a simple messenger," he whispered.

Iain did not take his eyes off the old man. "Tell me this," he said in a low, dangerous voice. "What did she tell you to say if I arrived on Thursday?"

"Thursday?" The porter scratched his head again. "Ahh...that's it. That she'd be gone to the lepers' village if ye came on Thursday. Or maybe that was for Friday. And Thursday she'd be ill to her stomach? I know Saturday and Sunday were the prayer days and she could not be disturbed. Ahh, I've muddled it all. The prioress will be able to explain much better, m'lord. She'd be waiting at the chapter house for ye."

"You said that before." Iain handed the man a coin.

"I'll show ye the way," the porter said, relieved.

Everyone but Luke and the laird headed for the kitchens. At the sound of another growl from his stomach, Brother Luke was tempted to head that way, too. But gauging his nephew's temper and having heard about the iron fist of Mara Penrith MacLeod, prioress of the Convent of Newabbey, he decided his presence and mediation could be needed. The good Lord only knew what Iain might say in his present mood. The last thing they needed was to leave without the McCall heir.

"Has Lady Marion always been kept to such a rigorous schedule of daily activities?" Iain asked the porter as they moved toward their destination.

"This is not the prioress's doing, if that's what ye are asking. Lady Marion has never been one to sit still. From the time the wee creature arrived, the lass has always been ready to put her shoulder to the priory wheel," the old man said with a smile. "The lass likes to work, be it here or at the village, or visiting a sick crofter or even the lepers."

"And the prioress allows her to roam all over Skye?"

"To be honest, that is the one thing that drives the prioress to distraction. She doesn't care to have her charges out on their own... particularly Lady Marion."

"But she allows it nonetheless."

"Skye is far safer since the laird Alec Macpherson took young Malcolm MacLeod under his wing. They watch over us, to be sure, but the truth is, m'lord, there are still some rogues that pass through every now and again."

"So when did this regular daily schedule of Lady Marion's begin?" Iain asked. "Monday no travel, Tuesday fasting...and the rest of it."

"I'd say just about a month ago. About the time yer messenger first arrived to let her ladyship know she'd be traveling south."

The man stopped dead, going red in the face. Brother Luke figured the porter was smart enough to recognize his error in telling the truth. He looked up at the laird.

"I shouldn't have said as much."

"You told me what I needed to hear." Iain gave him another coin. "Where can I find Lady Marion?"

"She's a good lass, m'lord. She's got a heart as good as gold. I shouldn't have said..."

"Where is she?" he asked sharply.

"I'm sure I don't know, m'lord. I've been at the gate...minding my duties...not hardly running my mouth to guests." The porter visibly cringed under Iain's hard glare. "The convent is little more than what ye see. You ask any of the nuns, and they'll be sure to tell you where she might be...or which way she was heading."

"Perhaps we should introduce ourselves to the prioress first," Brother Luke interjected, hoping to calm his nephew before he met with young Marion.

"You'll do that," the laird replied. "Give her my regards. And inform her that I intend to leave with my betrothed today."

Only a mean and tightfisted master would starve his people, Marion thought, watching the servers head off for the third time to the dining hall. Each time they'd gone, they'd been carrying heaping trenchers of food. The way everything was disappearing, it looked like the men had barely eaten in a fortnight.

Marion and Sister Beatrice moved to one of the tables near the back door of the kitchen. The two women had been working in the kitchen since dawn. They'd baked all the bread they had rising. Since the onset of the feeding frenzy, they had been measuring flour, mixing and kneading dough, preparing more batches for tomorrow's baking. But at the rate food was being consumed right now, Marion figured the men would be eating the uncooked dough in another hour.

"You cannot avoid him forever, child."

"Forever might only be one or two days. Perhaps a week," Marion answered, adding more flour to the huge bowl she was using to mix the dough. "I can avoid him for that long."

"Do you really think the laird would give up and leave without you?" Sister Beatrice asked gently.

"Of *course* I do. He doesn't care a straw about me. Twelve years he's left me here. It might as well be a hundred twelve. The only reason why he's here now is to complete the business of a contract made between our kin when I was but a child."

"You're his betrothed."

"He can find another wife," she said stubbornly. "The McCalls and the Armstrongs have been trying to find a way to combine their land for nearly a century. But the timing has never worked out to the satisfaction of the families, and it will not work now, either. I will make sure of it."

"But you're saying it yourself. If it has taken a century to match a lass of your place and an Armstrong laird, he is not about to meddle with such an arrangement."

"Indeed, he will," she said confidently. "He doesn't care anything at all about me, and when he realizes I don't want him, either, he'll go right back to the Borders."

"But Marion, what about the land your family--"

"That's no issue at all. He has been controlling it for twelve years. He can keep it, so far as I care. He can have the whole of Scotland, for that matter, down to the last sheep and pig. I give it all to him and my blessing with it. But he will *not* have me in the bargain."

"But he's come all this way for you. He must want you to be his—"

"No, he doesn't. He doesn't care for me, and he doesn't care for my family. He *doesn't* want me, I tell you."

"But what makes you say that?"

Marion stood with her hands on her hips and faced the nun. "Because he thinks there is madness in my blood."

"Madness?" The wrinkled face of Sister Beatrice creased into a smile. "Are you talking of the little peculiarities you've occasionally mentioned about your uncle? About him acting as if he was William Wallace?"

Marion nodded, thinking about Uncle William's 'little peculiarities.' No one at Fleet Tower thought anything of it, but Iain Armstrong had used it to send her to Skye.

"My 'betrothed' has no respect for my family. My uncle is loud and talks and acts strangely at times, but the important thing is that he is quite kindhearted. Sir William is very sweet. Funny, even."

The nun motioned to one of the kitchen helpers to bring them more water. "An uncle who acts peculiar at times. That is certainly not enough reason to think your entire family is mad. I believe you're imagining the worst about Sir Iain."

"No, I'm not. You don't know the man," Marion argued. "He is very serious. Twelve years ago he was old before his time. Withered in spirit. He sees people as he wishes to see them, no matter how innocent that person's actions might be. He thinks even worse of the rest of my family, too."

Sister Beatrice straightened gingerly and wiped her hands on a rag. "But, how could he? Your father is dead. Your two aunts are gentle old ladies, and from the letters you have been reading to me that they regularly send, they love you like their own child."

"I agree. But Iain twists things to suit himself. He finds something wrong with everyone," Marion explained. "Starting with my father. John McCall never imagined he was William Wallace like Uncle William. But in bravery he was no less than that great hero. After all these years, I still remember him so vividly. He was fearless, bold, a giant of a man who was a master in wielding a sword. He died in Flodden Field beside King Jamie."

"Your father, the Earl of Fleet, was a hero, to be sure. Now, why would your betrothed think something was wrong with him?"

"Because of rumors," Marion said quietly. "I was young but not deaf. And I never witnessed any of this. But there were stories of my father...well, liking to roam around the village at night."

"And what's wrong with that?"

"He..." Marion hesitated. "They said he often walked about at night wearing nothing but his cap...a tam with a great feather rising from it... and his sword."

Despite her advanced age, Beatrice's face turned three shades of red.

"They were surely just ugly rumors," Marion said passionately. "No doubt tales invented to besmirch the man's name. He was a powerful man. Now that I'm older, I understand it much better. His enemies, our neighbors the Armstrongs—probably the present laird's father, in fact —were no doubt the ones that invented such nonsense."

Marion picked up a nearby bowl and sprinkled more flour into her mix. She dug her fingers into the dough and kneaded furiously. "And then my aunts. They like to talk...sometimes ceaselessly. But that comes from being so close to each other in age, in life. They are almost one spirit in two bodies. They have to think aloud so the other can hear, too. Of course, Aunt Margaret was getting hard of hearing when I was there. And Aunt Judith liked to repeat what her sister said. But that can happen to anyone. There is nothing wrong with that, is there?"

"And your betrothed does not think too highly of them, either?"

"He sent me away, didn't he?" she replied shortly. Marion could feel the heat of her anger rising up her neck into her face. She tried to fight it, but it was the same burning feeling she felt every time she thought of home. "And not once, during all these years, did he send for me or arrange for my family to come and visit me here. I was discarded and forgotten. Banished."

"You were cared for," Sister Beatrice said softly. "You still are. Every one of us here loves you. Things could have been a lot worse."

Marion blushed, feeling suddenly embarrassed. "I am sorry. I did not mean to sound ungrateful. For the past twelve years, you and the rest of the sisters here at the abbey convent have kept me safe beneath your wings, nurtured me, made me feel at home." She straightened, wiping dough off her fingers. "And this is all the more reason why this marriage should not take place."

"Why would that be?"

"I need to stay here. I *want* to stay here," she corrected herself. "I want to take my vows, become a nun, do for others what you have done for me."

Beatrice sat down on a three-legged stool beside the table. Her expressive face reflected her distress. "You haven't been built for this kind of life, Marion. You're too much of a free spirit...far too headstrong for the life of a nun. Your many battles with the prioress over the years should have made you realize that this cannot be a permanent home for you."

"I can change. I can be what everyone here wants me to be," the young woman cried passionately. "The prioress is a compassionate woman. She'll not refuse me shelter if I promise to obey her orders."

The older nun reached over and took the young woman's hand, stopping Marion from battering the dough lifeless. "Would you want the same thing if marriage were not a condition for returning home?"

"Well, I..."

"Is it possible that you might be using the convent now as a way of punishing the laird for sending you here to begin with?"

Marion closed her eyes and threw her head back in frustration.

"You miss your family, lass. You always have," the old nun said gently. "Your roots are there in the Borders. You belong with your own folk. The time has come. You should go to them."

"Not with him. Not as the wife of the Armstrong laird." Mist gathered in Marion's eyes when she looked at her friend again. "And it's not just for myself that I feel this way. I'm doing this for Iain, too. He has never wanted this marriage. I'm going to set him free and let him have his land in the bargain."

Marion's heart skipped a beat as she suddenly saw a giant of a man standing in the doorway behind Beatrice. The sun was behind him, so she could not see his face. But she knew him immediately from the tartan, the laird's broach, and the long brown hair touching his shoulders. He was larger than she remembered him, though. Wider in the shoulders. Taller. She wondered for how long he had been standing there and how much he might have heard.

Time was of the essence. Escape was impossible. Marion picked up the wooden bowl of flour sitting beside the dough and turned it upside down on her head.

3

A DUSTING of white powder covered Marion from head to toe. The old nun jumped up from her seat and stepped back, gaping in shock at the young woman. Iain masked any reaction he might have had and strolled into the kitchen. A few of the workers looked up from their tasks, immediately bowing slightly in acknowledgment of his presence. As their eyes turned then to the white statue standing by the kneading table, there were a few gasps and even hushed chuckles.

The older nun was quick to recover from her surprise. "You must be Sir Iain. Welcome, m'lord."

"And you are?" He took a step farther into the kitchens.

"Sister Beatrice." She stepped in front of him, effectively blocking his path to Marion. "You must have lost your way to the chapter house."

"No, I have come to the right place," Iain answered, watching his future wife. She stood motionless, still wearing the ridiculous bowl on her head. Beneath the inane mess she'd created, however, it was impossible to miss how much she had grown since he'd sent her here. Unlike the rest of her family, she was tall and slender. Looking at her now, he realized he was eager to see the rest of her, too. She was going to be his wife. It would be much better if she did not have her fathers and her Uncle William's pear-shaped noses or her aunts' pointy chins. Even with the little he could see of her face, though, it appeared she lacked both distinctive features. Her face actually looked well proportioned. He caught himself looking down at the brown habit that might have doubled for woolsack. The white veil covering her hair was no finer.

"Ah, you mean the dining hall. You must be famished," the nun said, pretending relief. "Allow me to take you to the hall where your men are seated."

Beatrice motioned, but he didn't follow. She then took him by the arm, but Iain stood where he was, staring at his betrothed.

"Good morning, Marion."

She remained silent. The bowl didn't cover her eyes. They were open, watching him. There was defiance there, but interest, too. The long lashes were speckled with flour, as were the bridge of her nose and her cheeks.

"The food must be getting cold, m'lord. You must be starving," the nun persisted, tugging on his arm again.

"In good time."

Sister Beatrice shook her head. "Really, m'lord, after such a ride, you—"

"Leave us!" His bark had the desired effect. The older nun let go of his arm as if she'd burned herself. Immediately, she scurried past him and out the door. Iain decided she'd be back with her superior in no time.

The eyes of twenty workers were on them. Everyone in the kitchen had stopped working.

Marion took a step back, glancing quickly at another door beyond the baking ovens. She looked like a doe about to bolt. Iain approached, determined to mount a chase if he needed to. They would settle this nonsense right now, and he didn't care who witnessed it.

"Am I to receive any kind of greeting?" he said in a gentler tone.

"No!"

Another feeling of relief washed through him. She lacked the high-pitched voice of her aunt Margaret. "And why is that?"

"Today is my day of complete seclusion," she said, taking a couple of steps backward and glancing toward the door again. "I cannot entertain any company."

"Seclusion...with a score of kitchen workers."

"I have duties. I'm still in seclusion."

"Excellent. Well, it happens today is my day of seclusion, too." He followed her as she again backed away a step or two. "I will be in seclusion with my future wife."

"I'm serious."

"So am I."

She moved quickly around a table toward the door. With a few long strides, he crossed in front of the ovens and reached the door at the same time that she did. She hurried through and started along the path. He was beside her in a moment.

"If you recall, lass, our stars were made and matched in heaven. So many similarities exist between us. I've heard your aunts say so a hundred times."

"That is a lie. We have nothing in common."

The morning sun was shining through the clouds. As they turned a corner of the building, Marion nearly barreled into two nuns coming toward them on the path. The two women gasped loudly.

"What have you done to yourself, child?" one of them asked in distressed tones.

"The prioress wants to see you, Marion," the other chirped immediately. "But you cannot go to her looking like that."

"Why is that? You disapprove of her hat?" Iain asked, moving next to her.

The two women exchanged glances.

"It's quite lovely," the first nun croaked, biting her lip. "And you must be the laird we've been expecting."

"Lady Marion's betrothed," he corrected, taking his intended's arm. She tried to shake him loose, but he tightened his hold on her. "Did you say the prioress is looking for her?"

"She is, m'lord," the second woman answered. "She was hoping to greet you, too. She's asking that both of you go to the chapter house."

Marion sneezed, and the bowl tipped forward on her head. Iain took off her disguise and handed it to one of the nuns. "You can advise the prioress that my fiancée and I will join her as soon as Lady Marion has cleaned up."

"Kindly take the laird there *now*, Sisters," the imp on his side said pointedly as she tried to wrench her arm free again. "I shall join everyone later."

Iain held on. "I cannot stand our separation any longer, lass. I simply cannot let you out of my sight."

MAY MCGOLDRICK

"You tolerated our separation well enough for twelve years," she blasted at him. "Now let me go, villain."

Iain smiled confidingly at the nuns. "Lovers' quarrel. Please tell the prioress her charge and I shan't be too long."

He didn't see the blow to his shin coming. *She must have rocks in the tips of her shoes*, Iain thought. He hid his grimace, not wanting to give Marion the satisfaction of knowing that she had inflicted pain.

"On second thought," he said to the wide-eyed nuns, "my beloved demands some private attention. She has missed me far too much. We may take a wee bit longer than I intended. Which way to her chamber?"

The second nun pointed weakly to one of the buildings. The first woman, though, quickly pushed her companion's hand down. "Perhaps, it would be best if you let *us* help Marion. You don't know her disposition."

"Indeed, I know her temperament very well." He looped an arm around Marion's waist and drew her tightly to his side. "Let us go, sweetness."

She refused and dug her heels into the dirt. Scooping her into his arms, he began to carry her toward the building the nun had indicated. Half a dozen steps were all it took before she started fighting him in earnest.

"Let me go," she cried, battering his face and squirming to free herself.

"You've sprouted extra hands and feet in the past few years." He tossed her across his shoulder. "Much easier this way."

"I'm not six years old anymore, you barbarian. Villain. Put me down right now. You're embarrassing me."

"You asked for this."

"I did not." She landed a sharp elbow to the back of his head and grabbed his hair. Iain tilted her backward, and she gasped and clutched at his tartan. "I dare you to drop me on my head. When I'm free of you, I shall take out your eyes, tear every lock of hair from your head. I shall use your own dirk and cut out your ruthless heart and feed it to the dogs. If you even have a heart, that is. You're an ill-bred cur. Vile and disgusting. You have lived too long."

A lengthy string of threats and epithets continued to pour out of her. Priory workers and nuns and some of his Armstrong warriors were beginning to line the path ahead of them, watching them with amusement. No one approached or tried to stop him. They all knew. There had been plenty of warning. The men he'd sent ahead had been here nearly a month. Iain nodded and smiled as he passed them all, ignoring Marion's tirade. At the door to the residential building, he asked an older woman who was coming out which room was Marion's. She didn't hesitate to answer.

Iain climbed the steps three at a time to the second floor. The building was old, the hallway narrow and dark. As he shifted her weight on his shoulder, her head accidentally hit the wall a number of times. He had to give her credit, though. She didn't complain about that even once. At the same time, the curses and threats never stopped.

Her room was at the end of the corridor. He pushed the door open and walked in. Marion tried to raise herself on his shoulder and banged the back of her head hard as they entered the cell. Iain felt a fleeting moment of remorse as she actually did quiet down.

The room was small, but not uncomfortable. At the end, sunlight came through a narrow window that he figured she could slither through if she was given the chance. The shutter was open and the air wafting in was fresh and warm. A narrow, tidily made bed sat against one wall, and the red-and-green plaid of the McCall tartan spread across it brightened the chamber. A chest and a table and stool completed the furnishings. He kicked the door shut with his foot and dropped her on the bed. She immediately sat up.

"I am sorry about the bruises to your head," he said, seeing her rubbing a few of the spots and looking around in a daze. He crouched before her and lifted her chin. "But such blows can only leave a bruise...not incur madness or loss of memory or forgetfulness or the inability to speak. In so many words, lass, I am on to your sly tricks."

Her eyes cleared, and she pushed his hand away.

"I hate you."

"You don't," Iain said calmly. The white veil she had been wearing had dropped back onto her shoulders and for couple of moments, he found himself staring at the dark curls dancing around her face. Most of her hair was pulled back in a thick braid and bundled in a knot at the back of her neck. Her face was still covered with flour, her black eyes glaring beneath thick lashes. He realized he was very eager to see her cleaned up.

"You don't trust me nor care for me," she said in a low, husky voice. "There is no reason for us to wed. Why don't you just gather your men and leave me here?"

On his route here, he'd been tempted a number of times to do just that. He was fourteen years her senior. His taste ran to older women who brought some experience of lovemaking to his bed. Iain did not think he had the patience to deal with even a fraction of the trouble Marion had been as a child. Temperamental, stubborn, loud. He had hoped the convent life had beaten some of it out of her. Obviously, it hadn't. He was here, though, and it was too late to walk away.

"We can do this the easy way or the hard way," he explained. "You're coming back with me to Fleet Tower."

"Not as your wife."

"*As my wife*," he stated.

"Why?"

"Because our fathers and their fathers wanted it that way. Because it's best for our people. And because it's in the best interest of Scotland to do so."

"That is a lie." She shoved at his chest and tried to get up.

He pushed her back onto the bed. She landed hard on her buttocks. "Why are you being so difficult? You were ready to marry me at the age of six. Why not now?"

"I was a wee, blind simpleton at the age of six. I have grown, seen the world, learned about people."

"All from inside the walls of a convent in Skye?" he asked mockingly.

"Yes. And what I see now is that *you* are the simpleton, and I do not wish to marry you."

"My apologies, lass, but it's too late for such antics." He smiled smugly and put a hand on Marion's shoulder, forcing her to stay put. "Now, here is the plan. You may wash your face and change your clothes and pack whatever you need to bring in the same small trunk you brought with you when you came. Then, you and I are going to say our farewells to the prioress and whomever else you please. We'll be on the road by noon and if the weather remains clear, we'll be back at Blackthorn Hall in a week, just in time for our wedding. Is that all perfectly clear?"

She shoved his hand off her shoulder. "And here is my plan—"

"I am not interested in hearing your plans."

"You arrogant bully. How dare you!"

"My schedule is simply derived from plans already in place...plans your troublesome delays have jeopardized," he said seriously. "The date, the time, the list of invited guests...all of that...was decided by those at Stirling and Westminster. Both the Stewart and Tudor courts believe our little union will help put an end to all the troubles in our part of the Borders."

"By his wounds, what have you been doing all these years, marauding and pillaging helpless crofters? Why is there suddenly such interest in our wee patch of countryside?"

Iain crouched before her, trying to get through to her, hoping she would hear him and put an end to her foolishness. There was duty involved here. Responsibility.

"I have been trying to provide a peaceful existence for my people... and for yours, as well. The troublemaker in the Borders region has been your dear cousin."

"Jack Fitzwilliam?"

"The same."

"I cannot believe it. He was always a little wild, but—"

"Well, believe it. Your Uncle William's illegitimate son has been raiding farms and attacking travelers. He has gathered other outlaws to his band and avoided capture by terrorizing Border folk. They have even hidden him out of fear of his ruthlessness. You probably don't remember him well."

"I remember him. He used to come and visit sometimes...when my father was away."

Marion shivered slightly. In her eyes, Iain could see she didn't like the memories of her cousin that were coming back to her. After a moment, her eyes narrowed. "What are you, a coward? You cannot take care of one outlaw without the intervention of two royal courts?"

Iain fought his temper as heat rushed into his face. "I am no coward, but a considerate man who too many times listened to two old women's tearful pleas about sparing the life of their only nephew. Jack would have been dead a dozen times by now if it were not for your aunts."

Marion considered his words.

"He comes and goes," Iain continued, "preying on one part of the

Borders and then traveling south into England, only to return later. He is rarely in one place for too long. He is a creature of darkness, striking wherever he is least expected."

She frowned and shook her head. "My dear cousin has hated my very existence from the moment I was born. I hid from him whenever he came to visit Fleet Tower. What makes you think this marriage would have any effect on him?"

"He has been spreading it across the countryside that he himself is the true heir to the McCall title and lands," Iain explained. "He has told your people that you're really dead. If they don't support him and shelter him, they will face his wrath. As it is, I'm now just a steward of your land, and that makes Jack more dangerous. Our marriage at Blackthorn Hall will put an end to his claims and also assure the Crown that there is to be continued stability in the lineage."

She shook her head again. "No matter how grand a ceremony you've planned for this wedding, it will mean nothing to Jack. He will not change. So what are you going to do to him afterward? Kill him?"

"Drive him off," he said shortly.

Iain knew he would surely kill him if need be. But not before dragging Jack Fitzwilliam before a judge for his many crimes. After all, this was 1525 and not the age of barbarians. Modern Scotland had laws. He would be tried fairly his claims heard.

Then Jack would be hanged from a gallows and his head placed on a pike at Fleet Tower.

All Iain wanted was justice and peace for himself and his people. He had seen too much blood shed needlessly at Flodden Field. No more. Iain wanted a calm life. A wife, children, and the clans McCall and Armstrong living in peace and putting their disputes behind them.

"Enough of that." He stood up and grabbed Marion's hands, pulling her up to her feet. "You need to get ready to leave."

She shook him off and sat back down on the bed. "You have not convinced me."

He ran a hand through his hair. "Marion, you're trying my patience for no reason. What is it that you don't understand? Your people are being abused. They need you. Your aunts and uncle are advancing in age and are in poor health. They want you back, as well."

"They never said any of that in their letters," she protested.

"How could they? And why would they, when the last thing they want is to worry you? And what could you have done from here?" Iain saw the look of doubt creeping into her face.

She rubbed her forehead, but then stared in horror at the pastry flour falling onto her lap.

"And what do you have to lose by marrying me, anyway? It's not as if you have another suitor."

She was too transparent. Iain shook his head as he could see on her face the thoughts that were already forming in her head. He was out of his mind to give her ideas.

"In fact, there...there is someone else. A man closer to my age. Not old like you."

He smiled and shook his head. "Will you wash your face, or would you have me wash it for you?" He reached over and wiped the flour from the tip of her nose. "How about the dress? I'd be happy to help you change." He touched the coarse fabric at her neckline and let his finger brush against the silky soft skin of her neck.

As if she'd been burned, Marion slapped his hand away and jumped to her feet. Stepping off the bed, she moved to where a pitcher and bowl sat on the table. "You must leave my chamber. I shall wash and change."

With her words, Iain smiled at her back. "You will soon be my wife. There is nothing about you that I shall not soon see or touch."

She poured water on a small towel and started wiping her face with it. "'Soon' is your word. I want you to know that 'soon' may never come."

"I beg to differ." Iain moved behind her.

"What are you doing?" she asked nervously, looking over her shoulder.

"Helping you clean up this mess." He took the towel out of her hand and dipped it in the water.

"I can manage perfectly well without your help."

"I know you can." Iain turned her around so that she faced him.

Marion took a fistful of the veil and held it tight at her throat.

He shook his head. "This thing is covered with flour, lass. You're just making it worse." He tugged it gently from her hand and dropped it to the floor. He brought the towel to her face.

She stepped back but came up against the wall. He closed the distance until their clothes were touching. Iain used the towel to swab lightly at her brow and nose, and then her cheeks. Her eyes stayed open, watching him. He dipped the towel in the water again and ran it across her full lips, causing her to take a sharp breath.

"This is very unexpected," Iain said.

Her eyes fixed on his. "What is unexpected?"

"How beautiful you have turned out to be."

Color bloomed in her newly washed cheeks. "I wish I could say the same thing about you."

He laughed out loud and wiped at a spot on her chin. "You were not obligated to return the compliment."

"If you're looking for a compliment, then I would say you're ugly and venomous as a toad."

"A toad, you say?" he asked, lifting her chin, and studying every aspect of her face. It really was perfect, except for a tiny white scar near the point of her chin.

It was a blessing that she'd been locked away in this convent for her years of growing up. Iain could only imagine all the men he would have had to fight to keep them away from her. Her eyes were so dark that they were almost black. Her skin, the texture of silk. Her high cheek-bones and straight nose were perfectly proportioned, and her lips, rose-colored and moist and...well, her lips simply looked delicious.

He leaned toward her.

"What are you doing?" she whispered.

"I'm going to kiss you," he whispered back.

"I'll not kiss a toad."

His lips were inches away from hers. Iain realized that her breathing was unsteady. The blush had spread down her neck. And she had not turned her face nor tried to push him away. She was definitely affected by his nearness and he liked that.

"I take nothing that is not offered."

"Is that the truth?"

He nodded.

"Do you promise me that's the truth?"

"Of course," he asserted, focusing on her lips.

Her voice was a vague whisper. "Then there will be no marriage."

"Our union was determined when you were but three, Marion. You will be my wife."

"Then I am offering you no kiss," she said quietly. "And when it comes to the other...uh, duties that go along with being a wife, I'll not be doing any of those, either."

He rested a hand on the wall beside her head. Laughter rose up in him. "What duties are you talking about?"

Her face flushed scarlet. "All of them. Whatever they may be."

"Such as sharing my bed?"

She nodded. Red as it was, he could see in her face a look of confidence for the first time. She was a fighter.

"And I remind you of your honor, laird. Taking what I don't offer would break your promise. And what honor is there in a laird who cannot keep a promise?"

"You will share my bed, and you do so willingly."

She stared at him for a long moment. "You're quite wrong about that, and I know you will soon see how mistaken you are. But after a fortnight or so of travel to Fleet Tower, you will have ample time to consider the attractiveness of such a marriage. For I promise you there will be no heirs. No legitimate ones, at least." She smiled up at him for the first time. "And what tragedy for your clan, considering you were the only son."

Iain smiled back at her. "Talk as you will, my sweet. I have no worries that you will share my bed...and happily."

Marion placed her palm squarely on his chest and pushed him backward. "You may live your life in a fantasy world," she said, moving past him to the window. "But that is as far as it will go."

Iain crossed his arms and leaned a shoulder against the wall, watching her. Turning her back on him, she let her hair down and shook the flour from it. The waves of dark locks hung nearly to her waist. Without a glance back at him, Marion picked up a brush and began to run it through her hair.

He felt the tightening in his loins. Making a fantasy real would certainly make the journey to Blackthorn Hall very entertaining.

4

"You will obey the wishes of your future husband and prepare yourself for leaving today."

Marion squirmed but bit back her objection to the prioress's command. The Armstrong laird had gruffly and reluctantly agreed to wait outside while the two women exchanged some private words, and Marion had felt a moment of hope.

The moment had been short-lived, however. The truth was that there had been no exchange of anything. The older nun had not even paused for breath in her lecture on Marion's responsibilities as the McCall heir. The younger woman figured Brother Luke, who was also waiting outside with his nephew, had whispered a thing or two to the prioress before Marion and Iain arrived at the Chapter House.

To Marion's thinking, the prioress was the wrong person to make this decision, since the nun's entire life had been about sacrifice and responsibility. The prioress had been the undisputed overseer of these lands for more than forty years. From the time she had proved herself able at the age of twenty-two, no one had ever thought of challenging her authority. She had always been fair but strict in her administration. Over the years, she had earned the respect of those around her, but had demanded obedience as her due. Through times of turbulence and times of peace, she had drawn a straight line, and almost all had followed where she led. She liked the life in the priory orderly and serene.

Twelve years of insubordination on Marion's part had not made anyone's life easy. Without a doubt all the trouble she'd caused had made the prioress's decision simpler. Marion and the prioress had had many differences of opinion over the years. And it had all led to this. Marion now had to pay for her transgressions by leaving without further dispute.

"Go ask the laird and his uncle to come back in," the prioress said.

Over the years, experience had taught Marion that becoming emotional or throwing a tantrum would have no effect on the old woman. The prioress was at least a head shorter than Marion, but she had the force of personality that made others feel she towered over them, especially when she was displeased. Right now, Marion did not want her displeasure, for that was not the last memory she wished these people to have of her.

"Everything will work out, daughter. God's will be done," the prioress said in a gentler tone, seeing Marion's hesitation. She motioned toward the door. "Now bring them in."

Balls and chains dragged at each of her feet as Marion went to open the door. The laird was standing beside it, his expression arrogant. She wondered if he had overheard any of the lecture she had received.

"You may enter," she said in as condescending a tone as she could muster.

It was impossible to maintain a sour attitude toward Brother Luke, as he seemed genuinely happy to see her. And from the letters Marion had received from her aunts over the years, she knew the cleric was a frequent visitor to Fleet Tower. They exchanged a few pleasantries again at the door.

Marion was relieved to see Sister Beatrice join them, as well. The old nun was perhaps the most devoted friend she had at the convent.

"Marion and I have spoken," the prioress announced to the others once the door was closed again. Favoring a bad knee, the old woman limped around her desk to a chair and sat down. "She'll be ready to leave today."

"But I cannot travel alone with a group of men." The idea came out of nowhere. Marion figured it had to be a divine intervention.

The prioress paused over her concern for a few short seconds before turning to the Armstrong laird. "Marion is correct, m'lord. It would be completely improper for her to be in the company of all your men for such a lengthy journey."

Iain thought for a moment, then glanced at Brother Luke and Marion before looking back at the prioress. "May I have a moment to speak to Brother Luke...by the window?"

"Of course," the older woman said.

As the two men moved away to exchange a few hushed words, Marion strained to hear what they were saying. She didn't like the look on Iain's face as they came back toward them.

"Perhaps," she suggested quickly to the prioress, "I can have couple of the nuns accompany us on the trip south. Maybe Sister Beatrice would not mind."

She glanced at Iain. He was looking at Beatrice, and the pained look on his face was precious. The old nun was nodding enthusiastically.

"That is out of the question. Sister Beatrice's health would never withstand so long a journey, complicated by the fact that she would need to travel right back before the winter storms set in." The prioress shook her head adamantly. "Perhaps some of the younger nuns."

"I might suggest a more reasonable solution to Lady Marion's concerns," Brother Luke offered in a gentle tone.

The confident look on Iain's face told Marion that she was not going to like the suggestion, whatever it was.

"Pray continue," the prioress instructed.

"The betrothal is well established, and the banns have all been read," Luke said. "The wedding that is to take place at Blackthorn Hall in little more than a fortnight is ceremonial. It's simply an opportunity to feed hundreds of guests and to allow everyone to witness a momentous union of the Armstrong and McCall clans."

Marion felt like she was standing on the edge of a cliff, ready to be pushed. Or to jump. She watched Brother Luke wipe at the dust on his cloak before continuing.

"That celebration could still go on as planned, but what I would suggest is to have these two young people marry before we leave the convent."

"That is impossible," Marion cried out.

"Why is it impossible?" Iain asked coolly. "You're the one who brought up the inappropriateness of the travel arrangements."

"My intention was to have female companionship during what would surely be a very dull and arduous journey."

"Now you will have the company of your husband to keep you entertained," he said with finality. He turned to the prioress. "Fall is already here. The rivers are running higher, and the bad weather is nearly upon us. It will be impossible for me to arrange an escort to send your nuns back before winter. This suggestion is a good one. It will give Lady Marion and myself the opportunity to know each other better before we get back to Blackthorn Hall."

"I'll not do it." Marion glared up at him. "I'll not marry you with-out...without my family around me."

"You claim we have been like a family to you for these past twelve years," the prioress responded, turning to Marion. "Is that not so?"

The old woman's voice had become harsh again. She was ready to get rid of her.

"It is so," Marion croaked, fighting the sudden tears that were burning her eyes.

"Then we'll stand witness to this ceremony." She motioned to Sister Beatrice, not allowing Marion to say anything more. "Please alert the sisters and gather everyone in the chapel. I should like the ceremony to take place prior to noon prayers." She next turned to Brother Luke. "I expect you would like to assist our chaplain in the blessing of this union?"

"I would be honored," the cleric replied, beaming cheerfully.

"And you, daughter, need to change into something more suited to this joyous occasion than what you are wearing now."

Marion looked at her, trying to understand what was happening.

"She has no fine dresses," Sister Beatrice interjected.

"Well, find her something more suitable. Were there not some gowns left here when Lady Fiona...?"

Marion sat down and buried her face in her hands. Everyone had lost their minds. This did not make any sense. She had been a child when she was sent away from Fleet Tower. She didn't know Iain Armstrong then. She knew him less now. She didn't care for him. In fact, she despised him for separating her from her aunts. And his feel-ings were no different toward her. And what did she know about being a wife? *Nothing.*

That's it, she decided, standing up. She simply could not marry him.

5

SHE MARRIED HIM.

Just as Iain wanted, they were on the road by noon. No escort of shriveled and overly protective nuns, either, only the affable Brother Luke and a troop of grinning Armstrong and McCall warriors. The men were obviously entertained by the entire turn of events, never mind happy to be heading home.

Everything was finally going according to plan...with the little exception of three large trunks Marion had insisted on taking back to Fleet Tower. Twelve years of collected memories, she'd called them.

The wedding was behind them, but Iain had to admit that it hadn't been the most joyous of ceremonies. Throughout the proceedings, Marion had not once stopped grousing about her distaste for the arrangements. And not even a minute after Brother Luke and the wee mouse of a chaplain had said the final prayers, pronouncing them husband and wife, she had run out of the chapel alone. Iain had simply accepted the congratulations of the prioress and his own men for both of them.

Outside, the horses were saddled and ready. Her trunks were stacked and lashed on a cart. Marion, naturally, was nowhere to be found. Her absence, however, was not prolonged, and more than a few jaws dropped when she entered the courtyard. She had changed into a black gown with a black hood and veil. She appeared to be in mourning.

Iain looked over his shoulder at his wife, riding one of the spare horses he'd brought with him on the journey north. She had positioned herself toward the rear of the group. Her eyes met his and then she quickly looked away. He turned his face forward to hide his smile.

Several hours later, night was slowly descending on them. Since leaving the priory, she had spoken very few words, and none to him. He was certain that Marion's mood was every bit as sour as when they had left, despite Brother Luke's attempts to engage her in conversation. The cleric caught Iain's glance and separated himself from the mourning bride, joining him in the front of the group.

"I believe it's time to find a place to set up camp for the night."

Iain looked ahead at the road snaking through the mountains. They had been traveling at a slow pace because the ground was soft from the previous week of rain. "Not yet."

"Lady Marion is not accustomed to spending so many hours on horseback, don't forget," Brother Luke objected. "Why, the poor lass must be hungry and thirsty, too."

"You wouldn't be a wee bit hungry, now, would you, Uncle?"

"Not I," the monk said, scoffing. "I'm just thinking of the lass."

"Very noble," Iain said, smiling. "There are dry meats, oatcakes, and a skin of wine in her saddle, if she wants it."

"But that is not enough."

"Did she say so?"

"No. She is being shy and—"

"We continue to ride, Uncle."

"Show her some kindness, and perhaps you'll receive some of the same," the older man advised.

"I doubt it."

"Listen, nephew. This is no way to start a marriage. You're older, wiser. Consider her situation over the past twelve years. A woman needs to be wooed, lad."

Iain grunted. "We are not stopping. Not yet."

The curses mumbled under the cleric's breath might have seemed contradictory to his profession, but Iain took no offense. He knew his uncle was often directed more by his belly than by any higher power. Iain spurred his horse on.

Marion's behavior at the chapel and since then was beginning to bother him. There had never been any doubt in Iain's mind who would become his wife. It surprised him that she thought any different. He couldn't understand the childishness, the temper, the attitude. His uncle was correct in saying that this was no way to start a marriage, and Iain was getting too old to let this fester for long. Marion needed to learn a lesson. She needed to change her attitude before they reached Blackthorn Hall.

The temperature continued to drop, and the Highland air was downright cold by the time night was fully upon them. It was dangerous trying to push ahead after nightfall. Darkness hid many dangers. Putting his stubbornness aside, Iain decided it was time to stop for the night.

Leading his men down into a wooded glen, he quickly found a flat area covered with soft pine needles beneath a grove of trees. A river ran past, not too far down the hill. He could hear the burbling water through the encroaching gloom. The Armstrong warriors took care in looking about the area before seeing to the horses and starting to set up camp. It seemed to be a good place, and Iain was satisfied.

He looked around him for his new wife. In the midst of the commotion, no one was watching her. Just as a hint of concern began to rise in his throat, he spotted Marion, dismounted and walking by herself in the direction of the river. Iain handed his horse to one of his men and followed her.

Her pace was proof enough that she was made of hardy stock. She was definitely not as fatigued as Brother Luke thought she was. There was a break in the trees ahead, and he watched her cross a small meadow. Patches of heather looked like wild beasts crouching in wait, but she hardly gave them a glance as she passed. On the far side, Marion entered the line of trees, and Iain lost sight of her. A moment later, he reached the fast-running river. With the heavy rains, the surface was a raging torrent. Water rushed around and over the rocks that bordered it. She was nowhere in sight.

"Marion!" he shouted, looking down the river. If she fell in, she could be halfway to Loch Lomond.

"Don't turn around."

Her sharp words caused him to do exactly the opposite of what he was told.

"Can I not get a moment's privacy?" she yelled at him. She was crouched under a tree, not half a dozen steps from the river. He turned

around. "I'll have you to know that since our so-called wedding ceremony, my dislike of you has multiplied tenfold."

"I'm very sorry to hear that, lass. Perhaps tomorrow we could
increase that to twentyfold and cover twice the distance." He leaned a
shoulder against a tree. "You still haven't told me why I shouldn't be
watching you."

"You're an ogre," she replied. "Your complete lack of consideration
for anyone but yourself makes me think of strangling you with my bare
hands."

"I think you should pursue such thoughts. Do your worst."

"Really?"

"I've nothing to lose," Iain said. "And anyway, strangling me might
just improve your sour attitude."

"*My* sour attitude?"

"I promise not to put up a fight," he said encouragingly.

"You, Iain Armstrong, are a liar and a coward!" He heard her rising
to her feet and shaking out her skirts. "But you'd not be foolish enough
to let me get my two hands around your miserable throat."

She walked to the edge of the river and stepped onto a couple of
sizable rocks. She leaned down and washed her hands and her face.

Iain wondered if she knew how slippery those rocks could be. He
came up behind her.

"I think you're far too timid. Here I am giving you the chance you
claim you're looking for, but you refuse to take it."

She stood up and whirled about too fast. There was no way he
could reach her in time. She desperately waved her arms and fell backward into the river.

"Now, that was brilliant," he muttered, clambering over the rocks to
reach her. When Marion surfaced, she was in the middle of the river,
way out of his reach and moving quickly.

"Help me," she called before going under again. The moon moved
behind the clouds.

It didn't matter if she knew how to swim or not. The current was
strong. Iain unbuckled his sword and threw it on the riverbed. As he
flung off his cloak, he turned and dived in after her. The rush of cold
water nearly took Iain's breath away. Rocks scratched his legs as he
sailed by them. He tried to stay afloat and avoid smashing into the
boulders.

"Marion!" he shouted. The roar of the water was his only answer.

A sense of urgency seized him. All their differences aside, Iain was responsible for her. He was responsible for this accident. His stubbornness had caused this. She didn't deserve to drown. Her life had been placed into his hands by her father as the earl drew his last breath on the battlefield. He had to save her.

He didn't know what lay in their path, where the next bend in the river led. He wasn't sure if she was strong enough to keep her head above water.

"Marion!" he shouted again, swimming with the current and scanning both shores for some sign of her. The moon had once again emerged from the sea of clouds.

Iain thought he heard a scream from somewhere ahead. It could have been a bird in the night. He wished he could believe Marion was that bird, sitting on a branch of a tree and laughing at him as he bobbed up and down like an apple in the water. The river became narrower but deeper, and he felt himself drop down a number of levels. Where the current passed between large rocks, the flow of the water was stronger and faster. He tried to remember if there were any waterfalls ahead.

He found himself making promises with his Maker. *Please, let her live.* He would try harder. They *would* get along.

With its roots pulled loose from the bank, a tree stretched across the river ahead. His heart jumped with joy when he spotted the dark figure holding on to the very end of one limb.

"Marion!" he shouted, gliding in long strokes toward the figure.

She turned and stretched a hand toward him. The water was pushing him away from the tree. In a moment, he'd sweep past her. He swam hard across the current, trying to close the distance to her. But the river had a mind of its own, pushing him away.

"Stay there! Work your way to the shore," he shouted as the water carried him past her. "I'll find you."

To Iain's disbelief, she let go of the tree and got swept under the water again.

"What are you—" The breath was knocked out of Iain's body as he slammed against a large boulder sticking out of the water. He felt a few ribs crack, and his left arm went numb as his shoulder struck a submerged rock beside it. He hadn't been watching, hadn't seen it coming. He was nearly on top of another boulder and he winced, waiting for the next smashing blow.

"Don't worry. I have you." Small arms wrapped around him from behind. "Lean against me. I will carry you to shore."

Iain was relieved to have found her, but at the same time he wanted to laugh out loud. He couldn't, though. It hurt too much. And his nose and mouth were full of water.

"*I* will carry us to shore," he corrected. "I'm saving *you*."

"Say what you will," she cried into his ear. "But let's not waste any strokes or I'll have to drown you where you are and take off on my own."

Iain heard her grunt as she swung him around and wedged the two of them against another fallen tree trunk. He glanced toward the shore. It looked like the water was somewhat of an eddy beyond the tree. They were not too far from the water's edge. He turned in her arms. Marion was shivering badly.

"Hold on to me."

"I *am* holding on to you," she shouted. "If I wasn't, you'd probably crack that thick head of yours on one of these rocks."

"Have it your way. I'll hold on to you." He looped one arm tightly around Marion and used his other to start inching along the tree toward the shore.

Whatever strength Marion had left in her was quickly draining away as they tried to free themselves of the river. Iain wasn't much better. His shoulder throbbed. The cold had seeped into his bones, and a terrible sleepiness was beginning to cloud his brain. He knew that was a bad sign. They managed to work together, though, until their feet could touch the riverbed. A moment later, they dragged themselves out of the water.

Once ashore, she sank down on the cold ground and gathered her knees against her chest. She was shivering uncontrollably, and her teeth chattered incessantly.

"I don't know how far the water carried us," he said. "I don't think there is much chance we could find our way back to my men in the dark."

"I'm c-c-cold," she whispered brokenly.

Iain looked about them. They were both soaked. She had lost her cloak somewhere in the river. A stiff, chilly breeze was blowing from the west. He reached for her hand. "Come with me."

"I c-c-can't walk. I'm too c-c-cold."

"We won't be going too far, just out of the wind."

Marion allowed him to pull her up. Iain wasn't armed, and between his bruised shoulder and Marion, he felt very vulnerable. The terrain was rough upstream, and the briars grew right to the river's edge. It would be hard going.

"Maybe we should stay where we are. Your men should come after us."

"They will, but not before tomorrow morning."

"Do you really think they'd wait that long? We're missing, by his wounds."

"We're also newlyweds on our wedding night."

Her jaw dropped clear to her chest.

"You mentioned privacy a while back. Well, they may just think we have escaped into the woods for some...well, privacy. They would expect it, I should think."

She took a step back. "Is this what *you* were expecting, too? Is that why you came after me, you unfeeling brute?"

He shook his head. "I came after you because I wanted to make sure you wouldn't get lost or get hurt or jump in the river and try to drown yourself."

"I wouldn't have fallen into the river at all if it wasn't for you. You p-p-practically pushed me."

Iain forced back his words, thinking on his promise of getting along with her.

"Come on, vixen." A boulder-strewn hill to their right looked like a possible place where a cave or an overhang of some sort might provide shelter for the night. He tugged in that direction.

"S-s-so you're not denying it. You planned this," she said, still shivering.

He decided to let her have her way. "Absolutely. All of it. The water looked fine and I needed a bath. But the real reason I pushed you in was so that I could come after you. I wanted to save you and then take advantage of you."

"But I saved you," she corrected, digging in her heels and turning to him.

"Of course," he said, facing her. "And because of that, now *you* get to take advantage of *me*."

She stared at him for a long moment. Then he took her arm and they continued to climb the hill toward the most likely boulders. They moved side by side in silence until Iain was surprised to hear a small chuckle escape her lips. He gave Marion a side glance. She looked amused.

"And what is going through that troublesome mind of yours now?"

"I wish I knew how to take advantage of you." She crinkled her nose, looking up at him. "That would have been a perfect punishment considering everything that you have put me through."

Iain smiled at her innocence. They were definitely talking about two different things. "Perhaps over time, you will learn how," he said, bringing her freezing hand to his lips and pressing a kiss to her palm.

She fell silent and shyly withdrew her hand. Iain let her hand go, knowing that it was only a matter of time before the ice melted.

He helped her climb up the side of a large boulder. Just as he had hoped, there was a small protective clearing behind it. "We are spending the night here," he told her, helping her down ahead of himself.

"I'm *really* cold," she said through chattering teeth.

"I will try to make a fire. That should help things."

"But everything is so wet."

"Leave that to me. I'll be right back."

Iain left Marion there and went back to the riverside where he had seen some broken branches and deadwood that looked dry enough to use. By the time he came back a few minutes later, he was surprised to find her blowing gently on a small fire she had made of twigs and leaves from the gorse and heather dotting the hillside. He was impressed. She was certainly not helpless. He noticed that she had even made the fire in the perfect spot, a small corner mostly protected by the outcropping.

"G-g-good timing," she called to him. "I used whatever I could find, but it wasn't much. It's about to go out."

He crouched beside her. She held her hands near the flames as he began to feed branches to the fire. She was still shivering.

"You're cold."

"I'm not only cold. I'm hungry, too."

"I'm afraid if I turn my back for a moment, I'll find you roasting a wild pig."

"I have hunted boar before. Skye has many. I know how to dress them for roasting, too."

Iain smiled.

"You don't believe me."

"After today, I'd be a fool to doubt you," Iain answered.

She edged closer to the fire. "Do you think I'm accomplished, then?"

Iain studied her more closely. Her dress was soaked. She had streaks of dirt on her face. The ringlets of dark hair hanging around her shoulders still dripped with water from the river. She was a mess, by anyone's standards. And yet, she'd really done a minimal amount of complaining.

"Indeed, lass," Iain answered. "I'll give you that. You're an accomplished woman...in many things."

Marion nodded, appearing pleased.

"Who taught you to swim and ride a horse and make a fire in the open...and the rest of these things?"

"Some of it I learned as a child, of course, while I still lived at Fleet Tower. My father treated me no different than if I were his son."

Iain remembered this much, himself. Even as a wee child, Marion was allowed to accompany the Earl of Fleet on the hunt, to watch and even mimic the training of the McCall warriors, and to travel on visits to Edinburgh and other places. As far as Iain could tell, Marion had never been limited by any rules, and she'd been allowed everywhere. As a result, of course, she'd been a terror to anyone outside of her family.

"The rest I learned on the Isle of Skye," she added.

"With the prioress's blessing, of course," Iain said dryly.

"To her dismay, you mean." Marion rolled her eyes and shook her head. "The prioress didn't approve of the young women of the convent roaming the island with hunters from Dunvegan Castle. She also punished me numerous times for hiking the hills on my own and for getting lost in the woods for days at a time."

The larger pieces of the deadwood were now catching fire, and the yellow-and-orange flames were causing steam to rise off their clothes. Marion's hair was too close to it, though, and Iain reached over and tucked the hair behind her ear. She let him, but then tucked the other side behind her ear.

"And did you get lost in the woods frequently?"

She shrugged. "Not really lost. I made many friends in the villages and at Dunvegan. Life was not the most exciting at the priory, so when folk I was visiting asked me to stay for supper, I did. Then, if it were too late to get back to the priory, I might have stayed...or spent a night or two in a tree."

Iain now understood why the prioress was so agreeable in expediting the marriage ceremony. "You were a great deal of trouble for her, weren't you?"

"That is who I am. I am trouble." Her eyes sparkled with mischief when she looked at him. "There is still time for you to change your mind. Blessing or not, we've not consummated this marriage."

"But I will not be changing my mind," he said, leaning against the boulder. He unclasped his broach. Without hesitation, he then peeled off his shirt.

"What are you doing?" she asked, her shock registering on her face.

"It will dry faster this way." Iain spread the shirt on a smaller rock next to him and then reached for Marion again. "Come here."

"No, I'm cold." She crawled closer to the fire.

Iain noticed how hard she was trying not to look at his chest and his arms. "There is no wind. It is warmer here." He tugged on her arm. She lost her balance, and he pulled her to his side.

"You're a bold and arrogant brute," Marion scolded as she settled herself next to him. They were hip to hip. She continued to shiver, and he knew her heart was not really in her words. All was not the same as it had been earlier today.

"And you, m'lady, are incapable of following directions, even when you know it's good for you." Iain wrapped an arm around her shoulders, drawing her against him. His other hand felt her wet sleeves. "You need to shed this dress."

"You've lost your mind."

He picked up a fistful of her skirt and squeezed. A stream of water splashed on the ground. He touched her face. It felt like ice. The same was true with her hands. "Between the heat of the fire and the breeze, your dress will dry before the night is over. You need to get out of that dress before catching your death."

She shook her head stubbornly.

"You will do it, or I will take it off for you."

"You will *not* force me."

Iain leaned over her menacingly. "I didn't drag you out of that river to have you die on me somewhere between here and Fleet Tower. I will certainly force you to do *something* if I think it's necessary."

"Tyrant," she shot back, moving away from him and inching closer to the fire. "And you didn't."

"Didn't what?"

"Drag me out of the river," she muttered. "I dragged *you*."

Iain watched Marion's back as she pulled at the laces of her dress. His mind strayed to imaginings of a different night, a more comfortable arrangement, and Marion seducing him with these very same actions. It was an attractive thought, and he felt the familiar stirring in his loins.

"I can help you with that."

"You can help me by going away and giving me some privacy," she said in a frustrated tone.

He didn't need to go. But Iain actually felt some sympathy for her, so he stood up and made his way back toward the river to collect some more wood. The air was crisp, and he needed to keep Marion warm tonight... one way or the other.

By the time he came back, he was reasonably warm from the climb up the hill. Nearing the outcropping, he could see her dress spread out on two sticks beside his shirt. Her shoes and stockings were arranged neatly beside the fire. Marion had tucked herself into the corner where she'd been before. She was a bundle of long exposed arms and a thin linen chemise that she had pulled over her legs. She'd pulled her knees into her chest. Her chin lifted as he drew near.

"Do *not* look at me."

"I'm afraid that is impossible. I like looking at you." He put more pieces on the fire. Her shivering was worse than before. Iain moved beside her and sat down as the wood started to catch.

"Not so close," she said in a low voice.

"Not close enough." Iain pulled her into his arms and was immediately concerned. She didn't put up any fight at all, which meant the cold was getting to her or she was already dead.

"Don't touch me," she whispered. Well, she wasn't dead. But she still wasn't fighting.

He ignored her and ran his hands up and down the cold, clammy skin of her arms and back. The chemise was still wet. "You should have taken this off, too."

"I couldn't sit here naked."

"Why not?" he asked, smiling as she laid her face against his chest. Her hands pressed against his skin, trying to absorb his warmth.

"You know why. I wouldn't want to give you any wrong ideas."

No wrong ideas were necessary. Iain glanced down at his own lap. He was past mild stirrings. Her touch had him erect. Marion must have noticed where he was looking, for she immediately tried to pull out of his embrace.

"No, stay." His fingers fisted in her wet hair. He held Marion's head against his chest. When she stopped struggling, he eased his grip, and she looked up at him. He fought the urge to kiss her lips. "I told you I won't do anything you don't want me to do."

He could see the look of hesitation in her face, but in the end the warmth of Iain's body must have been too comfortable. She didn't move away.

"How's your shoulder?"

"It's sore as the blazes. But I think I'll live."

"That's too bad." She rubbed her cheek gently against his shoulder. "I think I'll try to go to sleep."

He nodded, watching her as she nestled herself closer against him, tucking one hand under her chin. Her other hand remained on his stomach.

Marion was exhausted, and it didn't take too long before her breathing slowed, her eyelids fluttered, and her legs jumped a couple of times as she fell asleep.

All Iain could do, though, was to watch the partially clothed woman who was his wife. His feelings were changing. He no longer was angry at her, and he no longer dreaded what trouble she would come up with next in her quest to torment him. Instead, he realized he was actually looking forward to it.

6

THERE WAS NO BEACH, no shoreline, no islands. For as far as Marion could see, there was nothing to relieve the vast expanse of water around her. In every direction, all she saw was the unending blue and gray of a choppy sea. Somewhere in the distance, the waters blended in with similar colors of the sky.

She didn't know how she got here. She had no clue how long she had been swimming. Her arms and legs, though, were so tired. They felt heavy, as if a millstone were tied to each. She felt her chin beginning to slip beneath the surface. Her body rose on a huge swell, the white crest of the wave slapping her hard in the face. She looked ahead at the next cresting wave as her body slid down into the trough. She was so tired.

No one wanted her. No one was coming to save her. There was no purpose in fighting. Her fate was sealed. She might as well end it all now, she thought in despair. The next wave would surely finish her anyway.

She saw the wave coming. It was higher than the last. It was as tall as the walls of Fleet Tower. She kept her eyes open but ceased trying to swim. Her body was not rising on the swell. As the wave approached, she saw it start to crest over her. She saw it ready to crash down on her head.

She held her breath, but just as sprays of water reached her, strong hands reached up from beneath the surface of the sea, taking hold of her waist and drawing her under.

As the water churned around her from the force of the wave, Marion felt herself being drawn ever deeper. The surface was strewn with bright foam far above her, and she struggled to get back up for air.

Breathe, her rescuer's voice whispered.

She paused, stunned by the sound of the voice in her ear. The voice was so confident, so reassuring.

She breathed in and found she could breathe like a fish.

She turned around to look at her rescuer. Half man, half fish...the creature's magnificent muscled chest drew her gaze. The sinews rippled as she was drawn closer to him. She looked up into his face.

It was Iain.

Startled, Marion opened her eyes at once. She took a breath to test the air. Wisps of steam escaped her lips. She stared at the blue sky above. The loud twittering of a bird drew her eye. The wee noisy beast was sitting on some gorse not far from the boulder.

"You need your feathers plucked," she murmured.

With the sound of her own voice, reality began to dawn on her slowly but surely.

She was not floating in any sea but lying on top of hard and uneven ground. She was no longer wet. The skin of her face was nearly numb from the cold, but the rest of her was comfortable and warm. There was, however, the small problem of the weight that was about equal to a boulder sitting on her chest and trapping her arms and legs.

She tried to lift her head but found her efforts to be futile.

Now fully awake, she recognized the source of the warmth and the weight. Iain's body was draped across hers. His rough, unshaven face was buried in her hair, his breath tickling the skin on her neck. His legs had hers trapped between theirs. His hand, flattened against her stomach, was a source of incredible heat.

The image from her dream danced in her head. She had believed him enough in a dream to do the impossible. She had breathed beneath the sea. She had trusted him.

She looked around at his powerful arm, his muscular back, the wide shoulders. She had been attracted to him in her sleep. She couldn't lie to herself. He was a very attractive man. For years, anytime the prioress was at odds with her, Marion had dreamed of Iain coming for her. Taking her away to where she belonged, where she was wanted.

And he *had* come. Perhaps, she thought with a frown, it wasn't too late. Perhaps she was creating a ruckus for nothing. Rather than dwelling on what she found distasteful about the situation, perhaps she should focus a wee bit on the positives.

Iain Armstrong was a very handsome man. He was also a patient one, when he chose to be. Marion knew he had an excellent sense of humor. Aside from these, she could add courage, independence, intelligence, and dozens of other virtues. It was true that he was an excellent catch for any woman of marriageable age. Too bad for them, she thought somewhat smugly. He was already *her* husband. And that was no surprise, either. This marriage had been arranged long before she was old enough to know of it.

Marion tried to clear her thoughts. These things were too serious to be thinking while she lay half naked in Iain's embrace.

She turned her head and saw her dress and his shirt where they'd left them last night. The fire looked to be out. There was no escaping the human blanket without awakening him.

She tried to think of some clever way to escape, but her stomach immediately sounded the alarm, growling loud enough to awaken the dead. Iain stirred. Stretched. His body rolled more fully on top of hers. His hand moved over her chemise, caressing her skin with it.

A feeling like lightning shot through her, making her cold and hot at the same time. Instead of pushing him away, Marion found herself frozen with anticipation. They were husband and wife, she reminded herself again. It was perfectly understandable that she would want to know where his hand might drift to next. It was natural curiosity.

His hand drifted toward her breast. She caught his wrist.

"Enough pretending, brute," she told him. "I know you're awake."

His head slowly lifted off her neck. His blue eyes were sleepy; his hair stood up in every direction. He desperately needed to shave. Despite all his flaws, though, he looked more handsome than he had any right to. There were butterflies raging a full-fledged battle in her stomach.

"Good morning," he whispered, keeping his hand where it was, just beneath her breast. His thumb moved in a small circle on her ribs. "How did you sleep?"

"I couldn't sleep," she lied. "Not a wink."

"Why is that?"

"You're far too heavy. I couldn't breathe."

A smile danced on his lips. "You'll get used to it."

He rolled to his side before she could answer, and Marion immediately felt the bracing cold on her warm skin. She tried to get up, but he didn't let her, instead draping one leg tighter over her thighs, entrapping her.

"Not yet. Your dress is still wet."

"How do you know?"

"This thing is still wet." He put his hand on the chemise where it draped across her hip.

Maybe it was a bit damp. Marion caught his other hand, keeping it from straying. She felt that fluttery feeling in her stomach again.

"It will have to do," she said. "We have to get up and dress. Your men could arrive anytime now, and we cannot have them see us like this."

"You're right about that. No one can see you like this...but me."

He was staring at her chest. She followed the direction of his gaze and was appalled to find the chemise pulled down and too much of her breasts exposed. She immediately pulled up the neckline, but things didn't look much better. The linen undergarment was too thin, and the tips of her breasts too dark. She struggled to get up, but he held her firmly in place. His arm wrapped around her back and pulled her closer to his side.

"Why are you fighting it?"

"Fighting what?"

"Our marriage," he said seriously, looking into her eyes.

"Didn't you hear anything I told you yesterday?"

"No," he said.

She landed a halfhearted punch on his chest. "And why is that?"

"Because you were throwing a temper tantrum...much like the ones you used to throw as a child."

"What I did yesterday was no temper tantrum. I was angry."

"How are you today?" he asked.

"I'm still angry."

"Why?"

"Why?" Marion repeated incredulously as she raised herself on one elbow. "You left me in that convent for twelve long years. No visitors, no family, no trips home even for short visits. Twelve bloody years," she drawled, leaning over him. "Don't you think I should be angry at you over that?"

"You probably should be angry." Iain reached for a strand of her hair and a defector curl looped around his finger. "But I had my reasons."

"What were they?"

"You will find out soon enough."

"That is hardly an acceptable answer. I want to hear your reasons now." She shoved at his chest again, this time with more vigor, and he rolled on his back. Marion had forgotten he was holding her curls captive, so she had to go with him.

A roguish smile broke across his lips. "You're very physical. We'll have a lot of fun with that."

Fun? Marion thought. *Doing what?* She shook her head, forcing herself to not get distracted by his comment. "Tell me your reasons for banishing me to Skye."

"Very well. Our families, to begin with."

She shook her head. "I have stopped blaming our families for putting me in this predicament of having to marry you. I only blame you. It's time you took responsibility for your actions. You're at fault for everything."

He put a hand behind his head. The other one continued to play with her hair. "Say what you will. But however horrible living in a convent was for the past twelve years, you would have fared much worse at Blackthorn Hall."

She winced. "Your mother never liked me."

"She never disliked you. She's just terrified of your family and likes to keep her distance."

"You should have listened to her and stayed away, too." She shuddered. "She'll probably try to drown our firstborn child, thinking him mad for crying."

He smiled. "No chance."

His smile was too boyish and distracting. Marion realized she had said the wrong thing. She'd admitted that they might have a future together. Even have a child. She forced her face into a frown. "I would have never stayed at Blackthorn Hall, anyway. I belong at Fleet Tower."

"Not the way your family has been behaving."

"You told me all your lies about my aunts and uncle getting older, yesterday. I don't believe any of it."

"Your aunts are fine. They're harmless enough."

"But they talk too much," she finished for him. She tugged hard enough to free her hair. She jumped to her feet. "That's it. You're doing it again. Just because my aunts are not as silent and dull as your family. So what if they talk? Well, I'll have you know that I like to talk, too. I even talk to myself, and to the trees, and to animals. I even talk to *you*. I must be insane."

Marion started pulling her dress over her head. He was right; it was still damp. Marion didn't care, though.

"I have no problem with them."

"But my uncle is another matter, is that it?"

He said nothing.

"What does it matter if he pretends to be someone else? Perhaps the rest of us should be a little more like him. Live in our dreams. Actually be happy!"

"I'm telling you that people are talking about Sir William. They're beginning to fear him. He is much louder than he was when you were a wee sprite. Your uncle is now completely oblivious to the possibility of being anyone but William Wallace. Sword drawn and calling them 'bloody English,' he's chased many servants from the tower."

She shoved her arms into the sleeves. "It must have been their own fault, then. He was not always so contentious. When I was there, we all knew that, even in his worst moments Sir William wouldn't hurt a mouse."

"He doesn't recognize most people he meets." He sat up and stretched his legs out before him. "As fine a place as Fleet Tower is, Marion, there is no servant left who will stay there after dark. The McCall villagers who work there refuse to stay at the tower house. They're all afraid he'll murder them while they sleep. Your aunts are forced to take care of your uncle all on their own."

"I cannot believe you're telling me this now."

"You aunts are not as strong as they once were. Lady Margaret's hearing is getting worse. The same goes for her eyesight. Lady Judith, well..." He reached for his shirt. "They are a credit to your family, though. Despite their own troubles, your aunts visit the needy and sick in the village almost daily. They think nothing of all that work."

"I should have been there to help them." She started pulling the laces tight. "But that will be rectified as soon as I get back."

"You'll be staying at Blackthorn Hall with me."

"I think not," she snapped. She bent down to put on her stockings and shoes. "My home is Fleet Tower."

"You're my wife, Marion," he said, standing up. "You're the new mistress of Blackthorn. There are new responsibilities that will go along with your position. You can only visit Fleet Tower. Our son...in time...will inherit Fleet Tower and Blackthorn, as well. He can decide where he--"

"You've said yourself that my aunts have no one. I'll not leave them alone there. I will be staying at Fleet Tower."

"I wanted to bring this up later, but since you insist on pressing the issue..." He yanked on his shirt. "I've found a safe place where we can send Sir William. He'll be well cared for. And your aunts can go back to their normal life, with cooks and servants and whoever else they want to make the last years of their lives comfortable."

"A safe place like the one you sent me to?" she asked, looking up at him. He was only a step away. She felt like striking him.

"It's a monastery. Cracketford Abbey. Brother Luke has already spoken to them. They're known for—"

He didn't finish, as she delivered a sharp kick to his shin and walked away.

7

"You don't even know where you're going."

Iain might as well have directed his words at the rocks or the heather. They certainly were having no effect on her. Arms swinging at her sides, her dress beginning to steam in the cold air, Marion marched along the riverbank, trying to ignore him. Her hair was a tangle of dark curls that swept from side to side across her back as she walked. Her beautiful face was glowing from the exertion.

As he strode along with her, it occurred to him that she'd grown up to be quite a woman.

"We need to do something about your temperament," Iain told her. "We have been married only a day, and I already feel as battered as old Noah."

She looked straight ahead, but he could see the color rise into her cheeks. "You started this."

"I had no intention of saying anything about your family. You wanted to know."

She stopped and whirled on him. "And you think I should be happy about seeing my poor, harmless uncle sent away?"

"Marion—"

She interrupted before he could explain. "Perhaps you think that would be a fine wedding present for me?"

"Let me—"

"I'm only surprised that you didn't arrange it so that he'd be gone before I arrived at Fleet Tower."

"Listen to me, Marion." He put a hand on her shoulder. She shook it off. He took hold of her shoulders. She was not going to shake him off. "If you'd listen a moment longer, you would understand that I have *not* made any firm plans about Sir William. What I told you was that I have found a safe place where we can send your uncle. *We* can," he repeated. "You deserve to be a part of that decision...when we see fit."

"You must be daft," she shot at him. "You think I would send away my own kin. That will never happen."

"You're being hasty. You have not seen him for a long time."

"All the more reason for me to be more feeling toward him. I'm not a heartless brute, like you. You think he is too much trouble for my aunts. Well, then, I'll take over his care. Fleet Tower is his home. I'll do whatever needs to be done, so that he can remain there."

"You speak without having any idea what you—"

"And Fleet Tower is my home, too. So don't ever think that I'll live at Blackthorn Hall. That will simply not happen..."

She continued to pour out her anger, and she was certainly not short on words. Iain let her. She was like a wounded boar, frantic and bleeding, spinning and charging at anything that moved around her.

He should have followed his instinct and not said anything until Marion saw her uncle for herself. There were times when Iain simply stood in awe when it came to Sir William's peculiarities.

Before heading to Skye to bring Marion back, Iain had stopped with Brother Luke at Fleet Tower to pay his respects to the aunts and tell them of his plans. As he and his men rode from the courtyard, however, the laird was surprised to see Sir William on the thatched roof of the stables, decked out in kilt, sword, chain mail, and blue face paint. As Iain raised his hand in greeting, William returned the salute—turning, bending over, and raising his kilt to give them a good long view of his portly, lily-white arse. Then, they had not even left the McCall farms behind them when a crofter approached the travelers to complain that Sir William had shot arrows at his sons from the castle parapet the day before as the lads tried to deliver cheese to the kitchens. There were too many stories.

Iain had hoped that Marion would change her opinion once she saw her uncle.

She paused for a breath and he seized the opportunity to put in a few words.

"I regret I mentioned any of it. I'll not speak of this again until we arrive at Fleet Tower."

"You're almost correct," she retorted. "We'll not speak of this *ever* again."

Her tone sparked a strong desire in him to put both his hands around her neck, but he fought back the urge.

"You're in no position to be making demands, minx," he said firmly. "If you want something, then you better be prepared to hear what *I* have to say."

She crossed her arms against her chest. "I'm in no mood for idle prattle."

"Then put yourself in the mood," Iain growled as he loomed over her. "I have been patient, considerate, and more than understanding of your predicament."

She responded with an unladylike snort.

"But I tell you now that my patience has grown thin. Unless you concede to *one* demand, all of that liberality is going to come to a halt, as of right now. You're my wife. That makes you mine now to do with as I wish."

"Ha!" Marion retorted.

"The same goes with your affairs and with the future of your family. And with anything else that has to do with you and the McCall clan. I'll now be making all the decisions. You'll have no say in any of it," he said firmly. "So if you believe I have been unfeeling and brutish in my treatment of you since yesterday, from now on, you'll find me a hundred times worse. And the same thing applies to my decisions about your aunts and your uncle. And where I decide they will spend the rest of their lives will be my choice. No one else's. Understand?"

Men three times her size would have conceded in the face of his anger. Iain Armstrong was a dangerous man when riled, and he was now good and riled. Naturally, Marion showed no such inclination. Cheeks flushed, dark eyes blazing, she met his stare, arms still crossed against her chest.

"Do you have anything to say to that?"

She continued to glare at him.

"Make your choice. But know that there are consequences."

She paused for another moment, and when she spoke, her tone did not convey a note of concession. "One demand?"

"One."

"Very well. I will agree to one, and only *one*, bloody demand. And in return, you will forget all this other nonsense," she told him firmly. "I *will* be involved in any decisions having to do with the future of my family and their whereabouts."

Iain gazed intently into her face. It sounded as if he had won. But had he? He studied her, trying to decide if he should press her further.

"One demand," he repeated. "And no resistance whatsoever."

She shrugged. He released her but didn't move.

"Very well," Iain said. "This is it. You will abide by the marriage vow you took."

Her eyes narrowed. "You expect me to become submissive to you?"

"I don't entertain much hope in that regard," Iain explained. "But I do expect you to respect me and our marriage and treat our union as permanent."

"And that is all?"

"And in that you will share my bed and bear me children."

The color in her cheeks became a few shades darker.

"You made a promise to me back at the priory," she said in a low voice. "Are you going to break that promise?"

"I will not force you to do anything. It's you who must willingly put an end to the ridiculous notion that our marriage counts for nothing."

Her gaze flickered from his face. For the first time, Iain sensed indecision in her. The devil in him made him push further. He reached out and took her chin in the palm of his hand, raising her eyes to his again.

"And we'll consummate our union before we reach Fleet Tower," he said.

———

From a bluff looking down over the valley and the tumbling river, Brother Luke watched the newlyweds. They appeared to be having a pleasant discussion.

Iain and Marion's disappearance last night had been perceived as a very positive step. For both of them to spend the night away from the camp boded well, in the clergyman's opinion. As dawn broke, though, one of the men had found Iain's cloak and sword beside the river, and Brother Luke had become concerned. At first, he feared that the two had been attacked and taken. Since there was no sign of struggle, though, and no tracks leaving the riverbank, it was decided that the two had somehow been swept away by the river. Luke couldn't see Iain willingly going for a swim at this time of year.

Luke and the others had been searching since first light, working their way down the rough terrain along the river. Leaving most of the men waiting at the riverside, Brother Luke and two of the Armstrong warriors had climbed a narrow path on foot to the top of this bluff to get a better view of the countryside. Their effort had been immediately rewarded; they spotted Marion and Iain right away. Luke had no luck drawing their attention; the two of them were too far away.

"Shall I take their two horses and go down to them?" Alan, the laird's most trusted warrior, finally asked.

Luke looked up at the blue sky. There was a slight chill in the air, but the weather was still quite good. He looked down the valley beyond where Iain and Marion stood. No travelers were visible in any direction that he could see. The Highlands were so beautiful, and so wild. He spotted, at the base of one gorse-covered hill, a farmhouse, but there were no sheep or shaggy red cattle grazing near it. There was no smoke rising from any hearth. The place appeared deserted.

"I see no reason to rush," he replied with a smile at the men. "Those two might just benefit from more time alone together. We shall just take our time and circle around them—you can see where the terrain is less wild—and see if we can catch up to them by nightfall. By that cottage, I should think."

Alan shook his head doubtfully. "But what about food or weapons or dry clothing?"

"We'll be near enough to respond in case of any real danger. As for the rest of it, they have obviously survived the night. A few hours more will only do them good, my friend. The sustenance they each need right now is more for the... er, soul than for the body."

The Armstrong warrior stared at him as if Brother Luke were reciting the Psalms in Latin. But the cleric didn't care. As far as he could see, all was well. Iain and Marion had not killed each other during the night.

Perhaps, Luke thought, *we can hope for more.*

8

A PEBBLE she'd picked up in one of her shoes dug into her foot. Her skirt insisted on getting caught on every bramble bush she passed. Branches hung down and poked Marion in the head anytime she walked beneath a tree. The way her dress felt so coarse rubbing against her neck and shoulders, a bucket of sand, at least, had to be trapped in it. And this was all on top of being so hungry she was sure she'd pass out before she walked another ten steps.

The silver lining in the cloud she was tramping through, Marion thought vaguely, was that she might just die before she had to worry about Iain's expectations about her and her "wifely duties."

"Your men's dislike of you must be even worse than how I feel," Marion noted, dragging herself up yet another hill. They'd left the river an hour ago to find an easier way back to the camp.

"What makes you say that?" The blackguard didn't even seem to be winded, never mind hungry or tired.

"I cannot think of any other reason for them not being able to find us, even though it's now well past midday."

"It might have nothing to do with me and everything with you, I should think," Iain answered. "Perhaps they were insulted by your treatment of them after our wedding."

"My insult was directed at you, and everyone knew it."

Iain held back the branches of a spiny shrub and let Marion go by.

"And how would they know that, Marion? Do you think most of these Armstrong warriors remember you?"

She wasn't going to feel guilty. "Brother Luke knows me well enough. He must have explained it all to them."

"Short of all the complaints he heard from the prioress, what my uncle remembers about you is that you were a spoiled child that everyone did their best to stay away from. Even as a wee thing, you had a formidable reputation, and you haven't changed anyone's opinion on this journey."

"You make me sound like a monster."

"I don't make you out to be anything. However these men see you is your own doing."

As torturous as it was, Marion walked faster. She didn't want to hear any more. She was no monster. There were reasons for her actions. One had to care about her enough to see and understand. None of these people cared at all.

Iain didn't.

She wanted to be with her family. She was going back to Fleet Tower, and she wanted to enjoy that thought. This was what she'd dreamed of for years. Now she had to make it work. Even if some sacrifices needed to be made.

Oh, Lord. She didn't want to think about that.

There was no getting away from him. Iain caught up to her again. "As we draw near the Borders, a couple of my men will ride ahead to bring the news of our approach. Now, I suggest you make some small effort to win everyone's affection before we arrive, or it will be a rather chilly reception at Blackthorn Hall. Perhaps you don't know this, but men gossip more than women."

"Everything that you say is based on the assumption that they find us before we die," she said, the thought giving her some comfort.

"They will," he said confidently.

"Too bad," she murmured.

The sound of the water reached her ears. Marion pushed through a thicket of gorse and found herself standing beside the river again. She looked up at a rocky promontory. The river dropped in a series of steps through this gorge. She hardly recalled being carried down the rushing water through this. At any rate, there was no path that they could travel on. Marion glanced up at the jagged boulders and shook her head.

"I cannot do this anymore. I don't know why we don't wait right here for your men to find us."

Hearing no answer, Marion turned around. Iain was nowhere to be seen. For a moment, a knot of fear lodged itself in her throat, and her heart pounded in her chest.

A pebble struck her on the head.

"Ow!" Looking up, she saw him a few feet above her, climbing the rocks with the agility of a goat.

"Are you leaving without me?" she called up at him.

He gave no answer and continued to climb. Marion decided he wouldn't leave her. He was made of hardier stock than to give up on her after a day.

Knotted vines of wild grapes were growing near the edge of river, and when she spotted them, she stopped dead. Food. She walked to them and searched in between the leaves for the fruit. The large clusters she found could not be more delightful to her eye if they were made of gold. She picked a handful and stuffed some in her mouth. They were juicy and sweet and perfectly ripe. Marion pulled off more clusters, gathering them in her skirts until she'd stripped the vine bare.

Her face and arms were scratched when she turned back to the rock wall. Iain was climbing back down to her.

"I found us some breakfast," she called up excitedly to him.

He paused on a rock halfway down. "I found a place with a roof where we can stay until my men reach us."

"Walls, too?" she asked.

"From a distance, it appears to have walls. It looks like a deserted croft just down into the valley."

"How far? I cannot walk any farther."

"You can. It's not too far. We only have to work our way around this bluff." He jumped to the ground.

Marion turned to show him her treasure. "Breakfast first. I picked these for us."

She saw him stare at her face and hair and not at the grapes.

"I know I'm a mess. But there is nothing I can do about it now. Eat some. They're good."

"You eat them. You're hungrier than I."

"I cannot stand it when you try to be nice." She walked toward him, chose a large grape, and brought it to his lips. "These are so juicy. They taste like heaven on your tongue."

She held the grape to his lips, and he took a bite. The juice dripped on her fingers. A tight knot of heat formed in Marion's belly when he took her hand and brought it to his mouth to finish the rest of the grape. His warmth was suddenly all around her. She stared at the chiseled lines of his face, the fullness of his lips. She looked up into his blue eyes, and her heart drummed madly.

Marion pulled back her hand, despite the attraction she was feeling. She was a jumble of contradictions. There was something in his eyes. His face. A look of barely constrained danger. Her insides were in turmoil. As nervous as he made her, she wanted to unleash it, feel it, taste the fire. She took another grape and reached for his lips.

He caught her wrist. "There is something other than grapes that I crave to taste right now."

"This is all I—"

Marion was barely conscious of his face descending to her, but suddenly his mouth was pressed to hers. His lips were stealing her breath away. She moaned with shock and delight when his tongue delved between her lips.

The hem of the skirt dropped and the fruit with it. Forgotten were the fruit, the hunger, the discomfort of the dress and shoes and everything else. All she could think of was Iain, his mouth, and the delicious warmth that was spreading through her. All she could do was to hold on to him, as her legs had lost their will to support her.

"You *are* hungry," she heard herself whispering as his lips moved around her face, tasting, nibbling.

"Starved," he said hoarsely. His mouth sank to the side of her neck.

His attention felt so right. Heavenly. She wrapped her arms around him, tilting her head to the side as his mouth traveled down her neck.

"I dreamed you'd be just this," he whispered into her ear.

"A monster?"

"Hardly."

"Something horrible, then?" Marion asked, smiling.

"Passionate, beautiful, full of life. And you are mine. My wife."

Marion, holding him tight, looked up into Iain's handsome face. What had happened? What had changed? Something inside her felt so different. She welcomed his attention. No one had ever kissed her before. She loved everything that he was doing to her.

"I'm your wife," she repeated, for the first time accepting the vow.

He kissed her again. This time tenderly, encouraging her to explore. It was a fascinating thing to experience so many tastes and textures in the simple joining of their mouths. Marion let her curiosity guide her actions. She touched the rough beard growing on his chin and face. His lips were firm and yet soft. She rubbed her mouth against his. Inside of his mouth was an abundance of heat. She reached with her tongue and mimicked what he had done to her before, tasting, rubbing.

Her entire body tingled. It had come alive, and she felt wetness in unmentionable places. She was melting. She pulled back to catch her breath and she smiled. "Why didn't you tell me that I would like kissing? We could have done some of this before."

He laughed and stole another kiss before tugging on her hand. "Come with me."

"Where are you taking me?"

"To that cottage I saw from the top of this hill."

"What for?" She planted her feet, eyeing the grapes where they fell.

"To be more comfortable while we wait."

Marion looked up. There was a mischievous twinkle in his eyes. "Is that all?"

"No. I intend to show you a few things more that you may like." He tugged on her hand again.

Entranced, excited, her body followed. "Can't this wait until we are at the Borders?"

He shook his head from side to side. "I cannot have you complaining to me that I've slighted you."

Her throat became dry. "About what?"

"About making love."

Her belly tightened. Her heart pounded in her ears. A flash of panic washed through her.

"But Iain, I don't know anything about it." That was the absolute truth. Back at Fleet Tower, she had been too young to know what love-making entailed. At the priory, she'd certainly seen animals mating, but the nuns didn't consider it a suitable topic of discussion.

"I'll teach you," he said, continuing to lead her down the path.

"I'm a slow learner."

Iain gathered her more closely to his side. He kissed her hand. "Don't be afraid. Trust me in this. You'll enjoy it."

"What if I don't? What if *you* didn't? You're just assuming that making love to me will be the same as...as with some other woman you've known." As they entered a grove of oak trees, Marion planted her feet in dirt again, and he stopped. Actually, it bothered her to think of Iain giving this kind of attention to any other woman. "How many times have you done this before?"

"This is the first time I've been married."

"That's not what I mean."

"I know what you mean. Not many."

"How many times since we've been betrothed to each other?"

"I haven't been keeping track. That is nothing you should concern yourself with right now."

"I *am* concerned," Marion said sharply.

"Then there were none. There were no other women. Put it out of your mind."

She didn't believe him. Jealousy bubbled up inside of her. She freed herself from his hold and crossed her arms on her chest. "I don't believe you."

"The number of times is a senseless measure. This is all new to me, too," he continued. "This is a first time for me. This is the first time I'm going to make love to my wife."

Marion thought about that for a long moment. She recalled the scores of young women who used to stare at him and follow him around when she'd been too young to know what their intentions were. "You have experience. I don't. I believe we should wait on this love-making until we are even."

His jaw clenched. "And how do you expect to get this experience?"

She looked around her at the deserted woods. "I don't know, but I'll think of something. Perhaps I might run into someone before reaching the Borders. I think we should wait until—"

Marion gasped as Iain grabbed her by the arm, hauling her against his body. "What are you doing?"

"Does the word 'adultery' ring any bells? You might have heard it once in a while in your religious training."

"Of course, but—"

"No *buts*. You're a married woman. You're *my* woman."

His hands were around her waist, pulling her tightly against him. She could feel something hard pressing against her belly.

"What are you doing?"

"Giving you the experience you long for."

"Here? Now?"

"Here and now."

"But I don't want it from *you*." Her complaint barely escaped her lips before he was kissing her again. She kissed him back with the same intensity.

His hands were all over her back, her buttocks, her sides. A soft moan escaped her throat when he kneaded her breast through the dress. Marion couldn't believe it, but she welcomed the touch. She wanted more. He pushed her back against the solid trunk of a tall oak.

She didn't know what he was going to do. But she was too afraid to ask. She didn't want him to stop, though. Her entire body burned with anticipation. Iain's mouth had become rough again, demanding. His kisses were deeper, more ardent.

She gasped with shock when he lifted her skirts and chemise to her waist and fitted one leg between her thighs.

She managed to break her mouth free. "What are you doing?"

"Ride me, Marion. Let your feelings loose."

Twelve years living in a priory, and there was not one single thought of shyness or caution in her head. Iain was taking her body on a bold, new journey, and she had to follow. He placed her hands around his neck and she tightened her hold. He pressed his muscular thigh into the junction of her legs, and she gasped as the excitement rushed through her.

His mouth stole her breath, and the pressure between her legs increased until she had no choice but to do what he was encouraging her to do. Her hips began to move, and she was riding the sinewy hardness of his thigh.

She freed her mouth to catch her breath. Her back, her head, pressed against the tree. Iain's body surrounded her. She was becoming light-headed and yet she continued to ride. The woods around her were a blur; the pulsing sound of the river filled her ears, pushing her to a destination she couldn't move fast enough to reach.

Vaguely, she felt Iain's fingers on her naked buttocks, pressing her tighter against his loins. "From this day on, I'm the only one who will give you this. And you will be the only one for me."

There was no argument in her. Not after this. Not after what she was feeling now. Still, she was totally unprepared for what was beginning to happen to her. She had no idea about the wave of sensations that was beginning to carry her away.

Iain moved one hand and slid two fingers into the moist cleft between her legs. Marion threw her head back as she felt herself stretch. But as he stroked, her breaths started coming in ragged gasps. As she rose higher and higher, he continued to hold her tightly to him, teasing, stroking.

Her release caused her to twist and arch in his arms. She cried aloud before wrapping herself tightly around his frame. As her shudders of pleasure began to subside, he gathered her tenderly into his chest.

"My wife."

9

Rocks, rocks, and more rocks. It was a field of rock, softened only by the yellow meadow grasses and fading wildflowers that sprouted between the stone outcroppings and small boulders.

The croft was a wee stretch of the legs from the river, and there appeared to be no well. The land around the low cottage was not fit for planting. The rock that had been used to build it had come from a single space where it appeared there must have been some kind of kitchen garden some time ago, but that was overgrown now. The surrounding area looked to be good for raising sheep, if that. But there was not one of those left, either. A crumbling wall that looked older than the cottage stood a short distance away.

Why someone had built the inconveniently situated cottage here was beyond Iain's understanding, but built it they had.

The furnishings that remained in the place were scant and filthy. A dirty pile of straw in one corner, a low stool from which two legs were missing, and a small iron pot with a hole in the bottom the size of his fist. The cottage had to have been sitting empty for at least a year, he thought. Like so many other crofters scratching out a living in the Highlands, Iain figured, these people had finally given up and moved on.

No windows, there was only a hole in the sagging thatched roof to let out the smoke. Still, Iain thought, the place would do quite nicely for the two of them until his men arrived. He stooped and came out through the low doorway to find her standing and staring wide-eyed by the cottage. He let the stiff hide that served as a door flap shut.

"Didn't I tell you to stay hidden in the trees on the far side of the meadow?"

"I was too far away," she told him. "How was I to save you from harm at that distance?"

There were a few things he would have liked to lecture her about such as who would save whom and the danger she put herself in by behaving so. But Iain couldn't bring himself to do any lecturing now. Not after the way she had come apart in his arms in the woods. Not when he wanted her so much.

My God, she was beautiful.

"By the devil," he cursed, pulling her inside the cottage and into his arms. He kissed her long and hard.

"There is no one in here?" she asked, tearing her mouth free.

"We have the place to ourselves."

"Not for long," she said, peering through a tear in the leather door. "I wasn't jesting about saving you. I heard horses."

Iain pushed her behind him and looked out, too. There was no one out there. "It could be my men."

"It could be," she whispered. "But in case it's not them, is there another way out of this place? Some way we could escape?"

He looked at her. "I'm relieved to know that you do have some common sense."

"This is hardly the time to be critical of me," she scolded him. "I have a very uncomfortable feeling about how friendly these riders are."

This was the first time that Iain was seeing her nervous. He decided to trust her instinct.

"How large a group?"

She shook her head. "I didn't see them. But there seemed to be as many horses as there were in yours. They were watering their animals by the river."

"More proof that the mystery riders are Brother Luke and my men. There cannot be too many groups of horsemen here in the Highlands. Even the occasional bands of outlaws up here travel mostly on foot."

She shook her head again. "With the exception of your uncle, your men speak little, treating words like precious gold. This group was downright chatty, and their accents I haven't heard."

"They were close enough for you to hear their voices, and you couldn't get a look at them?"

"One moment, you're mocking me for thinking safely and the next, you're criticizing me for not asking them for a bloody ride!"

He smiled and kissed her softly on the lips. "You did fine."

Iain looked around the cottage for anything he could use as a weapon. The couple of broken legs to the piece of furniture was the extent of it. He peered outside. Near the ruined stone wall, something metal glinted in the sun. Most likely a tool, he thought.

"I want you to stay inside. Don't let anyone see you."

"Where are you going?" Marion clutched his arm.

"I have to find something I can use as a weapon. Also, I need to climb that brae to see for myself what we might be facing."

"I'm coming with you," she suggested.

"You are not, Marion," Iain said curtly. "I don't want them to see you. If they see me, I don't want them to know you're here. We don't want to tempt anyone who might otherwise just pass by."

"You think I'm tempting?" There was a note of genuine surprise in her voice. He caressed her cheek.

"Very much." Iain cleared his head and looked outside again. He hated leaving her. But the landscape around here was too exposed, and he didn't think the woods would be any safer for her if they spotted her. He turned back to her. "If you hear any noise, talk, horses arriving, anything at all, you hide under that old straw. If they think no one is inside, they'd have no reason to linger here."

She glanced at the dark corner of the cottage where he pointed. She frowned.

He cupped her chin, forced her to look into his eyes. "Will you promise to do as you're told?"

She nodded.

Iain kissed her lips and slipped out.

10

BLACKTHORN HALL WAS CERTAINLY BLESSED with many helping hands, Judith thought. Marion's aunt glanced at her sister and Lady Elizabeth, Sir Iain's mother, and marveled at how lovely an afternoon they were spending.

It was so different from Fleet Tower, where they were pretty much alone these days. So different from the old days, she thought with a sigh.

Here at Blackthorn, she and Margaret had seen an army of grooms and servants working near the stables and tending to things in the courtyard when they'd arrived for their visit. Just as many people were crowded in the great hall, bustling about and acting as if they had a purpose for everything they were doing. And that had not been the end of it. In Lady Elizabeth's chambers, a manservant stood by the door and a lady-in-waiting sat beside her, and a maidservant hovered behind the Armstrong dowager's chair, adjusting her shawl whenever Lady Elizabeth leaned forward or back, or moved side to side in her chair. Another serving lass stood beside them with a tray of sweet pastries and cakes. Yet another stood by with a pitcher of spiced cider. All Judith had to do was to stretch out her right hand, and her cup was filled with the warm sweet brew. Stretch out her left, and her plate received one of the baked delights.

When the McCall sisters first sat down with the dowager, Judith hardly knew which to try first. Dainty gingerbread cakes and tarts made of apple, pear, quince--all looked so tempting. Now that she'd sampled them all, she couldn't decide which she liked the best. By the saints, she thought, she felt the way she had on feast days when she'd been just a wee lass.

Judith glanced across the small table that had been placed by the fire for them. Lady Elizabeth was still talking. She'd spent time in France before she was married, and she knew so much of the ways of the world. What were they talking about? Well, it looked like Margaret, the dear, was listening.

Judith didn't want to let on, but she was getting a little bored. She'd been helping Margaret prepare elderberries for wine the past few days, and she wondered now how long before the present batch would be ready for the casks.

Still talking. Judith relieved her boredom by stretching out her left hand and then right, only to switch the sequence a moment later. She repeated the action, receiving yet another cake. Well, if they ran out of cider and cakes soon, perhaps it would be time to go home.

She realized Lady Elizabeth was talking to her.

"Pardon?"

"I asked if either of you had any questions for me."

Judith looked at her older sister, who was looking at her and smiling brightly.

"No questions," Margaret replied somewhat loudly in her high-pitched voice.

"No questions," Judith repeated in a whisper, looking back again at their host.

"I'm so happy." Lady Elizabeth clapped her hands in her lap and nodded approvingly. "I'm so relieved that you see no problem in allowing us to manage the arrangements. Preparing for a wedding ceremony and feast is a great deal of work that we really didn't want to burden you with. We are so much better prepared here at Blackthorn Hall to see to an event of this magnitude."

"Indeed," Margaret repeated, "much better prepared."

"Indeed," Judith added.

"And, as you know, there are some very distinguished guests who are traveling all the way from Edinburgh and London to attend the wedding."

The two sisters looked at each other and nodded simultaneously, pretending they knew.

"Very distinguished," Margaret responded.

"Indeed," Judith agreed. "Very distinguished."

Lady Elizabeth leaned forward in her chair and looked with discomfort at one sister and then the other. The servant in charge of the shawl jumped to her task.

"Which brings me to the sensitive topic of your brother and how he would feel about leaving Fleet Tower and coming here for the ceremony. I know the last time he journeyed here was twelve years ago, right after my beloved husband and the good Earl of Fleet died heroically at Flodden Field. If I recall correctly, he didn't take too well to Blackthorn Hall."

"Oh, no! William will not be coming," Margaret quickly offered.

"William is not coming." Judith shook her head adamantly.

"Our brother is very particular about his routines, Lady Elizabeth," Margaret continued. "Excessive company distresses him."

Judith stretched her plate out for more sweets. The servant glanced in distress at the four cakes and two tarts already on it but said nothing and carefully placed another tart on top.

"No company," she finally said.

Lady Elizabeth let out a deep breath and sat back. For the first time since the two sisters had arrived, she actually smiled. "Excellent. This is going so far better than I had ever hoped."

Margaret and Judith looked at each other first before turning their attention to their host.

"Far better," Margaret agreed.

"Far better," Judith repeated.

"I believe this is all we'll need to discuss, then." The Armstrong dowager shifted in her chair. The servant was quick to adjust the shawl again. "I'll take care of everything and make sure you are informed of each arrangement. The wedding guests should begin arriving within a week's time. Hopefully, we'll see our future bride and groom arrive back at Blackthorn Hall before then." She waved reassuringly. "In the meantime, I'll station servants on the east and south roads to direct our guests here rather than to Fleet Tower."

"Sir William doesn't do well with guests," Margaret added.

"No guests," Judith agreed.

Their host nodded. "I agree wholeheartedly. We don't want anyone causing Sir William any undue distress."

"Excellent," Margaret said.

"Excellent, indeed," Judith repeated.

There was no room left on her plate for more cakes and her cup was full to the brim, so Judith placed both of them on the table and stood up. Her sister followed suit.

Lady Elizabeth seemed to have far more pleasantries to share than when they had come in, but Judith was impatient to leave. The manservant opened the door and led them through the clusters of servants down a circular stairway out through the great hall. The younger sister waited until she and Margaret were out in the stone-paved courtyard before she asked the question that was hanging on the tip of her tongue.

"Margaret, did you understand what all of this was about?"

"Indeed, Judith." Her older sister nodded and leaned down to whisper in her ear. "The English are coming."

11

————

IT WAS ALMOST MORE than she could bear not to run out or shout a warning to Iain. Before Marion broke her promise, though, she saw him start down the hill he'd climbed before. He had spotted the new arrivals before she had. A dozen of them. All on horseback. Marion didn't like the way some of the men immediately looked toward the cottage.

She rushed toward the old straw mattress, pushed it up against the wall. She was happily surprised to see a space hollowed out beneath it. She was even more surprised to see a slab of rock partially blocking a hole at the base of the wall. Marion could see light filtering in around the edges. Climbing into the hollow, she pulled the rock back. There was a hole large enough for her to wriggle through. She could crawl through it, come up behind the cottage, and stay out of the intruders' sight.

Twelve to one. Iain was badly outnumbered. Never mind having to fight with a bruised shoulder. She looked around and picked up a small, rusted iron pot with a hole in the bottom. She rushed back toward the doorway. Peering out, she could see Iain had stopped some half dozen steps up from the bottom of the hill, talking to the leader of the group. She couldn't hear anything that was being said, but there had been no weapons drawn, and there was no shouting or sign of an argument.

Marion knew there was no way these men would mistake Iain for a crofter. She tried to decide if that was good or bad. They were dressed in a variety of plaids—most unrecognizable to her. She recalled the stories she'd heard of bands of men who got together and robbed travelers. She hadn't run into any of those on the Isle of Skye. But on the mainland, Highlanders were very different.

She didn't stand still and contemplate the situation for too long. Two of the men near the back of the group dismounted and started toward the cottage.

Just then, Iain shouted something at the leader and a dozen short swords appeared. Marion stared at what looked like the broken end of a hoe in her husband's hand. Totally insufficient to do battle with a gang of outlaws.

Panic at what they were going to do to Iain stunned her momentarily, but relief came as a rush when she recognized the McCall tartan on one of the two men coming toward her. The rogues had stopped halfway between Iain and the cottage.

"McCall," she cried. She pushed the leather flap aside and rushed out. "We are of the same clan. I'm Marion McCall, daughter of the late Earl of Fleet. I'm on my way back to—"

Iain shouted a warning, and Marion bent to the side just in time to hear the *ffffitt* and feel the rush of air on her neck as an arrow passed. She turned to see the arrow quivering where it had lodged deep in a crevice between two stones in the cottage wall.

"You shot at me!" she gasped in shock. She had no doubt that the shot had come from one of those on horseback. She turned around and found that pandemonium had broken loose on the field. Iain had pulled two men to the ground. One was lying still amid the stones, and one was staggering groggily. Against three others, Iain was battling heroically. Two men remained on their horses, obviously willing to get involved in the fray only if needed. Several others had dismounted and were approaching the fighting warily. The two heading toward the cottage turned and rushed toward her.

Marion stepped forward to meet them, holding the pot behind her.

"It's about time someone taught you some manners," she shouted. "This is no way you greet your own kin."

She swung the pot at the head of the man wearing the McCall plaid, and connected with a thud, sending him to the earth with a surprised look on his face. Before she could swing the pot again, though, the second outlaw, a filthy cur with the round face of a pig, grabbed her by the hair and threw her to the ground.

Marion saw the drawn sword in his hand and didn't waste any time. As he went to grab her hair again, she delivered a sharp kick to his groin. The villain bent over with a grunt, and Marion jumped to her feet, swinging the iron pot at his head.

There was great satisfaction in hearing the resounding crunch the metal made as it struck his thick skull. The man's short sword fell to the ground as he sank to his knees. Marion picked it up and turned to the first brute. He was holding a hand to his bloody head and backing away, not toward the horses, but toward another line of trees.

"Coward!" she shouted. "You are no McCall. Hear me? You're a cheat, a villain, spawn of the devil. I dare you to come back here." Turning around to face her other foe, she found him, too, on his feet and dragging himself back toward the horses.

She remembered Iain and looked past the two brutes. The reason for the two men's escape immediately became apparent. The Armstrong warriors had arrived and were quickly subduing the attackers. Marion didn't remember a time when she'd been happier seeing anyone. She searched the group for her husband.

Iain was holding one hand to a bloody shoulder—his same bruised shoulder—and shouting orders to his men. The outlaws were all on the ground now, and their hands were being lashed with leather cords. Only the two who had run off into the woods had escaped.

Iain turned around and looked at her from head to toe. She looked down and realized she was still holding a sword in one hand and the iron pot in the other. She threw both of them aside and walked toward him.

His shirt was bloody. She wondered how deep the wound was and if he was hurt anywhere else. He had been practically unarmed, taking on all of those villains. Despite his injury, she thought, Iain looked magnificent. Dirt or blood, nothing lessened the force with which he ruled the situation.

His eyes swept over her again, and Marion felt the tightness deep in her belly. Something primitive, something beyond her understanding and control, made her move more quickly to him. She wanted him, needed him. She had to touch him and assure herself that all was well. The intensity of the feeling made her want to run.

"Lady Marion." Brother Luke made the mistake of stepping in her path. "I am so relieved you're—"

"One moment, Brother," she said, pushing past him and running toward Iain.

He left the throng of men and came toward her. Marion didn't care how many people watched. She didn't care what opinion these people might have of her after the foolish way she'd acted. She stepped into her husband's arms and buried her face into his chest.

"I told you to stay inside the cottage."

"It was easier to fight them outside."

"My little warrior," he whispered into her ear.

The tone of approval warmed her. He wasn't angry at Marion for not hiding or running away. She pulled back to tell him just that, but his bloody shirt caught her eye. "You're bleeding from the same shoulder you bruised before."

"It's nothing. A slight wound."

He was lying. She saw him wince when she tried to touch his shoulder through the shirt. "Let me see it. I know how to clean and mend wounds. I was taught by the prioress herself."

"In a wee bit. Let me finish here first."

Patience wasn't one of her virtues, but she looked at the group that now sat bound on the field of stones and understood. He wanted some answers and she did, too. Marion wanted to believe that the arrow coming at her had been a mistake. She wanted to believe the McCall tartan the rogue was wearing was stolen...that the man had no ties to her clan. She didn't for a moment think she was going to get what she wanted.

She nodded. "How long will it be before you come? We should bind your shoulder soon."

Her insides turned to molten liquid when he bent down and brushed a kiss across her lips. He smiled. "I'll have someone bring your trunks inside the cottage. You need to change. After all this, I think it would be best if we had a roof over our head for the night."

She nodded. "Who will be sleeping inside?"

"Only you and I," he growled in a low voice. "And don't plan on doing any sleeping."

12

THREE LARGE TRUNKS. Twelve years of collectibles. Treasures that she could not live without, the laird had been told.

Iain stared in disbelief at the opened trunks lining the three inside walls of the cottage. A hodgepodge of rubbish had been haphazardly pulled out of each one of them. Broken furniture. Tattered wool cloth. Broken china. He bent down to touch something large wrapped in a blanket. It was a rock.

He looked up when Marion, carrying a pitcher of water, walked inside the cottage. She was all cleaned up. Her dress was changed. Her hair was gathered on top of her head, held by a pair of combs. He missed the wild woman warrior of a couple of hours ago.

"These are your trunks?" he asked.

She nodded.

"You call these treasures?"

She nodded. "What else would you expect a person to collect living inside the walls of an abbey?"

"We had to bring a cart along just to carry all this. Do you know how slow and dangerous that made our travels?"

"You only had to carry them for a day. Fine. Two days," she corrected as he gave her an incredulous look. Marion walked inside to a blanket she'd laid on the floor. She knelt on it and put the pitcher down. "I had the option of hiding all of this from you until we were at Fleet Tower. You would never have known."

He heard the note of vulnerability in her voice. "Maybe you should have."

She shook her head. "I wanted to punish you before. I don't anymore. Now, come and sit here so I can poke you with these needles."

He couldn't even pretend to stay angry with her. "Didn't you just say you were done punishing me?"

She patted the blanket next to her. "Stop acting so frightened. It won't hurt much."

For the first time he looked around the room. She had pushed into a dark corner what little the cottars had left. The blanket she was kneeling on was clean, and she also had started a fire with wood that Iain had seen one of the men carrying in for her.

"I guess not everything in those trunks is rubbish," he said, motioning toward the clean dress she'd changed into. "Black wool and twice your size. Was that one of the chaplain's?"

"Keep it up if you like, but it really doesn't matter. I'm not forgetting about that shoulder of yours." She reached for his hand, tugging him down beside her.

Iain sat on the blanket. "This scratch has already stopped bleeding."

Marion apparently didn't believe him, for she immediately began peeling the shirt off of him. It was true that his shoulder hurt like hell, but Iain had weathered enough battles and carried enough scars to know this *was* a minor wound.

He let her have her way. He liked watching her. He liked the feel of her hands on his skin. He also would have liked to do anything right now rather than tell her what he'd learned from the group of thugs who'd attacked them.

"So, what did you find out from those wandering curs?" she asked, as if reading his mind.

He pretended to wince in pain.

"What are you doing," he lied, "tearing my bloody arm off?"

She looked into his face and smiled. "I'm only taking your shirt off, you wee bairn."

"Oh, that's all right, then." He paused for a moment. "Can I take your dress off?"

Even in the dim light he could see the blush that crept into her cheeks. He reached up and ran his finger down the silky softness of her neck.

"I promise I shan't complain about your fussing, so long as I can help you out of this black tent you're wearing."

He saw her bite her lip in an attempt to hide a smile. She finally managed to work the shirt off his shoulder. He was impressed to see she was not squeamish at the sight of blood.

"I want my wedding night, Marion."

"Hush! Your people are just outside."

"Good. That means we'll have an entire night with no interruptions," he said, slipping an arm around her and bringing her mouth to his. She immediately opened up to his kiss, and he felt the tingling heat in his loins. After a moment, though, she pulled back, breaking off the kiss.

"I have to clean away this blood first. I need to know if there is any need for stitching."

"You can wash anything you want," he said, leaning back on his good arm and watching Marion dip a cloth in the pitcher. She moved around him and gently dabbed at his shoulder.

Excitement. Contentment. Hope. The feelings curled around him like wisps of smoke and filled spaces inside that had been empty for a long time. And they all had to do with this woman. Marion was filling his mind. She was under his skin.

Iain couldn't remember ever wanting a woman as much as he wanted Marion. The image of her in her dirt-stained dress, armed with the weapon she'd taken from her attacker, wild hair flowing around her shoulders, was too fresh in his mind. From that very moment, all Iain had wanted to do was to bring her inside this cottage and make love to her. Make love to his wife.

He reached up and pulled at one of the combs. Her hair spilled down to her shoulders.

"You're distracting me," she said, inching closer to him but not moving her gaze from the wound.

Laces ran down the front of her dress, and Iain reached out and untied the top lace. He heard the breath catch in her throat.

"Iain, let me finish," she whispered.

He reached up again and slowly pulled the laces out of the first pair of holes, running his finger along the silky skin of her throat.

"You just keep on with what you're doing." He slowly pulled the next pair of laces free, and the next.

She shifted her weight from one knee to the other. He saw her hand tremble slightly as she dipped the cloth into the pitcher again before taking it back to his shoulder.

Undoing the next pair, Iain gently spread the neckline of the dress open until the tops of her breasts were exposed. She shivered as he trailed his fingers along her throat and chest, slipping his hand inside the fabric of the dress and chemise. He cupped one of her breasts, lifting it and stroking the hardening nipple with his thumb.

A soft gasp escaped her. He saw the hand with the wet cloth withdraw from his shoulder, but she didn't move away. Sitting there, with her eyes wide and uncertain, she stared at him.

"I'm not done with you."

"I know," he whispered back, leaning down and kissing her neck. "I'm not done with you, either."

"What do you mean?"

"Remember what I told you? You can do whatever you want, so long as I can help you out of this dress."

"But what I'm wearing underneath is hardly proper."

Marion's words trailed off as he pressed his lips to the top of each breast. He pushed the dress and chemise down and gently suckled her nipple.

She softly cried out his name, and her fingers delved into his hair. After a moment of teasing, Iain found she had no objection left in her as he loosened the rest of the laces and slipped the dress off her.

Her neck and throat were a pillar of ivory, her arms long and graceful. Her breasts were perfect, and the thin chemise did little to hide them.

"If anyone comes in here, I'll die," she said shyly.

"Anyone comes in here, I'll kill him," he replied, unable to stop touching her.

She knelt close to him again and picked up the cloth, washing his wound.

Iain's hand moved up her leg and beneath the chemise. Her skin was like silk, her legs strong and smooth. His fingers reached the juncture of her legs and she gasped again, her hand stilling. She was moist, ready for him. He stroked the feminine folds for a moment before withdrawing his hand. Marion's face was crimson, but she held her head high and cleared her throat.

"You're still bleeding," she said in a husky voice, "though less so. Unless I sew up the wound, it may bleed again when you ride."

"I like your powers of concentration," he said, slipping the chemise off first one shoulder and then the other. The linen fell and gathered at her waist. "But my shoulder is not the part of me that needs your attention right now."

Her gaze moved down his chest. "You'll need to tell me what to do, where to start."

Iain threw the towel aside and rolled her onto the blanket. "We've already started."

13

More than a hundred candles lit the great hall of Fleet Tower and logs crackled and blazed in the wide fireplace.

Torches had been set up along the top of the square tower house, at the corner bartizans, in the courtyard, and even along a section of a road leading in and out of the seat of the area's McCall clan. Because of the lack of available house servants, the two McCall sisters had each taken on so much to keep everything ready and festive for the impending arrival of their niece. At the last minute, they had even decided to give their brother a job to do...just to keep him from stealing food and retiring to his room or escaping to the castle's dungeons. Sir William had been given the responsibility of keeping the candles inside lit and the torches outside burning, a responsibility that he fulfilled with the air of a warlord inspecting his legions.

Margaret had been in and out of the kitchens for most of the day. The help she'd been able to muster had run for their lives around the middle of the afternoon. Sir William's appearance in full armor had seen to that. In spite of the shortage of help, Margaret wanted to have a meal ready for whenever the travelers arrived, which to her understanding could be anytime. Sir Iain's mother had sent a message over but had not given them any specific time.

Other than assisting Margaret, Judith's chief responsibility today was to keep their brother, William, from stealing away with all the food to feed his "army." She had been somehow negligent this forenoon, however, for she'd found two large platters of roasted mutton missing. That is, in addition to a large platter of cheeses and dried fruit. And three loaves of bread. She was being a lot more careful tonight.

"William, you will take only what you eat," Judith scolded him when he returned from his inspection of the parapet. To show him what she meant, she prepared a plate for him and placed it at his assigned seat, motioning to him to sit down.

The array of weaponry strapped to William McCall's shoulder and belt and legs made it difficult for him to sit.

"I'll eat standing," he announced after several attempts. He tried to reach for his plate.

Judith slapped his hand away. "You will sit, Sir William."

"You will sit," Margaret repeated.

"I shall stand!" he replied authoritatively.

"Sit," both sisters announced simultaneously.

"Women!" William blurted the word like a curse before starting to disarm. "No wonder my band of merry men and I prefer the quiet of Leglen Wood."

A cacophony of pings and clangs rang through the great hall as the various weapons fell in a heap on the floor.

Margaret poured their brother a cup of wine, and Judith dragged the bench closer for him to sit on. The sisters liked to fuss over him, and despite his grumbling, they knew he enjoyed the attention.

The first bite was rising to his mouth when the sound of horses arriving in the courtyard outside reached them.

"Are we under attack?" Sir William cried, rising from the bench. "Is it the damnable English? Sound the alarm! Call out the men!"

Judith and Margaret ran off to check. As they knelt on one of the window seats and looked out, Sir William hurried to arm himself.

"Is it Marion?" Judith asked excitedly, pushing the shutters wide open.

"It's too dark out there. I cannot tell," Margaret responded.

Both sisters leaned farther out the window.

"Only two riders," Judith announced.

"It must be our Marion and the laird," Margaret explained.

The crash of at least fifty pounds of metal behind them caused both sisters to jump. They turned around and scowled at their brother. A belt appeared to have snapped, and Sir William, cursing under his breath, was scrambling to retrieve the fallen arms.

There was a call of greeting from the courtyard. Margaret and Judith waved excitedly.

"It's Marion, and she is dressed in...in armor!" Judith exclaimed as the two travelers moved into the light of the torches.

"That must be part of the nuns' habit on the Isle of Skye," Margaret whispered, unable to see that far. "Very different from the nuns here, I must say."

"*Very* different," Judith repeated before calling out. "Halloo!"

There were no grooms or servants to run out and greet them or see to their horses. She looked over her shoulder at William, but he was once again tangled up in his weapons, which were continuing to drop noisily at his feet. Turning back, she was relieved to see the two had dismounted and were tying their steeds.

"And she is armed," Judith whispered. "Do you see the size of the sword strapped to her belt?"

Margaret squinted at the moving objects in the courtyard, but quickly gave up. She was too excited to attend to such details.

"Perhaps the sword was a going-away gift of the prioress," she said as she leaned out the window. "Welcome! Come in...come in!"

"She is rather round in shape," Judith noted somewhat hesitantly.

"It must have been the food they fed her on Skye."

The two travelers were exchanging a few words on the steps leading up to the tower. Both voices sounded deep, even to Margaret.

"I cannot believe my ears," Judith whispered in shock. "Did you hear her voice just now?"

"She must have gotten a chill on the journey. I'll give her some of my honey-ginger brew, and she'll be all better before the wedding."

The portlier traveler threw back his hood, and the two sisters stared open-mouthed as a hat fell to the stairs. Beneath it, a shiny bald head reflected the light of the torches.

"Marion?" they both exclaimed loudly with shock.

The traveler looked up and waved. "My dear ladies, would you be so kind as to offer two lost travelers shelter for the night? We rode ahead of our party as sunset came upon us and appear to have lost our way. Our destination is Blackthorn Hall, but I don't believe it would be wise to venture any farther on this dangerous road until morning."

Judith and Margaret turned to face each other. Their whispers were simultaneous. "Englishmen."

Judith smiled. Margaret leaned out the window and called an enthusiastic welcome, inviting them again to come in.

The sisters turned away from the window seat. William had finally succeeded in strapping on all his weapons.

"Up to your room, Sir William," Judith ordered.

"I need to inspect the men, kind lady."

"Later."

"You can do that later," Margaret agreed, rushing to the table to set things right.

"I'll visit them now," William asserted.

"Sir William, as the great Wallace, you know that you must be prepared to train any new recruits."

"Indeed."

"Well," Judith said reasonably as she took her brother by the elbow and turned him toward the arched doorway on the far side of the great hall, "you must rest and prepare yourself to train some new men who will be arriving quite soon."

"New soldiers?" William asked excitedly.

Judith nodded, a twinkle shinning in the depth of her dark eyes. "We just received word."

"How many?"

"Two to start with. But there could be a dozen more at any moment."

"I must say I'm elated at the prospect, m'lady."

The two sisters stood together and watched Sir William stride through the doorway to the base of the steps. Pausing there, he drew his sword and raised it high.

"*Freedom!*" he shouted, charging up the steps.

14

SHE HAD NOT BEEN *ASKED* her feelings. She'd simply been *told* the plans.

Early this afternoon, the travelers had ridden down out of the Trossachs. The sun was still high when they'd arrived at this inn. But they would not all be staying, she was told.

Brother Luke and four of the men would be riding on ahead with directions to continue on to the Borders. The rest of the group, including Marion, would remain with Iain at the inn, which was only an arrow shot from the shores of Loch Lomond. She knew that to the south of the lake, the Lowlands stretched out all the way to the rising hills surrounding Fleet Tower. How long the party was to wait here, however, had not been discussed.

Glaring down at Iain, Marion was too exhausted to care who witnessed their exchange. She refused to dismount from the horse. She couldn't understand his logic, and he definitely wasn't being very forthright in his explanations.

"For four days," she said, "you've pushed us through long days in the saddle with practically no rest and no time for eating anything hot. You've led us on like a madman, as if the devil were on our heels. Now we are only two days away from Fleet Tower, and *you* decide we should stop here in the middle of nowhere and wait?"

"I believe you have it exactly right," he replied. Then he had the nerve to smile and reach up for her. "And did I tell you how wonderful and agreeable you've been during these days of hard riding?"

"Agreeable?" she snorted, pushing his hand away. "My complaining has been lost in the wind. And for the couple of hours we've camped now and again, I've been too exhausted to do anything but sleep."

He took her hand. "More reason for us to stay at this inn, my love. Here you can rest, and I can fulfill the husbandly duties I have been neglecting for most of this journey."

He knew how to fluster her. Marion had no control over the blush that warmed her face. Their night together at the hut had been beyond anything she'd imagined possible. She had been agreeable for several of the following days, occasionally reminiscing about all they had done to each other. All she had learned. She'd spent many hours anticipating and daydreaming about the next time they would be alone together.

The pain in her buttocks, caused by too many hours in the saddle, had gradually drained her of any romantic thoughts...for now. Marion also recognized that she was bone tired and irritable. And Iain was responsible for it.

"Why here? Why now? Why not stop at a larger village? Or a real town? How far are we from Glasgow?" she asked. "I know there must be some reason behind this apparent madness. Explain it to me, and in return, I shall sit here, docile as a wee lamb...for about the count of ten."

He shook his head, obviously amused. "No other woman in Scotland would think to be interrogating me. They would be thrilled at my proposal."

She leaned forward in the saddle and lowered her voice. "You had your chance at other women, but you lost that when you married me. Now kindly explain yourself."

"Wouldn't you at least get down from the horse? Never mind my men and everyone else in the stable yard. I believe I'd be accurate in saying you're entertaining the innkeeper and his entire staff with your scandalous behavior. You can see them all standing by the door and windows, wondering what you'll be doing next."

Marion glanced at the inn and then at the stables. The place wrapped around this central yard and definitely looked familiar. She wondered if she'd passed by it with her father as a child. From the moment they'd arrived, she was impressed by the orderly way of the place and the many hands helping in the yard. Of course, no one was working now. And they weren't even being discreet about their nosiness. She was definitely the entertainment.

"I'll get down, but that's as compliant as I plan to be, Iain Armstrong," she grumbled under her breath, allowing him to lower her to the ground. "I am not going inside until you explain yourself."

Her knees buckled momentarily as her feet touched the packed earth of the yard. Iain held on to her, making sure she was strong enough to stand on her own feet. She did, sooner than she should have, but she was not going to show any weakness.

They'd certainly traveled quickly during the last few days. The men they'd subdued at the stone cottage were left late the following day at the town of Oban on the coast. Iain told her they'd be well cared for in the responsible and just hands of the Duke of Argyll, Colin Campbell, an ally and friend of the Armstrongs. The three trunks Marion had insisted on bringing from the Isle of Skye had been left behind at the cottage, along with the cart.

Some of her "more useful possessions," as Iain called them, were tucked into two saddles of the McCall and Armstrong riders. When they'd arrived here, Iain had ordered those few items to be taken in. He also ordered his man Alan to see about fresh horses for Brother Luke and the four men who were leaving with him. Marion knew the clergyman was already inside the inn, having a meal and taking a short rest before his cruel nephew had the chance to shove him out onto the road south. Luckily for Brother Luke, the weather looked clear.

Iain started for the door, but Marion dug her heels in. Once she climbed down from the horse, their audience appeared to have lost interest and were drifting back to work.

"We are starting this marriage on the wrong foot. You need to understand that your life will be much easier and infinitely more pleasant once you accept the fact that I deserve answers for my questions and my concerns."

"I must say, the prioress has taught you some curious things there in Skye." He held up a hand. "But I have every intention of answering all your questions."

"Then do so," she encouraged.

"What do you have against continuing this conversation inside?"

"You know perfectly." She felt the heat rising in her face. "You will only manage to distract me...with other things...if we go in before I get my answers."

"What kinds of other things?" He caressed her cheek.

"Stop it. You're doing it now." Marion pushed his hand away half-heartedly.

"Does everything have to be your way?" he asked, amusement in his voice.

"No. But for twelve years you've had everything *your* way. This is my chance to make up for that lost time." She appreciated the fact that, despite her complaining, he was maintaining a good sense of humor about things. Marion tucked her arm into his, leaned against him, and whispered in his ear. "You realize you're wasting precious time by not explaining things to me. Just think of everything else that we could be doing with our time."

His blue gaze smoldered as he looked at her. "You need to promise me that you will continue to be this enthusiastic after hearing what I have to say."

She tensed. "There's something wrong with my family."

"*That* we all know. Everyone in the Borders knows there's something wrong with your family." He smiled. "But that is not what I have to tell you right now."

She punched him in the arm. It was like punching a rock. "You've married a McCall, Iain. McCall blood will run in the veins of any child we bring into this world. It's time you stopped ridiculing us."

He brought her hand to his lips and brushed a kiss over it. "I promise to try."

It wasn't exactly an apology. But he was so charming that Marion thought it was good enough. She tucked her arm into his again and nodded. "What you have to reveal has something to do with the rogues that attacked us at that cottar's hut in the Highlands. Am I right?"

He glanced around them. "Too many people are eavesdropping on our conversation."

Marion saw he was correct. The stable yard was crowded with workers and travelers. Although no one was gawking like before, the two of them were still the object of everyone's interest.

"Come for a walk with me."

She nodded. After so many hours of feeling the bumps and bruises of riding, it felt like heaven to stretch her legs. Iain led her toward a brook that ran by the inn. The land began to slope downward to the lake, and with it, the brook tumbled down a series of falls before flowing into the loch.

"It must be that. You refused to answer any of my questions about those villains the night of the attack," Marion reasoned. "And since then, you have avoided the subject entirely."

"Would you like me to explain, or do you plan to deduce the answers all on your own?"

"Would you like to jump in that lake all on your own or would you prefer that I push you into it?" she retorted.

He hugged her tightly. "I'll jump in willingly if you come with me."

"I don't think I'm in the mood to save you today," she said sweetly.

"No?" He kissed her on the neck, his lips teasing her earlobe. He kissed her mouth.

She had to clutch at his shirt to keep her balance when he ended the kiss.

"Now will you save me?"

"Maybe." Her gaze drifted toward the top of the hill. She was dismayed to find people standing and watching them again. "Don't they have something better to do than watch us?"

He looked up at them and smiled. "They are not watching us. They're watching you."

"And why is that?"

"Your reputation precedes you. They know who you are, and they're curious to see if you're as wild as you were the last time you stopped here."

Marion took a step up the hill, taking in the scene of the buildings and the countryside around them. She turned to face him. "The inn looks familiar. But when was the last time I was--oh, no!"

He smiled. "Indeed. Twelve years ago. The escort who took you to the priory on the Isle of Skye made the mistake of staying the night at this inn."

Marion turned to look up the hill at the buildings again. She remembered all too well. Twelve years ago when they'd arrived, it was already dark. And within a couple of hours, the inn had erupted in total chaos. She and her entourage had left before dawn.

"I tried to run away."

"You tried to burn the place down."

"That was after getting caught for wanting to run away," Marion corrected him. "And only after none of the people working here would listen to my pleas or take my side."

Of *course* she hadn't initially remembered the place, Marion thought. She was six years old at the time, and the entire world she knew had been taken away from her in a single afternoon. Accompanied by a group of strange, surly men wearing Armstrong plaids, and a nun that she knew no better, Marion had been sent on her way. But that wasn't the end of it, and she wasn't about to give in so easily. She had been angry and determined to get back to Fleet Tower, even if she had to go on foot. Her first opportunity, though, had occurred when they'd arrived at this place a couple of days into their journey.

"They say you tried to jump out of the second-story window."

"I wasn't going to jump. I was climbing out very carefully. Your warriors made far more of it than it was," she said, waving it off nonchalantly.

"And dumping a brazier of hot coals on the floor and starting the fire. Did everyone make more of it than it was, too?"

"That started as an accident. I tripped over it when I was running across the room to get away from the nun and the tray of disgusting food she was forcing on me. But to be truthful, I did try to take advantage of the mayhem afterward."

"So you admit that?"

"Indeed I do. I stole one of the horses. But they stopped me before I reached the stable doors." She looked into his face. "I speak the absolute truth about not intentionally starting the fire."

He nodded.

"Do you believe me?"

"I do. When it comes to creating disaster, you like to take credit for more and not less."

He understood her and that made Marion oddly happy. She scrunched up her nose, looking back up toward the inn. "How much damage was done to the place by the time I left?"

"Well, the most important thing was that no one was hurt. But the bedchamber you were staying at on the second floor was pretty well scorched. In the end, it was all definitely fixable...at some expense, though."

Marion struggled to fight down a flush of embarrassment. In a few moments, she would climb back up this hill. She wondered if, after so many years, there was something she should say to the innkeeper.

"Considering my reputation, Iain, how did you manage to convince them to allow me to stay here again?"

"I paid for the damages twelve years ago, so he trusts I'll look after you this time."

"He is brave," she whispered, recalling more clearly the terror she had been at that age.

"Naturally, we'll be taking the same bedchamber," he added.

"The same one that was burned?"

"They fixed the place up long ago," Iain said.

Marion looped her arm into her husband's. She knew she would be much happier inside the walls of that bedchamber this time around. Seeing Alan at top of the hill reminded her why they'd walked down here to start with.

"You've managed to distract me again. We've talked of everything else, but you have yet to answer my questions. Why are we stopping here?"

Iain took both her hands and faced her. Behind him, she could see the brown hills rising sharply beyond the loch, and lake water was glistening in the afternoon sun.

"The men who attacked us intended to shoot that arrow at you." Iain's face was in shadow. "I was able to get two of them to talk afterward. It appears they were hired by your cousin."

"Jack?"

He nodded. "Jack Fitzwilliam."

Marion felt as if someone had stabbed her in the back. Her breath and her voice struggled to the surface. "What do you mean?"

"They were hired to stop you from returning to the Borders."

"And how were they going to do that?" she asked, already knowing the answer.

"They were instructed to kill you," he said solemnly.

It hurt. It really hurt to learn that someone whom she had never wronged, someone who was her own kin, wanted her dead. Marion struggled to stay calm. "Because of your courage, Iain, they didn't succeed."

"*Your* courage was what turned the tide. Granted, it was good timing that Brother Luke and the men were not far off, but you gave those fools a lesson about how to treat a woman." He brushed away a tear that Marion didn't know she'd shed. He leaned down and pressed a kiss where the tear had been.

"What happens next?" she asked brokenly.

"I'll find Jack Fitzwilliam when we get back at the Borders. He'll be punished for his treacherous scheming."

"And what do we do for right now?"

"I'm not going to endanger you any longer. We are safe enough here. The innkeeper will lend a hand if we're attacked again. On the other hand, Jack could have more men out looking for us between here and Fleet Tower, so we'll wait here until Brother Luke and the men traveling with him reach Blackthorn Hall. They'll send back a larger group to escort us home."

"Aren't you worried about your uncle's safety?"

Iain shook his head. "You probably don't remember much about your cousin, but for all his peculiarities and a bloody streak of violence, he'd never attack Luke."

"Why?"

"Jack Fitzwilliam apparently sees himself as devotedly religious. That is the only reason I think he never sent a group to harm you on the Isle of Skye."

"Because I was staying in a priory convent?"

"That's right. For the same reason, I'm certain he wouldn't harm Brother Luke, either."

Marion tried to remember the stories she'd heard about Jack's mother. They were always spoken in whispers. One story claimed that the woman was a Gypsy, passing through the McCall land. Sir William had fallen in love for the only time in his life. But there was another tale about a lass on her way to a convent, having already been disowned by her Border lord father for something. And another about her being a scullery maid in the kitchens at Fleet Tower. Marion couldn't exactly remember the stories, but they all had the same air of romance to them. There was nothing Marion knew for sure about Jack's mother.

"So Jack Fitzwilliam intends to stop our marriage?" Marion asked.

"I think that's his plan. The scheming dog believes he's the rightful heir to the McCall lands."

"But we're already married," she reminded him. "Perhaps if he knows, he'll give up."

"I don't know what he'll do once he hears that news," Iain said. "He is not in his right mind. He might give up and disappear, or he might try to seize Fleet Tower. If he has it, we'd need to take it back by force, and he probably figures that the McCall clan will rally behind him against me."

Marion thought of how defenseless her aunts and uncle were at Fleet Tower with no one protecting them. But they were no threat to Jack. So, she reasoned, he wouldn't hurt them.

Hopefully.

"I want Jack to know we're married," Iain continued. "So I told Brother Luke to spread the word once he reaches the Borders. He'll make sure to get the news out."

Marion looked up toward the inn. "I'd like to speak to Brother Luke before he leaves. I want to make sure that he relays the news of our marriage gently to my aunts. I don't want to hurt their feelings or have them feel excluded from my life. They are very sensitive and so conscious of every slight. I'm like a daughter to them."

"They *were* sensitive and conscious," Iain said. "Now they are two forgetful old ladies who don't remember a thing from one moment to the next."

"You're being condescending again."

He put both hands up in self-defense. "I'm not. I'm only speaking the truth and trying to prepare you for what you'll have to face soon. Your family has aged, my love."

Marion let out a sigh. There was no point in arguing with him. She had changed, so it was only natural for the same thing to happen to her family. She wished she were going to Fleet Tower now...today. She wanted to get past this initial meeting. She wanted to be home. But none of that was possible. She turned to Iain.

"Do you think Brother Luke will be ready to meet with us now?"

He motioned up the hill with his head. Marion looked. Brother Luke and a group of Armstrong men were standing at the top.

"I believe he's ready."

15

TWO MEN WERE MISSING, but after just half an hour with the elderly McCall sisters, Sir George Harington, adjutant to the Marquis of Dorset in the Borders, was thinking only of self-preservation. The two women were nearly smothering him with their hospitality, and there was certainly no point in questioning these gentle people any further about the missing men.

Sir Francis Hastings and Sir William Eden, two members of the marquis's staff, had disappeared four days ago en route to Blackthorn Hall for the Armstrong and McCall wedding. The worst of it was that Hastings was a cousin of Dorset's wife. When Sir George had arrived from York yesterday, he'd been assured that search parties had been scouring the countryside every day. They'd found the men's horses grazing the land in the hills a half hour north of Fleet Tower two days ago, but there had been no sign of the two men.

This area in the Borders was notorious for its lawlessness. That was the reason why King Henry had directed the marquis to send trusted members of his staff to witness the wedding. This marriage between the two clans promised a chance to add stability to the region. In planning for this, neither Dorset nor Sir George had ever expected that their own men would fall victim to any roguery. The adjutant still held fast to the hope that the two men were perhaps resting at some manor house, since there was still a week until the wedding. The problem of the horses didn't help to buoy those hopes, though.

"Would you care for another of these pastries, Sir George?" Lady Judith offered, holding the platter before him. "They were made fresh this morning."

This was his third serving, but the food was far too tempting. George Harington smiled up into the round and gentle face of his host. "If you don't mind, I might just help myself to one last serving."

"Mind? I insist." The lady placed not one but two pieces on his plate and carried one to his attendant and the Armstrong man, who were standing by the great fireplace.

How peculiar it was, he thought, that there was no sign of servants here. He knew that the estate attached to the late earl's castle was fairly extensive. And yet these sweet old women appeared to be fending for themselves. No servants. No kitchen help. No steward, it appeared, to run the farms. Not even a bloody gatekeeper. No one. Very odd.

"We insist," Lady Margaret, the older sister, repeated as she poured more warm cider for Sir George.

"Are you certain the three men waiting in the courtyard wouldn't care for something?" Lady Judith asked.

"I'm certain," he replied as he took a bite of the pastry. It was delicate and superior to anything he'd tasted in the months since he'd left the south of England. The spiced cider was also sweet and left a delicious sensation in his mouth.

"So is it only the two of you who reside at Fleet Tower?" he asked, though he already knew the answer. Lady Elizabeth Armstrong had warned him about Sir William, the Earl of Fleet's peculiar but harmless brother.

"Only us...and our brother," Lady Judith replied, sitting on the edge of her seat.

"Sir William," Lady Margaret added, nodding cheerfully.

"Our brother," Judith clarified again.

"Am I going to have the pleasure of meeting the gentleman today?" George asked.

"We're dreadfully sorry, sir, but our brother is not accepting visitors," Lady Margaret responded, shaking her head solemnly.

"No visitors today," the younger sister repeated.

Harington's men had been hearing some entertaining stories about the man and his fascination with the legendary Scottish blackguard William Wallace. He would have liked to meet this creature that everyone talked so much of. "Perhaps if I made an appointment and returned another day. Would that be any better?"

"Oh, no!" Margaret poured another drop of cider into his cup, even though it was already full.

"Sir William doesn't like to plan that far ahead," Judith explained.

"Our brother's schedule is quite unpredictable," the older sister added.

"Unpredictable," Judith repeated.

"Perhaps I shall meet him during the wedding festivities, then," he said politely, not intending to fluster these gentle ladies.

Judith shook her head, "I should doubt it, Sir George."

"No, indeed," Margaret added. "Our brother doesn't like crowds."

"No crowds."

Their resistance was intriguing. Sir George's curiosity with regard to Sir William McCall was definitely piqued. He finished off the second piece of pastry before asking his next question. "Will Lady Marion not be offended if her uncle fails to participate in the festivities?"

The two sisters looked at each other as if the thought had never crossed their minds. A moment later, they both shook their heads simultaneously.

"Marion will understand," Margaret replied.

"She will definitely understand," Judith agreed before getting up and serving Harington two more pastries.

He could have behaved in a more mannerly fashion and refused the pastry, as the Armstrong man had done. These sweets were too good to pass up. "I really shouldn't finish all of these. I mean, you're probably expecting the arrival of other company for the wedding."

"No company," Judith said with a heavy sigh.

"No company," the older sister added somberly. "We're only waiting for Marion to return with Sir Iain."

Sir George found himself actually feeling bad for the two aging sisters. They appeared so accomplished in their courtesy and their conversation, but it was obvious they were very lonely. He knew that in London, ladies such as these two would have busy schedules and productive lives. He ate another one of the pastries.

"Besides, Sir George, we like to bake," Judith explained.

"Baking and cooking," Margaret added.

"We do both," the younger sister chirped in.

"But there is only so much food that we can eat."

"And we like having guests." Judith sent him a gentle smile.

"But there are few."

Harington sipped his cider. "Do you get many travelers who stop here?"

The two sisters again looked at each other first before Margaret answered the question. "No travelers."

"No one stops here."

As quiet as Fleet Tower was, he thought, perhaps they wouldn't know if someone came and went.

"What about your tenants? Don't you see them regularly?"

"Heavens, no!" Lady Margaret said.

"Sir Iain has looked after the tenants for years," Judith explained, sitting back in her chair and folding her hands demurely in her lap.

"And your villagers?"

"Oh, we sometimes have help from the villagers, but very rarely." Margaret thought for a moment. "And only for a short time."

"Usually only for a day or two," Judith added. "But when the villagers come to the tower to help, we do like to send them off with pastries and sweets."

Sir George looked at them. They were truly all alone here. "And that's all?"

Margaret nodded. "That's all."

"That's all," Judith repeated.

"No one else?" he pressed. "Not even an occasional rider or two who have lost their way?"

"No one, Sir George."

Harington exchanged a look with his attendant. He had his answer. These ladies had not seen the missing Hastings and Eden.

"I suppose I should be going before I finish *all* of these delicacies you have worked so hard to prepare." He put the plate and cup on the table and stood up.

"We do this every day." Judith stood, as well.

"Do please come back to visit," Margaret encouraged.

"Anytime at all, Sir George. It was lovely meeting you."

Harington smiled, very pleased with his hostesses' warmth. "If you don't mind, ladies, I might just do that. I don't know when. But perhaps I might ride over one day...before the wedding festivities begin."

The two sisters exchanged another look, and they were both beaming when they turned to him.

"We'd be delighted," the two replied together cheerily.

16

"YOU SHOULDN'T HAVE TOLD your uncle before he left that we'd be going first to Blackthorn Hall. I've told you time and time again, Iain. I'm going to Fleet Tower."

When Marion slowed on the inn's steep, narrow steps, Iain placed a hand in the small of her back and gently pushed to keep her moving upward. He was actually impressed that she had waited this long to say what was on her mind.

Brother Luke and some of the men had left in the early afternoon. Iain had been able to distract his bride with a feast of a dinner that the innkeeper had produced for them. An aging former soldier, he had fought the English kings in France and in skirmishes along the Borders under the banner of the late King James. Rewarded for his service with a tract of land and an inn on Loch Lomond, the man had settled in to a quiet life. That is, until a wee lass from the Fleet Tower had arrived.

Nonetheless, the innkeeper had been jovial and quite entertaining, with dozens of stories about peculiar guests he'd given shelter to and the damage they'd done to his inn and people over the years.

"Iain, you're ignoring me."

"Could we call a truce for one night, lass?" he asked.

"Not until you give me some answers."

She tried to stop halfway up the steps. Iain didn't let her. "You mean, not until you get your way."

"Say what you will. But I've conceded many things during my lifetime of betrothal. This is one thing I'll not accept," Marion pressed. "I'll be staying with my aunts and uncle until the day of the wedding."

"That ceremony is to fulfill some formalities. We *are* already married. You are my wife, and as such, you will stay with me."

She shook her head. "Fleet Tower is my home. Those people are my only family. It's only right that I should return there after being away for so long."

"You can visit them. I'll take you over there myself, every day if you wish it."

"That is not enough," she said, shaking her head stubbornly.

"Do you remember what happened in that hut in the Highlands? You might not be safe there."

They reached the top of the stairs, and she planted her feet, refusing to go another step. "I was safe there for all my years of growing up. Jack would not sink so low as to try to hurt me in the place where his father lives."

They had been married barely a week, and Iain already knew her so well. The stubborn set of her chin, the blazing eyes, the folding of her arms across her chest--all told him she was not about to lose this skirmish without putting up a bloody battle.

Iain crossed his arms, too, mimicking her. He glowered at her. "I have not taken all these precautions to have you get hurt at the last minute."

"You said it yourself. We are already married. You are now legally the master of all McCall and Armstrong lands. What does it matter if something were to happen to me now?"

"It matters to *me*," he said in a gentler tone. "Don't you see that I truly care for you?"

His honesty was genuine. Iain spoke his heart, and he was surprised to find Marion flustered because of it. She stepped away from the top of the stairs. He fell in beside her, and she appeared to remember which room they would be staying in.

"I would still like to go to Fleet Tower first," she said much less combatively, stopping by the door. "Think of it as a moment's respite that I need in my life right now. There is no way I can go directly to Blackthorn Hall and face your mother and dozens of strangers, and still have the confidence to play my role beside you."

He ran a frustrated hand through his hair.

A smile touched the corner of her lips. She reached up and pushed the hair out of his face. Her fingers traced the scar on his forehead. "You came home from Flodden Field with this. I hated you for bringing the news of my father's death."

"I hated to bring that news."

"I know that...now." She paused a moment. "Iain, I want to go back there, to my home, to the tower, with my new feelings for you."

"Feelings that are stronger than hate?"

Her fingers moved down and touched his lips. "I harbor no hate. Only affection."

Marion's words warmed his heart. He couldn't refuse her this. He kissed her lips, pouring out his own affection.

"Please, Iain," she whispered, pulling back. "Give me this time with my family. You can certainly spare me for a couple of days."

"You should know I hate the thought of giving you up for even an hour."

She stared at him, obviously unsure of what to say.

"I'll make this concession." Iain braced himself for her denial. "We shall *both* go to Fleet Tower. I'll stay there, as well."

Marion hesitated for a long moment. "It will be awkward. You're not accustomed to them."

"And you have been away from them for quite a long while. You don't even know how awkward it can be."

Her eyes narrowed. "Are you making fun of them again?"

"No." He laughed and took her hand. "I've made a concession, and I'm asking one in return. I only grant you your wish if you grant me mine."

Marion jumped when the door to their bedchamber opened. Three servants came out, carrying empty buckets. An ample-bosomed redhead followed the rest out. Her hair was long and loose and cascaded down her back. She smiled broadly at the sight of Iain and gathered her hair in front, stroking it as she addressed him.

"Everything is prepared, m'lord. Just as ye required. Is there anything else I might be doing for ye tonight?"

Iain peered inside the room. Steam was rising from the water in the wooden half-barrel tub. Clean towels had been placed beside it. The wool blankets and quilt on the bed were folded back and the clean linens glowed in the fading light. On a table by the fireplace, a platter of cheeses and fruits sat next to a decanter of wine. It was a chamber fit for a queen.

He flipped the woman a coin. "Exactly what I wanted."

She paused before him, turning her back on Marion and totally ignoring her. "I'd be happy to stay around and help ye with your things."

Iain was relieved that his wife couldn't see the wench's saucy expression and the direction of her gaze. "No..."

The rest of the response never left his mouth as Marion pushed past the woman and stood in front of him in the doorway.

"I'm certain that I can see to anything else my husband needs."

If the tone of her voice sounded somewhat territorial, there was no question that the message got across. The wench curtsied, turned, and tossed her hair over her shoulders. The two watched her as she marched off and disappeared down the stairs.

Taking him by the hand, Marion pulled him inside the bedchamber. Iain pulled the door shut and latched it. The room was warm, and a golden light streamed through the two small windows.

"Is that vixen one of your women?"

"One of my women?" Iain smiled at the sight of her fists planted on her hips, the same gesture she'd made when she was six years old. "I have no other woman. None but you." He unbuckled his sword belt, undid his broach, and hung his weapons and cloak on a peg on the wall.

"She acted as if she's known you a while."

"Didn't they teach you in that priory that jealousy is a sin?"

"I'm not jealous." She flushed slightly. "I'm...I'm curious."

"Ah, well. That's different."

"So?"

"If you really must know, Marion, I saw the wench today for the first time. The innkeeper called her in to see to the preparations for our bedchamber." He peeled off his shirt.

Marion's gaze fixed on his wounded shoulder. She had been changing the dressing every time they made camp. The last time, he hadn't let her. There was a healthy scab forming, and he was healing fine.

"What are you doing?" she asked, her gaze moving over his chest.

"Undressing. Getting ready to take a bath. You should do the same."

"With you here?"

He nodded, taking off his boots.

"I can't do any such thing. It would be totally improper."

Iain realized she was watching every movement of his hands. "We are husband and wife, my love." He undid his belt, and his kilt fell to the floor at his feet. He smiled, watching her gaze follow that movement, too. Her face had turned a few darker shades of red.

"It's really quite warm in here. Perhaps we should open the windows."

"Take your dress off, Marion. After so many days on the road, we both need it."

She wiped her brow and tried to look away, but her gaze returned to his body. "I...I think I'll wait until you've finished."

"No, lass. We'll take a bath *together*."

She looked over her shoulder at the tub, then at the bed. "It's too small. We won't fit."

"Oh, we'll fit. In fact, we'll fit perfectly. Don't you remember?"

She didn't have to answer. Iain could tell by the way her gaze swept down his body, and her eyes narrowed as they fixed on a certain part of him.

"Do you need help with that dress?" He started toward her.

She shook her head and backed toward the tub. Her hands drifted to the neckline of the dress. Slowly, she untied the laces and began to pull them free. Iain's gaze followed the movement.

"I've been thinking about this for the past four days," he said, his voice husky.

"I have, too," she whispered, sliding the dress down her arms. He looked at her long arms, following the movement of her hands.

"You are so beautiful."

"And you're growing," she whispered, staring downward. "I think we shan't fit today."

"We will. I'll show you." The back of her knees touched the edge of the tub. He took her hand. She stepped out of the dress. "I have been thinking of the things I'd like to do to you. The ways I could have you. The things I could teach you." He reached and untied the top of the shift and slipped it off her shoulders. It pooled at her feet.

Her firm, round breasts called to be kissed. Marion laid her hand on his cheek as his mouth approached her flesh.

"Before you make me forget everything, including my name, answer my earlier question."

She never forgot a thing, Iain thought, smiling.

"We'll stop at Fleet Tower first. You and I both. We'll stay there until our wedding festivities require us to go to Blackthorn Hall. Satisfied?"

"Yes," she replied softly. "I believe I will be."

Smiling, she took him by the hand and stepped back into the warm water of the tub.

17

SITTING on his horse and looking down at yet another hut in yet another glen, Sir George Harington thought yet again about the letter he had received the day before. He was no more pleased with it.

The Marquis of Dorset had condescended to make a personal appearance at the Armstrong and McCall nuptials.

"Blast," he cursed to himself, starting down the hill. The four men attending him followed wearily.

Dorset would be at Blackthorn Hall by the week's end. In the letter, his lordship had also directed that Sir George send Hastings and Eden south to Carlisle to attend to other business. Sir George, on the other hand, was to wait at Blackthorn Hall for the marquis.

This was a dilemma, to be sure. Should he go to Carlisle himself, since the two men were still missing, or remain at Blackthorn Hall? His lordship expected the two men to go south immediately. At the same time, Sir George didn't want to bring the marquis's disfavor down upon himself by not being here when he arrived. The nobleman was in the habit of sending an entourage ahead to any country estate to see that all his requisite comforts were provided for before he arrived.

He simply had to find the two rogues, Sir George had decided. Asking Lady Elizabeth for every able body that she could spare, he'd search every glen and hut and sheepcote within twenty miles of the place. And that's just exactly what they'd been doing.

Unfortunately, many of the Armstrong workers had been sent north as an escort for the laird and his future wife. Still, the dowager had given him as many men and boys that she had to join his own soldiers in the hunt. Accompanying one of the four groups of men, he'd left Blackthorn Hall at midday yesterday, stopping at every village and crofter's hut they passed, but to no avail.

He'd ordered everyone to continue the search through the night. Now, with the morning sun moving high in the sky, he questioned his decision. After all this, there was still no sign of the two men. Their unsaddled horses had been found north of Fleet Tower, but where the riders had gone was anyone's guess.

"Ye have been in the saddle all night, m'lord," one of the Armstrong men said, riding up beside him. "This is unfamiliar country. Perhaps ye should return to Blackthorn Hall to get some rest. We'll continue to look for your officers."

"No. My men will continue the search, too." Sir George was already preparing a defense for when the marquis arrived. His lordship would want to be assured that no stone had gone unturned. There would be the devil to pay for the loss of Lady Dorset's cousin, and Sir George wanted to be sure it was the bloody Scots and not he who would be paying.

"As ye wish, but perhaps ye yourself might return to Blackthorn Hall. I'll send a couple of men along to escort ye back."

It was true. Sir George wasn't adding any value to the search. These parts were totally unknown to him. He also had to admit that he was tired, in addition to being starved.

"I want every available soldier to stay focused on the task of finding these men. I know exactly where we are. That road we just left...all I have to do is to follow it south, and I'll be at Blackthorn Hall in little more than an hour."

"Well, that's very true, m'lord." The Armstrong man looked doubtful. "I don't know that it'd be wise for ye to be traveling alone."

"Do not correct me," he snapped. "It is daylight. And I'm quite capable of finding my way. Now, you do what must be done. I'll be looking for you to return with the missing men. Carry on."

Sir George gave some orders to the English soldiers and turned his horse back up the hill.

Fleet Tower lay between not half an hour out of the way. It would be practically on his way. Yes, he decided. A stop there would be just the thing. With the thought of some very fine pastries before him, he spurred his tired horse and rode off.

Alone.

18

JUDITH WAS CLEARLY TOO AGITATED to sit still. Brother Luke watched her put the decanter of the wine on the table. A moment later, she decided against it and put it back in the cupboard. Taking out a pitcher of spiced cider, she placed it on the table. Bustling back to the cupboard, she returned with goblets...two more than were needed. She put those back. One of the goblets on the table had something at the bottom. She took that away and returned with a clean one. She did everything but offer him the platter of honeyed nuts and bite-sized fruit tarts.

"You are a whirlwind of activity, Lady Judith," the portly cleric said. "Please stop fussing over me. Come sit down so we can visit."

"A whirlwind? Why, nothing of the kind, Brother Luke," she replied, sitting on the edge of a chair. She looked like a sparrow, ready to take flight again. "I'm so happy that you're back. Margaret and I were just talking about you this morning. We've both grieved over your absence since you went to Skye to fetch our wee lassie. Since you've been living at both the abbey at Cracketford and at Blackthorn Hall, you've been our only regular visitor at Fleet Tower."

"I've always enjoyed our visits together," he said, trying not to be too conspicuous about eyeing the platter of sweets.

"But I must tell you that your absence has not been the only thing grieving us."

"No?" Luke looked around. Nothing seemed to be amiss. The

descending sun was still shining in the windows of the great hall. "Have troubles found their way to your door?"

Judith paused. Luke waited, nodding encouragingly.

"Oh, my dear...what was the other thing?" She touched her lips, looked blankly ahead. A moment later, she seemed to cheer up again. "Yes, yes, we've always delighted in our conversations."

Brother Luke folded his hands over his stomach. "I feel exactly the same, Lady Judith, but what is it that has been bothering you?"

The gentle lady jumped up again and held out the platter of sweets to him. Luke selected what looked like a blackberry tart and popped it in his mouth. It was as delicious as he remembered, and he nearly sighed aloud as it melted in his mouth.

Luke had been somewhat embarrassed for not coming right over to Fleet Tower when he'd first arrived home earlier in the week. He knew Judith and Margaret would be looking forward to hearing some news of their niece. There had been so much going on, though, when he'd ridden in the gates of Blackthorn Hall. With all that was happening with missing Englishmen and wedding preparations, Lady Elizabeth had a hundred and one duties for him to see to. His visit with the sisters had simply needed to wait until this afternoon. He hadn't expected to miss Lady Margaret, though. Judith told him the older sister had walked down to a village on the far side of the glen to visit a sick tenant.

"You see," the younger sister explained, "living in the same tower house where our father and his father before him lived, we've always been so accustomed to visitors coming our way regularly." She sat down again, still holding the platter of sweets. "But no more."

"Only the bloody English intrude upon us now," a gruff voice boomed from behind him.

Brother Luke practically leaped out of his chair. He hadn't heard Sir William come down the steps to join them. The cleric stared at him. The brother of the McCall sisters was as odd-looking as always. Wearing a chain shirt over a kilt, he also had on an old-fashioned helmet with a visor that kept tipping forward over his face. It was not Monday, Brother Luke noted, so the man's face wasn't painted blue. He was impressed, however, by the length of the sword strapped at Sir William's side. The tip of the weapon was touching the floor.

"No, Sir William," Judith quickly corrected. "No one visits us now. How do you like these tarts, Brother Luke? I made them myself today."

"They are excellent," he said, turning to speak to Sir William.

The eccentric walked past Luke, ignoring him, and popped one of the sweets in his mouth. As he did, the visor slipped down over his eyes.

"Nearly inedible," he announced, sitting on a chair beside Judith and raising the visor. "Horrible things. Are they English?"

"No. I made these, Sir William," Judith repeated, extending the tray in Luke's direction. "Won't you have another piece?"

"No, I really can't. I have promised Lady Elizabeth to return for supper with an appetite. If you know what I mean?"

"Why, of course I do. But you should try one of these," Judith insisted, pointing to a small honeyed nut. "They are not filling at all."

"No, I really can't," Luke explained.

William reached over and popped that one in his mouth.

"Horrible," he asserted again loudly.

Luke suppressed a smile and turned to him. "It's wonderful of you to come and join us, Sir William. It's been so long, perhaps months, since I had the pleasure of your company."

The pleasantries did not appear to be heard. William never looked Luke's way. He reached for another tart and ate it again in one bite. His "horrible" was only a murmur, this time from behind the visor.

Luke felt for the aging McCall sisters. He couldn't imagine how difficult it must be to deal with a brother such as this. The man was obviously mad as a tanner.

"Why, I beg to disagree, Sir William. I believe these are excellent," he declared. "In fact, I must tell you, Lady Judith. Your talents were being discussed by one of our guests at Blackthorn Hall only yesterday."

"Really?" Judith's round face broke into a smile. "Who?"

"Sir George Harington," Luke explained. "The Marquis of Dorset's right-hand man in the Borders. He is the emissary from the English king's court."

"The English king, sir?" William asked sharply, acknowledging Luke for the first time and slowly standing up.

"Yes, Sir William," the cleric explained. "Sir George Harington was raving about your sisters--"

"Where are your weapons?" William asked in a menacing tone.

"My weapons?" Luke asked incredulously.

"Your sword, sir," he said, as if he were talking to an imbecile.

"I carry no sword, sir. But I certainly would not be prepared to fight. I'm a man of God and—"

Judith stood up, too, and placed a firm hand on her brother's arm. "This is Brother Luke, William. He is Iain's uncle."

He shook off his sister's hand and took a step toward Luke. "If you have no sword, laddie, how do you expect to help me when we go into battle against the English?"

Realization dawned on the cleric. William McCall was very much Sir William Wallace today, as he was every day. Luke should never have mentioned the English at all.

"Sir William," Luke responded, drawing himself up, "I'll fetch my sword before we go into battle."

"Why, Sir William," Judith scolded softly. "You're confused about—"

"Sister!" Her brother whirled to face her. As he did, the visor of the helmet tipped forward again. He raised it with a sweep of his hand. "Your cooking has caused the confusion. But where is the new recruit to be added to my ranks?"

"No more talk of battles, Sir William." She turned to the table, putting the platter of sweets down and picking up the pitcher. "Can I pour you some spiced cider, brother?"

"No, indeed. Horrible stuff," William grumbled, sitting down again as she poured it for him anyway.

"Brother Luke?" Judith asked.

He wasn't thirsty, but to bolster his hostess's mood, he asked for some. The smell of cinnamon wafted from the drink. Luke breathed the sweet smell when he was handed the cup.

"It's so quiet and pleasant here," he said, sitting down. "Blackthorn Hall is brimming over with people. One doesn't know if there is going to be room at the table during mealtime or a place to sleep at night."

"It's quite lovely here at Fleet Tower," Judith said. "Have you been here before?"

Brother Luke stared up at her.

"But of course you have." Judith looked about her contentedly.

"Margaret and I were very happy when Lady Elizabeth insisted on feeding us so many of her cakes. We like it much better this way."

Luke hesitated, trying to understand the connection between the cake feeding and the wedding arrangements. He knew Iain had asked Lady Elizabeth to consult with Marion's aunts and, between them, to take care of the preparations while he was gone. He learned upon arrival that everything was to take place at Blackthorn Hall. He sipped the cider and glanced at William, who was muttering something under his breath to no one in particular.

Everything stood a chance of going smoothly this way, he thought.

"Of course, our Marion might insist on sitting down with cake and Lady Elizabeth, once she gets back," Judith added.

"No, no, I think the laird and Lady Marion will be quite satisfied with the arrangements." Luke reminded himself that he was not to mention to the two aunts that their niece was already married to Iain. At Blackthorn Hall, Lady Elizabeth had ordered him to hold his tongue about it. She wanted to keep up the pretense of having the wedding taking place on the steps of the old Armstrong chapel. To her thinking, it would be more appropriate to formally unite the families in that way.

Luke decided that even if he had been given leave to share the news, there was no point in mentioning it now. With Lady Margaret away visiting, some confusion could easily arise with the younger sister.

"Lady Marion is very excited," he said, "about returning to her family. She's missed all of you dreadfully."

Judith reached over and touched William's arm, bringing him out of his trance. "Our niece, Marion, is coming back."

"Who is Marion?"

"Our niece," she repeated. "The Earl of Fleet's daughter."

William grinned broadly, showing even, white teeth. "Eee-lated. I'll have her work with me training the men."

"No, Sir William, Marion is a girl," Judith corrected him.

"She fought better as a wee one than my army do now," he complained. "They lack liveliness. They need that spark of life. They need—"

"You will not take her to visit your men," Judith ordered in a sharp whisper. "She'll be married to the laird and move to Blackthorn Hall. She'll have no time." Without giving William a chance to respond, she turned to Brother Luke. "Has our wee bairn grown at all since she left here?"

"Indeed she has!" Luke felt embarrassed at his lack of consideration in not offering this information before. "She has grown into a bonny lass. She has actually become a tall young woman."

"Taller than the laird?" Judith asked, obviously dismayed.

"No, not taller than Sir Iain. I tell you she has blossomed into a lovely young lady."

"How long is her hair?" Judith asked.

Luke had to think about that. "Quite long, I believe."

"And her eyes?" the older lady asked.

"They have not changed," he replied. "They are dark. The color of onyx."

"Does she still fart?"

"Pardon me?" Luke turned to William, unable to hide the mixture of shock and laughter rising up in him.

"The poor child," Judith continued, as if it were perfectly natural to discuss their niece's bodily functions. "She used to have such an unsettled stomach. Not too many things agreed with her when she was small. That was why she never grew. Has she grown at all?"

Luke stared at her.

"She farted all the time. Morning, noon, and night," William clarified, rising from his chair. He directed a sharp look at Luke. "Does she still do it, recruit?"

"No, Sir William." He struggled and managed to fight back his smile. "She does an excellent job of...uh, holding it in."

"We should just be happy that our Marion is coming home to us," Judith insisted.

"I've told you. I'm elated," William said to his sister before turning back to Luke. "Soldiers have been known to fart, you know. She can teach them how to manage it."

Luke took a long drink from his cup.

"Now, now, Sir William. No more talk of this before company," Judith scolded.

William snorted, taking a blackberry tart that Luke had been eyeing. The old knight mumbled, "Horrible" before sitting back in his chair.

The sound of riders arriving in the courtyard reached Luke's ears.

William and Judith were on their feet in an instant and racing toward one of the windows. Judith beat him there and then shook her head sternly at her brother, pointing to the chair. "You stay with Brother Luke, Sir William. I can manage this by myself."

Luke stood up, comprehending her concern completely. In Sir William's general state of confusion, he could very well draw his sword and chase after any visitors arriving at Fleet Tower, thinking they were English. William returned to the table, glowering at him.

Judith opened the shutters and began talking to someone below. Luke watched as Sir William stared down his nose at him. The visor was ready to drop over his eyes.

"No sword, no chain mail, no dirk, no helmet. You're not prepared for the battle at all, soldier."

"I couldn't afford any of that, sir," Luke said, trying to humor him and listen to Judith.

The older man put an arm around Luke's shoulder. "You come with me to the dungeon. I'll arm you with all you need to do battle against the bloody English dogs."

"No, no, William," Judith cried, hurrying back to join them. "Brother Luke is not going anywhere with you. He is *not* one of your soldiers."

Obviously disappointed, William released him and cast an eye back at the window. "Well, then...who's in the courtyard? Englishmen or soldiers loyal to me?"

Judith ignored the question and turned instead to Luke. "Two of your favorite warriors have ridden over from Blackthorn Hall."

"Who is it, woman?" William persisted. "There will be no fence-straddlers. They're either with me or against me. Who is it?"

"It's Tom and John, Sir William. Your own loyal men. They're seeing to their horses before they come in."

"I am eee-lated. They must be bringing me news from Leglen Wood." He strode toward the doorway, and Judith went after him.

Brother Luke shook his head with amusement as she tried to stop her brother. John and Tom Armstrong, two brothers who worked in the stables at Blackthorn Hall, were seasoned fighters, having served both Iain and his father for nearly twenty years. Good natured men, they were also tough, bearing scars earned of Flodden Field and a dozen other battles.

The two men walked into the room and were greeted warmly by Lady Judith.

William stepped in front of his sister and hugged each man. To their credit, neither flinched. "You're alive, lads. That's excellent. What news have you brought me?"

"All is quiet in Leglen Wood," John replied.

"Nothing to report, Sir William," Tom added.

"Eee-lated," William replied. He took a step back and inspected each man's attire and weapons. He tapped the side of his nose thoughtfully. "I have new swords for each of you, lads."

"We're quite satisfied with these, sir," Tom explained.

William shook his head in disapproval. "I'll fetch you what you need from the armory."

Judith tried to stop him, but William was already heading toward the arched doorway. As the four of them watched, the older man drew his sword.

With the shout "*Freedom!*" he charged up the stairs.

John and Tom strolled across the great hall as if there were nothing amiss.

Judith scurried over to the table to offer them something to eat.

"So," Brother Luke said with a smile. "Members of the Wallace's Merry Men, are you?"

They nodded and grinned.

"Indeed they are," Judith answered. "My brother decided several years ago that these fine men are John Somebody and Tom Somebody."

"John Blair, Lady Judith," John said.

"And Tom Halliday," said the other. "Don't you remember?"

"Oh, indeed. Now that you say it."

"We're two of the Wallace's most trusted friends, Brother Luke," John explained, taking a fruit tart off the plate.

"We're important men, don't you know," Tom laughed, looking over the sweets Judith was offering.

It was clear that the McCall sisters' excellent baking might have been added incentive for coming to Fleet Tower.

"What brings you here today?" Brother Luke asked of the two.

"Ah, well. There's a wee crisis over at the Hall, Brother," John explained.

"Sir George Harington seems to have gone missing," Tom added.

"How could that be possible?" Luke asked. "I thought the man was out looking for the other two lost Englishmen."

"He was," Tom said. "But we got back a couple of hours ago to change horses and were told that Sir George left his group this morning, heading back to the Hall. Never arrived."

"No surprise." John popped another tart into his mouth. "An Englishman couldn't find his own arse in a pile of millstones."

Brother Luke coughed, and Tom elbowed his brother.

"Beggin' your pardon, Lady Judith," he apologized, his mouth full.

"No need to, young man," she said. "We feel just the same here. Why, I remember when...when..." She paused and held up the platter of pastries to the two men. "You need to finish these. We have more in the kitchens, you know."

It *was* the baked goods that made these two volunteers to ride over, Brother Luke decided, as each man plucked a handful of the tarts off the plate.

"He could be wandering about," Luke suggested. "Has anyone gone out looking for him?"

"We sent..." John stopped as Lady Judith handed him a cup full of spiced cider. "You are a wonder, m'lady. How did you know how thirsty and hungry we were?"

The woman's round rosy face bloomed into a smile as she gave a cup to Tom, as well. She urged the men to sit down and rest themselves, and they both did as they were told.

"A group of the lads are already out searching for him," Tom managed to explain before Lady Judith turned to the table to pick up the platter of pastries again. "In fact, we should be out with them, as well."

"What are you doing here, then?" Luke asked.

"We heard Sir George raving about Lady Margaret and Lady Judith, so we hoped maybe he is not lying in a ditch somewhere, but sitting here instead, enjoying the day with you."

Any excuse to visit the sisters, Luke thought. "Well, as you can see, he is not here, and the evening will soon be upon us. So you fellows should be on your way."

"My army is growing, lads. The armory is short on swords."

William was beside them again. Luke almost laughed to see the two men jump. He wasn't the only one who never heard the older man come into the great hall.

"Perhaps we shall retire to the dungeons, where you can fight some of the other men for their weapons?"

"No, Sir William," Lady Judith scolded her brother. "They don't need new weapons. They have their own arms, as you can see. Now, sit and have a bite to eat."

The Wallace sat, but not without complaining and muttering, "Horrible" after he ate another tart from the platter.

"Brother Luke is right. We should be on our way," Tom said, pushing reluctantly to his feet.

"We should indeed be going," John said halfheartedly, following his brother's lead.

"You cannot be leaving empty-handed," Judith announced.

Brother Luke noticed that there were only two pastries left in the tray. Their host picked up the plate.

"All of you stay right here. I'll be right back. I'll just fill this plate and bring something for you lads to take along with you."

Both men called out their gratitude. Judith directed a warning look at her brother before rushing out toward the kitchens.

"This is all too strange," Luke told the Armstrong men.

"Indeed it is." John nodded. "Though I personally wouldn't mind if the whole lot of 'em disappeared off the face of this earth."

Luke nodded, thinking. "That aside. The two Englishmen before and today Sir George. Where could they be? If some outlaws had attacked them, then where are the bodies?"

William sat like a stone, silently staring at Luke. After a couple of minutes of being closely observed, the cleric realized his mistake. He had made another reference to the English.

"All is well. I am a friend," Luke said in what he hoped was a calm voice.

"Then join us, lad," William challenged.

"I *have* joined you. I'm one of your recruits."

Sir William jumped up to his feet.

"We'll take a wee walk to the dungeon, where I can question you."

Luke stood up and backed around the chair. "That won't be necessary now, Sir William." He glanced at the two Armstrong men. They were obviously not about to defend him. In fact, they looked as if they were finding this entire situation very entertaining.

"I can smell a lie," William said in a low menacing tone, stepping toward him.

"Now, listen to me, Sir William," he responded reasonably, putting both hands up in peace.

The sound of footsteps came from behind them. William whirled around, his hand grasping the hilt of his sword. Lady Margaret appeared in the wide doorway to the great hall.

"She must have been the one I smelled," William muttered under his breath, taking his hand off the weapon and stomping back to his seat.

Luke let out a sigh of relief.

"Well, well, how wonderful," Margaret announced as she shed her cloak and dropped it on one of the window seats.

The two Armstrong men were on their feet.

"Afternoon, Lady Margaret," Tom said cheerfully.

"Afternoon," John echoed.

"How wonderful to have all you gentlemen here," she said enthusiastically. "You all will be staying to eat, no?" She put a basket she was carrying on the window seat beside her cloak.

The three of them murmured their excuses, each stating why they couldn't stay.

"Excellent. It's been so long since we had so many people sitting around the table with us."

Luke realized she had not heard any of their explanations. "We cannot stay, m'lady," he said louder. "I'm expected back at Blackthorn Hall. So many guests have already begun to arrive. And these good fellows need to be out looking for one of the guests who's gone astray." Luke paused, looked at William. He wasn't going to make the same mistake twice. "One of the guests is missing."

"Oh, dear! That's quite dreadful," Margaret said in her high-pitched tone. "It's so close to supper, though." She addressed the two Armstrong men. "Why don't you have just a wee bite to eat before you leave?"

"We appreciate you offering, m'lady," John said pleasantly, "but we cannot stay, you see."

"Lady Judith is bringing out something to take along with us," Tom added. "That will hold us just fine until we'll get back to Blackthorn Hall."

"We made some pastries just this morning." Margaret walked to the table and looked at the pitcher and the cups. She glanced at the cupboard, picked up one of the cups and looked inside before putting it back. She turned around to the men. "I just took some oatcakes to a poor villager who has been suffering with toothache."

Judith walked back into the great hall, her arms full. Tom and John rushed over to help her and took the bundles she had for them, thanking her.

"Oh, you're back, Margaret," she said, spying her sister. "How was Duncan?"

"He is suffering, poor man."

"Poor man," Judith repeated. "That's hardly pleasing to hear."

"He told me the tooth puller from Dumfries is expected to be in the village tomorrow. He's going to see him," Margaret said, taking the platter of the cakes from her sister and putting it on the table.

"The tooth puller from Dumfries," Judith repeated excitedly. "Could we go and watch?"

Margaret nodded and smiled.

Brother Luke watched the two sisters giggle as something else was said that he couldn't hear. He thought, how kindly of them to want to be present and hold a suffering soul's hand while he was going through such an ordeal.

"We'll be on our way now, ladies," Tom said. "Thank you for the food."

"We might even share a bit of it with the rest of the lads," John added.

Sir William pushed to his feet. "I'll take something to share with *my* men." He picked up the platter of cakes. "I'll take these to them in the dungeon."

"No, Sir William," Judith scolded.

"Put it back, Sir William," Margaret ordered.

The older man held the platter protectively to his side. "They'll start pillaging on their own if I don't take this to them."

"William," both sisters said in a warning tone.

Brother Luke found it almost tragic to see how much trouble the older man was to his sisters.

"Perhaps I can assist with this." Brother Luke reached for the platter but immediately realized it was a mistake.

"Away, you bloody English cur. You'll be wanting to take this to your own men, I suppose." He reached for his sword.

Luke immediately stepped back.

"It's fine for him to have it," Margaret said, resignedly.

"He can have it," Judith repeated.

"Say good-bye to your warriors," Margaret told her brother. "They're leaving."

"They're leaving." Judith pointed to the two men who were standing wide-eyed near the entrance to the hall.

The platter stayed close to his side as William went to escort the Armstrong men out. Brother Luke watched the exchange between the three. This time, though, he didn't find it amusing. Today was the first time that he'd realized how dangerous William could be. The madness in him was apparent. Something needed to be done about it.

The two Armstrong men left, and Luke remained standing, keeping a chair between William and himself as the older man walked to the arched doorway on the opposite side of the great hall. If it was upstairs or the dungeons or the kitchens he was disappearing to, Luke couldn't know. He did notice, though, that there was no shout of "*Freedom*" as Sir William McCall went out.

19

MARGARET PUSHED ALL the dirty cups to one side. Reaching into the cupboard, she took out one that had a bit of liquid left in it. She looked into it thoughtfully and then turned around to ask her sister a question about the wine. She stopped. She'd forgotten that Brother Luke was still here.

"Are you certain you cannot stay for supper?" she asked.

"Do stay for supper." Judith clapped her hands in excitement.

The clergyman shook his head and picked up his cloak from the bench. "I have very much enjoyed your company and your cooking, ladies, but I cannot."

"That's disappointing," Margaret said.

"Very disappointing," Judith added.

"I promise to return very soon, however," he promised. A frown darkened his features, though, as he glanced toward the door through which William had disappeared. "But before I go, I'm very curious to know...I hope you don't think I'm intruding..."

"Of course not, Brother Luke," Margaret replied. "What is it you wish to know?"

"Well, have you ever tried to persuade your brother that he *isn't* William Wallace?"

"Oh, heavens, no!" Margaret cried out.

"Not at all," Judith stressed.

"And why is that?" Brother Luke asked.

Margaret looked at her sister first before answering. "Well, our parents named him William. I think they wanted him to be William Wallace, too. He couldn't be anyone else."

"No one else," Judith agreed.

"With a name like William he couldn't be Robert the Bruce."

"Not Robert the Bruce," Judith agreed.

"It would have been nice for a change," Margaret added doubtfully.

"But it wouldn't work," Judith finished.

"Lady Margaret. Lady Judith." Brother Luke shook his head. "Parents have many reasons for naming their bairn. But I sincerely doubt that your good father, the old earl, named your brother William with the idea that he should wander about frightening people by pretending to be the Wallace."

"But he's as gentle as a wee mouse, Brother Luke."

"As a mouse!"

"I know that, ladies. But what in heaven's name is wrong with being Sir William *McCall*? You two gentle ladies are yourselves. And your late brother, the good earl, was John McCall, Earl of Fleet. No confusion."

The two sisters looked in bewilderment at each other. Neither Margaret nor her sister really understood what the clergyman meant, or what they were supposed to do.

"But he's *happy* as Sir William Wallace," Margaret said finally, for the lack of anything else to say.

"Very happy." Judith nodded wholeheartedly.

"But are *you* happy?" Brother Luke asked the two of them.

The two sisters exchanged a look again.

"I cannot see as well as I did in my younger years," Margaret admitted. "But I'm quite happy, beyond that."

"My knee makes a wee cricking noise when I go up and down the stairs," Judith offered, pointing to her knee. "I'm happy, too, beyond that."

Brother Luke looked flustered. "Ladies, we're all advancing in age. What I was asking really had to do with Sir William. Are you two happy that your brother lives in a world of dreams? That he is no help to the two of you in running this tower house? That he scares off the regular help, causing you to be burdened with so much more than any gentlewomen of your age and station should be burdened with?"

Margaret didn't have to think hard to answer that one and shook her head. "I'm happy with William, Brother."

"I'm very happy," Judith agreed.

"He's our baby brother. It's our job to look after him," Margaret added as an explanation.

"Our baby brother," Judith echoed, smiling and nodding.

Margaret watched as Brother Luke's troubled face suddenly lit up. "This is all the more reason to be concerned. He's your baby brother. And what will happen to him when you two pass on?"

"We're not going anywhere," Margaret said.

"Only to the village, once a week." Judith explained.

"And to Marion's wedding at Blackthorn Hall," Margaret remembered.

"We are going to Blackthorn Hall to have some cake," Judith agreed.

"I'm not talking about going anywhere in this life," Brother Luke said grimly. "What will happen to Sir William after you die?"

Margaret looked at Judith, who was clearly surprised, as well, by the question. "We are not ready to die," she said miserably.

"No, we're not ready," Judith said with a choking sound in her throat.

The cleric ran a hand down over his face. He looked upset. All this talk of dying was clearly distressing him, Margaret thought.

"I'm very sorry to bring this up, ladies. I didn't mean to upset you. It's just as a friend and as someone who has great respect for your family, I thought you should begin thinking about such things."

"We're done thinking," Judith said firmly.

"I think we are done for today," Margaret agreed.

"Would you care for a wee bit of pastry before dinner?" Judith asked. "Did we ask you to stay for dinner?"

"Thank you both. You're too good, but no." Brother Luke shook his head and draped his cloak over his shoulders. "My apologies again, ladies."

Margaret nodded pleasantly, and Judith walked with him to the door.

"Please come and see us soon," Judith encouraged.

"Very soon," Margaret called out to him.

20

ALMOST THERE, and Marion wished she could grow wings.

At a fork in the road, the horses turned down the lane leading to Fleet Tower. She was again on McCall land. Finally. Her eyes drank it all in.

There was something dreamlike in the landscape as she looked around her. The countryside, the cottages nestled in the glens and on the sides of the hills, the farms—so much of it was almost new to her. It was all here twelve years ago. All just the same. She knew that. But she'd been too young when she left. It had slipped away from her memory like the mist on a morning slope.

Still, there was something familiar in all of it.

There was so much that she wanted to see, yet at the same time she was impatient to get to the Tower. The yearning ache of the years now became almost unbearable. She filled up her lungs with the cool autumn air, trying to recall the smell of the earth and the trees and the fading heather. She didn't even realize that she'd ridden past the front of the group until Iain suddenly appeared beside her.

"You need to promise to wear this same smile for all our married days."

"I promise." She smiled at him, happy that he wasn't slowing her down, but staying with her. "And thank you for taking me home first."

"I told you I'll stay the night with you at Fleet Tower, but I need to send most of the men back to their families."

"Send all of them away. I doubt my aunts would be ready to take care of so many new arrivals."

"We'll see. I might just do that," he said. "Tomorrow, though, you and I need to ride to Blackthorn Hall to see my mother. You cannot avoid her until the wedding."

She nodded reluctantly. Marion was not looking forward to meeting with Lady Elizabeth. All of the memories she had of the gentlewoman consisted of her looking down her nose disapprovingly at Marion. Correcting her whenever she was in her company. Lecturing her on how she should behave and what her responsibilities were. Lady Elizabeth treated Marion like a wild child who wasn't getting any instruction on behavior from her own family.

Well, perhaps she wasn't, Marion admitted to herself, but that wasn't any reason to try to make her feel so lacking.

"But I want to come back here to spend the night," she told Iain.

"Very well."

"And I want you to let me stop, visit, and get to know this countryside again on our ride over and back." She made a sweeping gesture that took in everything around them. "I've missed all of this so much."

"We'll do that, as well."

Marion looked at her husband and her heart swelled with everything she felt for him. He couldn't have been kinder to her since their stay at the inn. He could not have been more caring, compassionate, or understanding. Something had changed in him. She could see it in his eyes, in the way he looked at her, in the way he caressed her when he thought she was asleep, in the words of affection he murmured to her.

She showed him affection, too, but she hadn't spoken the words. She loved him, and that terrified her. Marion had to be herself. At the same time, she knew she wasn't good enough for Iain in the eyes of his mother, in the eyes of his clan. She was another of the mad McCalls. She wished he'd continue to think differently. She wished *she* could think differently about her family.

"There it is," Iain said as they topped another hill.

Marion had been so wrapped up in her thoughts that she hadn't seen Fleet Tower appearing in the distance. Emotions welled up in her, and she had to rein in and slow her horse. She looked at the great square tower with its parapet and bartizans at each corner. She had spent so many hours up there, daydreaming, keeping watch, or taking orders from Sir William as he prepared for his legendary victory, as the Wallace, at Stirling Bridge or for his march on York.

As they drew nearer, Marion spotted two men riding toward them along the road from the Tower. Alan, Iain's right-hand man, rode up to the front of the group.

"These are our men," Alan said to Marion.

"Regular visitors to Fleet Tower, these two are," Iain said. "You probably don't remember them. Their names are John and Tom. Your uncle considers them to be two of his 'band of merry men.'"

"Welcome, laird," one of the men called out.

The two greeted them warmly and paid their respects to Marion. She returned their greeting. She listened to the news they were sharing with Iain about the wedding. Some of the guests were missing and there were search groups out looking for them.

Moments later, the two men were riding back with them again toward the tower. As Marion got closer, the tower house began to show its age. The stonework needed repair in some places. She promised herself that she'd see to it with the help of her husband. She looked at the cluster of cottages along the road leading to the Tower gate. They all appeared to be deserted.

Finally, they rode through the gates. A thrill washed down her back as they passed beneath thick walls. She looked up at the pointed iron bars of the raised portcullis. There was an abandoned bird's nest on one of the crosspieces.

The courtyard, too, appeared to Marion to be as deserted as the village, and no one approached them to take their horses or even greet them. Marion looked around her. It appeared that there were no workers in the stables. In fact, if it were not for the smoke coming from the chimney of the great hall, she would have thought that Fleet Tower had been abandoned.

Just then, Brother Luke came out of the stables, leading his horse. The cleric lit up at the sight of them.

21

BOTH SISTERS WAITED until their visitor was gone, and then Judith walked back to the table. Margaret remembered the cup of half-drunk wine she'd taken out of the cupboard. She pulled out the pitcher and looked inside to see how much was left.

"Were you entertaining anyone today, other than the guests I saw here?" Margaret asked, curious.

Judith brought a hand to her mouth and giggled. "As a matter of fact, I was. I didn't get a chance to make anything for supper, so it was a good thing that no one accepted our invitation."

"And did you have any 'special' guests, Judith?"

"Why, yes! Didn't I mention it?"

"And how many 'special' guests did you entertain?" Margaret asked cheerfully.

Judith held up one finger.

Margaret smiled broadly. "And you did all that in the short time that I was out?"

Judith nodded. "I didn't want to wait, for I was afraid Marion and the laird would arrive in the middle of everything. And it was a very good thing I didn't wait, for Brother Luke dropped by for the visit. Did you know Brother Luke was here?"

"Yes, I just saw him."

"Well, I had no sooner tucked our special guest in before he arrived."

"You managed it all by yourself?"

Judith nodded proudly.

Margaret started across the great hall toward the arched door leading to the stairwell. "I'll just run down and have a look."

"Oh, no," Judith called after her sister. "There wasn't enough time. By the time Sir William came down to help me, Brother Luke was already coming up the stairs from the courtyard."

Margaret whirled in surprise and looked around the room. Everything was the same. She pointed to the fire in the great open hearth. "You didn't."

"Of course not. That wouldn't have worked at all."

Margaret circled the hall, glancing under tables, behind the tapestries, even under a blanket sitting on top of her basket of mending on a settee by the fire. "Well, where is he?"

Judith pointed with her finger. Margaret followed the direction and smiled.

"The window seat?" she asked.

Judith nodded.

Margaret went toward it to see for herself, and Judith joined her there. As the two women neared the window, though, they were suddenly aware of more visitors in the courtyard.

Judith leaned out the window. Margaret rested a hand on her sister's shoulders and squinted, trying to see.

"More English?" she asked in a whisper.

"No, lots of people. More than...more than a dozen," Judith answered. She leaned farther out. "Oh, Margaret, they're here! They're finally here."

"Who's here?"

"Marion and the laird. They've finally come."

Thoughts of the 'special guest' immediately fled, and the two sisters rushed toward the doorway to greet the laird.

22

THE TWO SMILING faces made this the sweetest of homecomings.

Margaret was the one nearest to her at the top of the stairs, so Marion embraced her first. "I've missed you both so much."

She moved from the arms of one woman to the other.

"Aunt Judith." She kissed the plump cheeks.

Marion found herself looking down into two bright sets of eyes. Her aunts seemed so much smaller than she remembered them. And they'd changed. Iain was right. They had definitely aged in the last twelve years. Margaret's face was a tapestry of wrinkles and Judith's back had bowed considerably. But to Marion, they looked wonderful.

"Our wee Marion has grown up," Margaret said, taking her hand and looking her over. "You've changed."

"Definitely changed," Judith said, taking her other hand.

"You've become a bonny lass, to be sure." Margaret patted her hand.

"Quite bonny," Judith mimicked her sister's motion.

"Tall, too."

"Very tall."

Marion was beginning to feel embarrassed with the attention. She knew it was useless to try to interrupt them, though, for they wouldn't hear her. Listening to them, she recalled that once they began a certain train of thought, it was almost impossible to break into it. This was very much the same as it had been before. The two repeated each other's words until a person wasn't sure which of them was saying what. She would just wait until it was her turn.

"You won't fit into your old clothes," Margaret was saying, shaking her head as if in regret.

Marion laughed. "I should hope not, I'm no longer—"

"She won't fit in my clothes, either." Judith shook her head, as well.

"The wedding gown!" Margaret looked at her sister with alarm.

Judith nodded. "Yes, the wedding gown will be a problem,"

"It belonged to your mother," Margaret said, turning to Marion. "We kept it for you."

"We kept your mother's wedding gown for you to wear to the church," Judith explained as if Marion hadn't heard.

Margaret pulled the front of her cloak back and touched her waist. "You're far too thin. But we can do something about that."

"We can definitely do something about that," Judith agreed.

"And too tall."

"Definitely too tall."

Marion slouched, but it didn't seem to make much of a difference. Compared with her aunts, she was too tall.

"We can't do anything about that." Still holding the edge of the cloak, Margaret looked down Marion's skirt, obviously disappointed.

"We'll add a panel of different material at the bottom," Judith blurted out. It was the first idea of her own. "I can sew it on, myself."

Marion hoped her Aunt Judith's aptitude with needle and thread had improved over the past twelve years. She remembered even from her childhood how ghastly her aunt's projects had generally ended up. When it came to the art of running different aspects of the household, Margaret had definitely been the more talented of the two. Judith was better at taking instructions and executing them.

"A panel of material will do nicely," Margaret agreed. "But we still have to put some additional weight on you."

"You two are the dearest aunts, but Iain and I…" Marion paused at the touch of her husband's hand on her back. She wanted to tell them that it really didn't matter, that she was already married to Iain, and she would be happy with any dress for the wedding. She looked at him over her shoulder. He gave the slightest shake of his head. "Aunt Margaret, Aunt Judith, you remember—"

"Her betrothed," Iain finished for her. "Of course they remember me."

"Indeed we do," Judith said, smiling. She let go of Marion's hand and took Iain's instead. "You told us you'd bring our Marion back."

"And you did just that." Margaret took Iain's other hand. "Now come and sit, the two of you. You must be starved after your journey."

Marion was not offended that the two women appeared more excited to see Iain than her. She took off her cloak and dropped it on a bench and followed the three to a table by the fire. Her gaze surveyed the great hall. The same long tables and benches, the same tapestries and armor on the walls. Everything looked a little worn, but everything still looked pretty much as it had twelve years ago. She glanced across the hall at the arched doorway that led to the kitchens and to the circular stairwell. She wanted to go and see the rest of the tower house, too. Especially her bedchamber. She'd just moved into it from the aunts' chamber when she was taken to Skye. And she wanted to go and say hello to her uncle William. But there was time for everything. This wasn't a dream. She was back at Fleet Tower. She was home.

"We have some meat pie left over for supper. You wouldn't mind such simple fare, would you?"

"Would you mind?" Judith repeated.

Marion noticed that the question was directed at Iain and not at her.

"Not at all." Iain said. He motioned to the table and the pitchers and cups. "But could I trouble you first for something to drink?"

"No, not at all," Judith said, reaching for one of the pitchers.

"No, not this," Margaret grabbed the pitcher out of her sister's hand and put it on a shelf in the cupboard. "We'll go and get you some wine and clean cups."

"Yes, clean cups." Judith took Iain's hand and led him to one of the seats.

Margaret began stacking everything up on a tray. Marion walked to her. "Can I help you with these?"

"No, dear. Judith is," the older aunt said, glaring over her shoulder at the sister.

"Oh, yes, I'm helping." Judith rushed over to help.

Marion wasn't a guest. This was her home. "Please, Aunt Margaret, just allow me to carry this for you to the kitchen."

The older woman shook her head firmly. "You sit here and entertain the laird. Judith will help me to bring back new drinks and some food for the two of you. Now be on your way. Sit down and keep him happy."

Marion heard Iain chuckling behind them. She could guess what was running through his mind. Entertain him, indeed.

"We want you two to feel at home," Margaret said.

"Yes, indeed. Feel at home, you two," Judith repeated as the sisters left the hall.

Marion waited until they were gone before turning to her husband. "They don't know, do they?"

He shook his head. "Lady Elizabeth appears to have intruded. She told Brother Luke to keep our marriage a secret. She didn't want the word of our hasty marriage to reach the ears of the two groups of emissaries from the English and Scottish courts."

"Then you cannot stay here with me. That would be totally improper."

"I'll show you what's improper." He took her by the hand and pulled her onto his lap. He kissed her long and deep.

"You heard your aunts," he whispered against her ear, biting on the lobe. His hand slid upward along her ribs and he cupped her breast through the dress. "Entertain me."

She reluctantly pushed his hand away. "I knew you'd be acting like this."

She tried to get off his lap. He held on tighter. She tried to glower, but with no success. He was too tempting. She kissed him again, and then whispered in his ear.

"I'll entertain you later. I promise. Now let me go. Someone might walk in."

He lifted her and moved her higher on his lap. She could feel the bulging evidence of his feelings. "How much later?"

"After our proper church wedding."

"That's far too late," he told her. "I'm staying here at Fleet Tower, you know."

"In a different bedchamber than the one I'll be staying at."

"I don't believe your aunts would mind at all if I were to sleep with you." He ran his lips along the skin of her neck. "They like me."

"Iain, either we're married or we're not. If your mother insists on keeping everything quiet, then we must behave appropriately until the wedding day."

"But we're staying at Fleet Tower, not at Blackthorn Hall." His hand slid over her hip, her stomach. His mouth continued to feast on her neck, his breath caressing her skin. "We can do whatever we want, wherever we want. This is the way things are at this house."

Marion should have objected, but the words never found their way to her lips. Iain could seduce her anytime, anywhere, as far as Marion was concerned. She loved him. The excitement of his touch and his words made her head swim. She thought about how good it would be to take him upstairs and make love in her bedchamber. It didn't matter that the bed was probably too short and too narrow. There would be plenty of room. They could make love standing against the door, the way Iain had taught her. Margaret and Judith could be in the kitchen for a long time. And it had been two whole days since she'd had him.

"Come with me," she whispered, taking his hand.

"Where are you taking me?"

"To my bedchamber." She smiled over her shoulder.

He didn't need any more persuasion.

The two of them were like excited children as they hurried toward the stairwell. They were only a couple of steps from the arched doorway, though, when a warrior, armed with a long sword and dressed in chain mail and a helmet, suddenly emerged and blocked their path. As he stopped, the visor dropped down over his face.

Marion knew in an instant who it was, but it still took her heart a moment to climb down from her throat.

"Uncle William," she cried out excitedly.

He didn't even look at her. It was as if she were not standing there, as if she hadn't spoken. He pushed the visor up and turned to Iain, patting him on the shoulder.

"How are you, my lad?" William asked.

"I am quite well, Sir William."

"Did you just get back?"

"Yes, sir. This very hour," Iain said. "I've brought back your niece, Marion, as I promised."

Marion smiled, waiting for William's recognition. The older man didn't look her way again. A sharp pain began to gnaw at her. This was not what she'd imagined their first meeting would be.

"What news you bring me from the men?" he asked Iain.

"Well, the men are all celebrating the arrival of your kinswoman. Your niece. Marion." Iain was holding tightly to her hand. "You remember Marion, don't you, Sir William?"

"Yes, a wee sprite she was."

"No longer, sir. She is right here, standing before you." Iain motioned toward her with his other hand. "She has grown a great deal since you saw her last. But she is the very same Marion."

William finally turned to her and she had to control her emotions. More than anything, she wanted to throw her arms around him, but there was no sign of recognition in his face.

"Uncle William, you must remember me."

He looked her up and down.

Marion studied him, as well. Of the three aging McCall siblings, William was the one who now looked the oldest. The wisps of hair sticking out from the helmet and the scraggly beard on his face were pure white. He had grown round in the middle. He was also shorter than she recalled. But there was no fooling herself; he obviously couldn't remember her at all. She tried again.

"I was your main watchman, standing guard on the parapet whenever you ordered," she said, hoping to prod his memory. "And you always said I was excellent at helping you to paint your face on Mondays."

"That's a difficult job," William said. "But it needs to be done. So who did you say you were?"

"I'm Marion, your brother's daughter," she said. "I lived here at Fleet Tower until the age of six. After the battle at Flodden Field, I was sent away to the Isle of Skye. Don't you remember me?"

"Marion," he repeated, looking up toward the blackened beams of the ceiling for a long moment, tapping the side of his nose with one finger.

She was too afraid to say anything and have him forget what was already said. Iain squeezed her hand, giving her courage.

There was a twinkle in William's eyes when he focused on her again. "You claim to be my brother's daughter. You claim to be Marion McCall."

"I'm Marion McCall," she said. "And twelve years have passed since I saw you last. I was a child then. I'm a woman now. I know I look different, but everyone changes in that length of time, even the Wallace himself."

Sir William looked suddenly startled. "By the devil, lass, you're right! I haven't lost at Falkirk yet, have I?"

"No, Sir William. Falkirk is still a long way off."

"Very good," he replied, looking closely at her. "And you say you're Marion."

"Yes, I am."

"I would know Marion anywhere. And I say you're not Marion," he said emphatically.

"And why is that?" she asked, feeling tears of frustration beginning to well up.

"Marion smelled." He leaned toward her and sniffed. "You don't smell at all. You're an imposter."

"I never smelled," she said, suddenly outraged.

"She farted. It's well known."

"I didn't. It was you who made wind. You just always blamed it on me."

"How dare you make such an unfounded accusation?" he asked, glaring at her menacingly. "Do you wish to step outside, sir, and fight this out honorably?"

"I'm only trying to defend my reputation," she said, glaring right back at him. "When I was six years old, I thought it was quite funny that you blamed me for your own transgressions. However, I am now at an age where I find it less amusing. So, Sir William, we'll put an end to it right now. We'll go outside right now and fight this to the finish."

His eyes narrowed. He looked at her up and down again. "You sound nearly as bad-tempered as Marion."

"Of course," she answered. "I sound just like you."

William turned to Iain. "Is she truly my niece?"

He nodded. "There is no one else like her. She is the one."

There was no change in William's expression, and Marion was surprised when her uncle put both hands on her shoulders and gave her a kiss on each cheek.

"Welcome back, lassie."

She'd hoped for a little more, but she told herself to be happy that at least he was finally acknowledging her.

"You've been away too long," Sir William continued. "There are a dozen duties that I expect you to take care of, now that you have reenlisted."

"A dozen duties," she repeated.

"Do you claim to be my sister Judith now?" he asked suspiciously.

"No! No, sir." She put both hands up in defense. "And what are my duties?"

He continued to glare at her warily for a long moment before turning to Iain again. "Who did you say she was?"

"Your niece. Marion McCall. I give you my word on that."

William uttered a low harrumph before turning to Marion again. "You'll be taking shifts on the tower, of course."

She nodded, following his game.

"And you'll help with polishing the armor."

"Naturally," she answered, happy that Iain was not objecting to anything.

"And you will again be in charge of mixing the paints," William ordered.

"With pleasure, Sir William."

"And bar and unbar the door from the courtyard," he ordered.

"As you wish."

"And there is work to be done in the dungeon."

"Tell me what needs to be done, and I'll get to it." She smiled at her husband after. Iain nodded.

Behind William, Judith appeared in the doorway. She was carrying a tray containing a pitcher and dishes. Marion went to take the tray from her aunt.

"Please let me take that." Marion was relieved when Judith handed over the tray.

"Sir William, did I hear you giving our niece jobs to do?"

"Yes, woman, I did," the armored man replied.

"Did I hear you tell her to bar the door from the courtyard?"

"So?"

"We told you we don't want it barred. It takes both Margaret and me together to lift the bar from the door."

"Of course," Sir William said. "Well, from now on, she is to help carry food for the army."

"No, she is not to do that, either," Judith scolded her brother. "You will stop wasting food by taking it down there, in fact."

"An army needs to eat, woman," he argued. "Do you want them pillaging the countryside?"

"No more carrying food to them, William," she said more authoritatively.

"Bloody hell," he muttered. He put a hand on Iain's shoulder. "Well, I must be off. There are reports of that vile dog Longshanks and his army in the valley. You're in command, lad, until I return."

Iain nodded.

William turned to the stairwell, drew his sword, and charged up the steps, shouting, "*Freedom!*"

Marion stepped back, looking up the stairs with a mixture of sorrow and amusement. With a quick glance at Iain, she carried the tray to the table. Either William was far worse than he had been twelve years ago, or the time Marion had spent at the priory had allowed her to forget the worst of her uncle's oddities. She had to admit to herself that most of Iain's warnings were warranted.

"You shouldn't listen to everything he says, dear," Judith told Marion, joining her at the table and helping to unload the tray.

"What's the new fascination with the dungeons?" she asked. "I don't recall him spending any time there before."

"He is raising an army to attack England," Judith said, laying a hand on Marion's arm.

The younger woman smiled. "And he is housing them in the dungeon?"

"You know we haven't too many spare rooms at Fleet Tower, so Margaret and I let him do as he wishes." Her aunt shrugged. "So long as he stops taking food and letting it go to waste down there."

Marion looked over her shoulder at Iain. He didn't have to say anything. She agreed that William had obviously become a challenge, even for his two kindly sisters. She promised herself not to ignore the issue. Perhaps with Iain's help, they could come up with some solution other than sending William away to some spital house. They clearly needed to do something other than leaving him alone here with his sisters.

"Food," Judith said aloud, turning to Iain. "I was supposed to ask you if *your* men would be hungry. Of all the days this week, we have no fresh dishes prepared. We have a wee bit of meat pie, of course, but we also have plenty of dried fish and cheese. I think we may have a bit of bread pudding and an oatcake or two about here somewhere."

Iain shook his head. "Thank you, m'lady, but I don't think that will be necessary. I'll be sending the men home to their families in a short time. They've been on the road for too long. If it's acceptable with you, however, I was planning on staying the night here at Fleet Tower. Tomorrow, I need to take Marion to Blackthorn Hall to visit with my mother, Lady Elizabeth."

"It would be lovely to have you stay the night," Judith said enthusiastically. She motioned toward the doorway that led to the kitchen. "I'm just going to run off and tell Margaret. She'll be thrilled, as well. And I'll see if I can get her to prepare something more for supper while she is in there."

"That won't be necessary," Iain said.

"Honestly, Aunt Judith," Marion added. "What you already have will be perfect. Please, we don't want to be any trouble."

Judith was already backing toward the door. "It won't be any trouble, dear. Your aunt Margaret is very adept at these things." She turned and disappeared through the door.

Marion looked helplessly after her.

"They'll do what they want," Iain said. "Taking care of people is what makes them happy." He walked to the table and poured himself the drink that he'd long wanted.

Marion looked up at her husband. She was impressed by the way he'd dealt with William and how kind he was to her aunts.

"I'm sorry for all the accusations I made. Of you not caring for my family, I mean. I was clearly so wrong."

He put down the empty cup on the table. "Do you understand now why this wasn't the perfect place for you to grow up?"

"I don't know," she answered honestly. "My aunts take some getting used to, but I was accustomed to their ways. And I am sure I'll feel comfortable after a day with them."

"And your uncle?"

"Sir William does appear to have grown more peculiar than I recall, but he's very sweet, and I'm certain that he's harmless." She smiled. "And after all, it takes a great deal of work to raise an army."

Iain frowned and lowered his voice. "Before coming inside, I took a moment to talk to Brother Luke. He told me that tonight, for the first time, Sir William actually frightened him."

"Frightened him?" Marion asked, suddenly concerned. "What did my uncle do?"

"He got it in his head that Brother Luke was English. You can imagine how Sir William behaves when he thinks there is an Englishman in the Tower." Iain glanced toward the back stairwell. "Your uncle is always armed. That is my immediate concern. Before I left, he was shooting arrows at tenants who were bringing food for your aunts."

"But he hasn't hurt anyone," she said.

"Not yet. But with his growing inability to remember people, it's possible that someone might get hurt." Iain frowned. "And don't forget, there are Englishmen in the Borders right now to attend a certain wedding."

As much as she hated to agree, Marion did. "But how are you going to take away his weapons without serious bloodshed?"

"I don't know. We need to talk about that more when I get back." Iain motioned to the courtyard. "The men are still waiting for me outside. My stable hands who have been serving as members of Sir William's army tell me that there's been no sign of your cousin, Jack, and his band of outlaws."

"Perhaps he heard the news of our marriage and decided to go away and leave us in peace," she said hopefully.

"Or perhaps he is preparing to create greater havoc through our wedding."

"What do you mean by that?" Marion asked.

"Brother Luke told me that in this past week, three Englishmen who were sent from the Tudor court have disappeared. All of them were last seen in the Borders, too close to Fleet Tower and Blackthorn Hall."

"And you think Jack is responsible for it?"

"Who else?" Iain shrugged.

"Doesn't he know that in doing this, he'll have not only you but the English army, as well, after him?"

"I don't pretend to understand Jack Fitzwilliam. I never have." He looked around the great hall. "All I know is that if we don't find them or the people responsible for their disappearance, there will be hell to pay."

He leaned down and kissed her lips. "I need to go out and send the men home to their families. We'll lower the portcullis, and Tom and John will stay the night and keep watch. They were supposed to be part of a search party, but they're needed here more. They should be enough until tomorrow. Alan will send back fresh riders to escort us to Blackthorn Hall tomorrow."

Marion walked with him to the entryway. "Won't Lady Elizabeth be offended that you're staying here tonight?"

"The way Brother Luke explained it to me, she's far too busy with all the guests who have arrived to worry about anything else. I'm not concerned about that. I have no interest in anything right now other than being here with you."

Marion certainly hoped so. She was in love with her husband. She looked forward to the lifetime they would have together. The children they would have. She wanted everything and everyone else around them to fit in with that life. She was so different from the woman she'd been a fortnight ago.

No conflict, only peace. This was to be her new motto. Almost over-whelmed with what she was feeling, she raised herself on her tiptoes and kissed Iain on the lips.

"I'll only be gone for a few minutes," he told her, smiling and caressing her cheek.

She waited until he went out the door to the courtyard before she turned to the room. Judith was standing by the table holding another tray. Marion hadn't heard her come in.

"I thought the laird was staying," Judith said. She looked disap-pointed.

Marion rushed over to help her. "He'll be right back. He wanted to send his men on their way before securing the gates."

"I saw you two," Judith said with a giggle.

"You did?" Marion put the basket of bread and the dishes on the table and glanced hesitantly at her aunt.

"I did. I saw the two of you kiss, just now, as I was coming into the great hall. The laird was going out the other door."

Marion felt her face growing warm, but she told herself she shouldn't be embarrassed. She and Iain were married. Still, her aunts didn't know the truth, and Marion didn't know why they shouldn't be told. It wasn't as if they were going to meet any of the guests in the few days left before the ceremony. And even if they did and the news got out, it didn't matter. If Lady Elizabeth hadn't involved herself, Iain and Marion were going to announce their news to everyone anyway.

"He is quite handsome, you know."

"Yes, I know."

"And I'm so glad you turned out so bonny and tall. He should be happy with what he is getting."

Marion thought Iain might have already felt differently on several occasions, namely the times she might have expressed her opinion too strongly, or acted a bit too single-mindedly, or behaved downright disagreeably. Other than those moments, though, he definitely appeared happy with what he was getting, especially in their more intimate moments.

When Marion looked up, her aunt was looking at her with a peculiar expression on her face.

"Is something wrong, Aunt Judith?"

"Well, yes, dear." She paused. "There are things that a young woman should learn from her mother before marrying, but you don't have a mother. And Margaret and I have never married, so there is much we don't know to tell you. And I doubt those nuns on the Isle of Skye knew much about these things, either. So Margaret and I were thinking of asking one of the McCall women from the village—"

"That really won't be necessary, Aunt Judith," Marion said in a rush. She felt her cheeks burning with embarrassment.

"But it will be very important," Judith said seriously. "You want to keep a man like the laird happy. It will be important not to be afraid and—"

"I won't be afraid. I'm not afraid," Marion said. "In fact, I have a secret to share with you, Aunt Judith."

"Really?" She smiled, coming closer. "I like secrets."

Marion looked around the empty hall. It was perfectly fine for them to know, she told herself.

"Iain and I are already married," she announced.

"No, dear. You're not." Judith shook her head. "You're *betrothed*. There is a difference. You'll be married after the church ceremony next week."

"No, Aunt Judith. We are married. The ceremony took place at the priory before we left Skye," Marion explained.

"You are *not*, my sweet." Judith shook her head adamantly. "I cannot blame you for not knowing, for I guess there are very few weddings that take place in a priory. And, now that I think of it, I don't remember ever taking you to a wedding when you were a wee bairn. But this is the way things are. There are betrothals and there are marriages."

Marion could not believe it when Judith began a lecture on how a wedding ceremony is conducted in a church, or on church steps. It was so much like her aunt not to hear what was being said. Unless, of course, it was being said by Aunt Margaret.

To her relief, Margaret appeared in the doorway, bringing in a platter of fruit and cheeses. Marion went to help her.

"Where is the laird?" she asked.

"He is in the courtyard, sending his men home. He'll be right back," Marion explained. "Aunt Margaret, I have a secret I'd like to share with you and Aunt Judith."

"We like secrets," Margaret said excitedly.

"We do indeed like secrets," Judith repeated.

Marion shook her head. She wouldn't dwell on each little peculiarity or she'd surely drive herself mad. "My secret pertains to Iain and me. We're already married. We were wed at the priory on the Isle of Skye. Since I was to be traveling south without a female companion, we felt it was more proper to be married."

She looked for Margaret's reaction.

Her aunt stared at her.

"Iain and I are already married, Aunt Margaret," Marion repeated.

The second time around was the icebreaker. The older woman's face blossomed into a smile. "You two are already married?"

"You two are married?" Judith repeated, acting as if this were the first time she was hearing the news.

Marion took a deep breath and nodded. "We are. But all of it is a secret, for Lady Elizabeth doesn't wish to offend the guests from court. So you can't tell anyone about it."

"We won't tell anyone," Margaret said.

"No one," Judith repeated.

Both women rushed to give her a hug. The little secret was out,

Marion thought. Now she had no hesitation about Iain staying the night. If they were caught holding hands or kissing, so be it.

"We were hoping you two would marry like this," Margaret said.

"We were hoping," Judith repeated.

"Now we don't need to worry about the wedding gown," Margaret announced.

"No need to worry now."

"Don't forget. Our news is a secret," Marion repeated. "You shouldn't tell this to anyone. I'll still be walking down the aisle and marrying Iain again next week."

Both women nodded.

"That is, if they find the missing Englishmen," Marion said in a lower tone.

"We must celebrate tonight," Margaret announced, clapping her hands.

"We love to celebrate!" Judith agreed.

"Come with me, Judith," Margaret told her younger sister. "I need your help in the kitchen to bring in the rest of the supper."

"I can help," Marion offered.

"No, dear. We can handle it."

"We can handle it on our own," Judith added.

Marion looked helplessly around the hall. "But I feel so useless. Please let me do something," she asked of the two women.

"Very well. We can set this table by the fire for our celebration, with all the finery," Margaret said. "The damask cloth to cover the table, and the silver knives."

"Damask and silver." Judith nodded enthusiastically.

"That was the way we used to entertain when your father, the earl, was alive," Margaret said. "Rest his soul."

"I'll set the table," Marion said quickly. "It will be lovely to have dinner the way we once did. Perhaps we can even get Uncle William to join us."

"Oh, I don't know." Margaret looked doubtful.

"I don't know," Judith repeated.

Both women started toward the kitchen.

"Where can I find the linens and the silver?" Marion asked them.

"The same place where they always are," Margaret said over her shoulder.

"The same place," Judith repeated.

As her aunts disappeared, Marion looked around the room, trying to recall where everything had been. When she'd been a six-year-old, there had been servants who saw to these kinds of things. There were only a few storage places in the great hall.

Marion opened a chest that sat beside the hearth. It was filled with what appeared to be garments needing mending. She went to a tall cupboard built into the paneling of another. As she opened one door, she remembered a small chest that had been locked away there. She wondered if it contained the silver knives. The shelf where the chest had been kept was bare.

She turned and scanned the hall again. Crossing the room, she went to one of the window seats and took off the cushions. Lifting the lid, she looked inside. Nothing but some scraps of cloth at the bottom.

Marion went to the other window seat. Margaret's cloak and a basket sat on it. Putting them on a nearby bench, she picked up the cushions and, tucking them under her arm, looked inside it. No chest, but there *was* a man inside. Marion lowered the lid and put the cushions back on before starting for the next window.

Two steps away, she stopped, whirled around, and went back to look again at what she thought she had seen. Marion's hand shook as she pushed aside the cushions and lifted the top a second time. There was no mistaking it. There was definitely a man inside.

Well dressed, but definitely, undeniably dead.

23

A TIGHT WEAVE of clouds filled the night sky, blocking any light from the waning moon. The air was heavy with the smell of rain. Iain hoped he still had time to do an inspection of the outer walls of the castle and send his men on their way before the storms moved in.

Twelve years ago, they had faced the possibility of the English following the wounded Scots after the devastating battle at Flodden Field. The victorious army had indeed moved northward but had bypassed the Borders for the easier going through the Lowlands. Still, no one knew what the English would do, so Iain had not bothered with defending the tower house. He couldn't, and with the McCall warriors almost wiped out in the battle, they couldn't defend it, either. Instead, he'd moved the remaining occupants and the unprotected villagers on McCall land to Blackthorn Hall for a short time. Iain hadn't worried about defending Fleet Tower then, but he was a little worried now.

He chose three of the men to go with him as he made his rounds.

Tom and John, the two Armstrong men, were frequent visitors to Fleet Tower. They were the most likely pair to walk with the laird and offer their opinion. Alan was the most experienced fighter of all of his men. He'd served Iain's father and he'd been a loyal friend and servant to Iain ever since.

"The only way anyone arrives at Fleet Tower is by traveling on that road," Tom assured Iain as they walked along the top of the curtain walls.

"To get in, they must come through the main gate," John said. "The ditch around the walls makes it difficult to scale them."

"And you'd see them," Alan said, "if we lit torches along the walls."

"Once we lower the portcullis, m'lord," Tom said, "there'd be no one coming in."

"We'll be snug here until Alan comes back with more men in the morning," John added.

Iain nodded. He knew Fleet Tower was not defensible against any attack by a large army. Walls could be scaled or battered down with the new cannon the English were so proud of. But the English weren't the ones that concerned Iain. It was Jack Fitzwilliam. Enough Armstrong men had been scouring these hills this past week, though, and there had been no reports of seeing Marion's outlaw cousin.

"The men are tired, m'lord," Alan reminded him as they continued their walk. "They're a wee bit anxious to get back to their kin before it's too late."

"I understand that," Iain assured his man. "I'll dismiss them as soon as I can. But before anyone leaves Fleet Tower, I'll be sure that every crack in the wall is sealed."

Everyone agreed.

24

MARION COVERED her mouth to stifle her scream. The man's eyes were open. He was staring at her. Partially propped up in the cramped area, his neck was twisted oddly. He was middle-aged. No one that she knew. Marion's gaze moved down to the dead man's clothing.

"An Englishman." She closed the window seat, pushed the pillows back over the top, and stood back. She couldn't tear her gaze away.

"But it can't be. I must be feverish. It's the excitement." She touched her forehead. It did indeed feel hot. She had to be imagining this. She stepped over to the window seat again and without removing anything, she lifted the lid a little and peeked in. It wasn't her imagination. He was still there.

"He's done it. He's finally gone through with his threats." She let the top drop and jumped back as it closed with a bang. Iain was right. All games and good humor aside, William had become truly dangerous. He needed to be taken away someplace where he couldn't harm anyone else.

"Oh, my God. Uncle William has killed a man." She put a hand on her pounding head as the realization finally sank in. This corpse was probably one of the guests at her wedding. One of the missing men from the English court.

Marion heard footsteps coming into the room. She whirled around. It was Judith carrying in another platter.

"Aunt Judith?" Marion called out in a strained voice.

Her aunt placed the platter on the table before turning around. "Yes, dear, I know. You haven't been able to find the linens or the knives. Margaret and I were just talking about it in the kitchen. She thought we might have moved them upstairs into the earl's old chambers, for safekeeping. But I said no, they're still down here."

"Aunt Judith," Marion said more sharply.

"Very well, dear, I'll help you look for them," she said pleasantly, looking for the first time at her. "What's wrong with you, Marion? You look as if you've seen a ghost."

She had. Not a ghost, but the body of a dead man. "There is nothing wrong with *me*," Marion said more sharply than she had intended. But it didn't matter. "I'd like to talk to you about Sir William."

"I don't think he'll join us for supper. You can ask him again, though, if you want."

Marion shook her head. "I don't care about supper. What I want to say is that I think it's time Uncle William was sent to a place where there are people who can take care of him. Watch him all the time."

"But why?" Judith asked, shaking her head. "We're not dead yet, you know."

"Yes, I know, and thank the Lord for that."

Marion's mind jumped to what William might be capable of doing. He'd killed once. He could kill again. Anytime, anyone...even his own kin. The poor man lived in a state of confusion all the time. Iain said Brother Luke had been frightened by her uncle just today. Then he hadn't recognized her, his own niece.

"Tonight! Perhaps we could have him taken away tonight." Marion realized she had said the words aloud.

"Who'll be taken away tonight?"

Aunt Margaret stood in the doorway, a platter of steaming meat pies in her hands. Marion was relieved to see her older aunt. It was so much easier to talk to her than Judith.

"Sir William," Marion answered.

"Marion just said thank the Lord we are not dead yet," Judith said pleasantly. "You see, Margaret? She is still the same affectionate child as before."

"That is so nice of you, my dear." Margaret put her platter down on the table.

Why was it that they chose to hear each other and not her? Marion wondered. She thought about the man in the window seat and decided to try again. The two were chattering away about the dinner settings.

"Oh, you haven't set the table yet," Margaret noticed.

"She couldn't find the linens or the knives," Judith answered.

"I told you, they're upstairs." Margaret shook a finger at her sister. "I'll go up and get them."

"No. No," Marion said, moving to block her aunt's path. "You're not going anywhere until we settle this."

"I can go up and get what we need," Judith offered.

"No." She motioned to them to stay where they were. "Neither of you are going anywhere until I'm done talking."

"She still has her temper," Margaret whispered to her sister.

"Definitely, the same temper." Judith shook her head in disapproval.

"Please," Marion snapped. She stamped her foot on the floor. "Please don't talk. Just listen."

The two women exchanged a knowing look. Judith tried to say something, but at the sight of Marion's finger pointing at her, she quieted down.

"You need to hear what I have to tell you about Uncle William," Marion spoke in what she hoped was a calm tone. Taking her aunts by the hand, she led them both to the settee by the fire. "Please sit down."

"Very well, dear. But I really think we ought to—"

"When Iain comes back in here from dismissing his men, I'm going to ask him to take Sir William away to a monastery he knows. I'm going to ask him to take him there right away. Now, I want your agreement to that."

"But why, dear?" Margaret asked.

"We're not dead yet," Judith added.

"No, we are not dead," Margaret agreed. "And Brother Luke said just this afternoon that someone should look after William after we are dead."

"Only after." Judith nodded with finality.

"Not after. Now." Marion shook her head adamantly at the two older women. "I'm going to try to explain everything once. Only once. So you need to listen. In fact..." She paused, remembering William, the person truly responsible for this havoc. "Let's bring Sir William into the great hall so that I can explain everything to all of you."

"But he won't come," Margaret said.

"He certainly won't," Judith agreed.

"If you ask him, he will. I'm certain you must know how to pique his interest. Please."

"Nothing will convince him," Margaret said, shrugging her shoulders indifferently.

Judith agreed. "He's down in the dungeon making room for a new recruit. He won't eat or drink or do anything else until he is done with that. His army comes first, you know."

Margaret nodded.

"Very well, then we'll discuss his fate without him," Marion asserted. "The time has come. You two have taken care of him for too long. He needs to be sent away to a place where he'll be safe." *And where everyone else will be safe, too*, she thought silently. "This has to happen tonight."

"No, that cannot happen. Not tonight, not tomorrow, nor a month from now," Margaret said, lifting her chin stubbornly. "He is not going anywhere until after we are gone."

"Not until we're gone," Judith repeated.

At least they'd heard what she'd told them, Marion thought. That was certainly an improvement. The image of the body in the window seat suddenly came to mind. After William's arrangements were made, there were much more serious problems that she had to see to. She had to use whatever it took to win this battle quickly, so she could start fighting the next.

Marion planted her hands on her hips. She pushed all the soft emotions she carried for her aunts aside and focused on the disaster she had to get all of them out of. Hurt feelings could be mended later.

"The decision is not yours, but mine. As the McCall heir and as the wife of the Armstrong laird, I say Sir William must be moved to a different place. That is the end of this discussion."

"That is a terrible thing," Margaret said brokenly.

"Terrible," Judith repeated.

Marion told herself she was a fool to assume it would be that simple.

Margaret took a kerchief out of the pocket of her skirt and dabbed under each eye. "Why are you doing this, Marion?"

"Why?" Judith asked in a grieving tone.

"How could you break up your family for no reason?" Margaret said tearfully.

"No reason," Judith repeated.

"And after so many years of us all being separated. Just when we could be a family again." The older woman wiped away more tears.

"I want my family," Judith cried, taking the kerchief out of Margaret's hand and blowing her nose in it. She handed it back.

Guilt clawed its way up inside of her, but Marion told herself to stay calm. Stay firm. This was the right thing to do. Everyone had to be kept safe. That was first and foremost.

The two women's sobs got louder. Marion glanced at the window seat. She supposed that it was inevitable that these two gentle souls would need to learn of the present their brother had left in the window seat for the family.

"Listen, Aunt Margaret, Aunt Judith. There is something else that I haven't told you."

They both stopped their tears.

"More secrets?" Margaret asked, interested.

"Good secrets or bad secrets?" Judith asked.

"Unfortunately, it's a bad secret. But there is no getting around it. You must know," Marion said calmly. Two pairs of red rimmed eyes were fixed on her.

"For as long as I can remember, we all have encouraged Sir William to pretend to be William Wallace. And we always thought of him as a totally harmless man."

"He *is* harmless," both sisters said at once.

"He *was* harmless. No longer." Marion shook her head. "That is why he must be taken away."

Margaret stuffed the handkerchief back inside her pocket. "You only arrived back tonight. What has he done to have you turn against him so quickly?"

"You are against him," Judith said accusingly.

"I am *not* against him," Marion replied. "Sir William has killed a man."

The silence in the great hall was complete. Only the sound of the fire in the hearth disturbed it.

"Killed a man?" Judith was the first to speak.

"He couldn't do such a thing," Margaret said passionately.

"Never." Judith shook her head.

There was no end to their denials. Marion walked over to the window seat and started removing the pillows.

"Aunt Margaret. Aunt Judith." She lifted the top. "There is a body in this window seat."

Again, silence reigned for a long moment.

"Is that all?" Margaret asked. She was obviously relieved!

"That's no reason to send William away," Judith said, waving her hand dismissively. "We know about the man in there."

The pillows dropped out of Marion's hands and the top of the window seat slammed shut. She wasn't sure she heard her aunt correctly. "What did you just say?"

"You are too young to be getting hard of hearing like me." Margaret smiled. "What Judith said is that we know there is a man in there."

"You do?"

"Of course! And that has nothing to do with William."

"Nothing," Judith said pleasantly, turning back to the table. "I'm glad that's settled."

"Yes, indeed."

Judith tapped her plump cheeks with one finger. "We still need to find the table settings."

The entire room seemed to tilt suddenly, and Marion's mind tipped with it.

"You *know*?" she asked vaguely.

"Of course. Now dear, just forget about it," Margaret advised. "Forget you ever saw the Englishman in the window seat."

"Just forget it," Judith said over her shoulder.

"*Forget* I saw a dead man? A dead *Englishman*? In my family's great hall?" Marion asked.

"We never dreamed you'd look in there," Margaret said gently.

"Never." Judith shook her head.

"Who is he? How did he die? I didn't see any blood. If William had nothing to do with it, then how did he get there?" Marion realized she was asking too many questions at once. Her aunts weren't listening anyway. Their attention was back to the table.

"Who is he?" she repeated more forcefully.

The two older women exchanged a look. There was a slight whispering, and then Judith answered.

"If you must know, his name is Harington. Sir George Harington. He's an Englishman who was sent here to the Borders to attend your wedding." Judith shrugged. "That's all I really know about him."

Marion remembered the name. This was definitely the Englishman Iain's men were searching for. She'd heard that much from John and Tom.

"What is he doing here?" she asked.

"He liked our cooking," Margaret answered. "He dropped by for a visit."

"Your Aunt Margaret's fruit tarts were his favorite," Judith said with a smile.

"What happened to him?" Marion asked, praying that there was a sane explanation for this. He could have died naturally, she thought hopefully.

"He died," Margaret said.

"Just...died," Judith repeated.

"While he was visiting?"

"Of course, dear. You don't think we'd go out *looking* for him!"

"So he died while you were...eating?" Marion asked, still hopeful.

"Just afterward, dear," Margaret answered.

"After," Judith agreed.

"Did he just climb into that window seat and die?"

Margaret and Judith exchanged a look again, and there was some more whispering.

Marion had no patience left. "Well, who is going to answer me?" she asked sharply.

"He drank some wine and died," Margaret said in a matter-of-fact manner.

"Drank some wine." Judith nodded as this should have explained it all.

"And he choked on the wine?"

"Well, no, dear. Not exactly." Margaret paused. "Actually, the wine had a touch of poison in it."

Judith made a motion with her hand showing how much a touch was.

Marion looked at the table and the pitcher sitting next to the cups. She remembered Iain taking a drink before going out. She moved frantically toward the table. "Does this have poison in it?"

"No, dear. Don't be silly!" Margaret said as if speaking to a child.

"Of course not." Judith shook her head. "We keep the *special* wine in the cupboard."

"For special guests." Both women pointed to the cabinet. Marion looked over her shoulder at a pitcher and cups, sitting on the shelf.

"May I ask another question?" Marion asked.

"Certainly!" Margaret replied brightly.

"Ask." Judith nodded happily.

"How did the poison get into the wine?" she asked.

"We put it in the wine," Margaret said proudly.

"*We* did it," Judith agreed.

"You...two...poisoned the wine?" Marion stared at her aunts in disbelief.

They both nodded happily.

"We tried it with cider and ale, but it didn't taste right," Margaret explained.

"Wine works perfectly," Judith continued. "Margaret wasn't here when I offered a cup of it to Sir George. He liked it immensely."

He liked it so immensely that he died, Marion thought. She looked at Judith, her murderous aunt. But Margaret knew about it, too, and clearly thought nothing wrong with killing a visitor.

Marion hoped someone would slap her right now and wake her up. She glanced toward the window seat.

"I put Sir George in there when I heard the noise in the courtyard," Judith said cheerfully. "Brother Luke was arriving for a visit, too."

"I was at the village," Margaret said, obviously disappointed. "I missed it."

Marion told herself she had to deal with one of them at a time. She faced Judith. "You knew what you did was wrong, isn't that right? That's why you decided to hide the body."

"Well, we hadn't seen Brother Luke for so long. We had a great deal to talk about without a wee distraction like that," her aunt explained.

Murder was only a *wee* distraction? Marion stared at the two women, seeing them for the first time. William was not the only crazy one in the family.

Margaret motioned to the food they had brought out. "You should call in the laird. You two must be starving. Judith and I will take care of setting the table."

"I have no appetite," Marion said in confusion. She didn't know what to do next.

"You look pale, dear," Margaret noted. "I know this was a lot to share with you. But now you know it all. So I suggest you just forget about the whole thing."

"Forget about it?" Marion asked in shock. "There is no way I can forget that my aunt has murdered a man and put him in with the linens in the window seat."

"So you *did* find the damask table cover?" Judith asked excitedly, going to where the body was.

Margaret's frown, though, was stern. "You really are becoming upset about nothing, Marion. I think Judith and I have the right to our own little secrets. You have yours, after all."

Judith removed the cushions from the window seat and poked around the body, looking for the tablecloth. "And I don't think you should share our little secret with the laird. Sir George was Lady Elizabeth's guest, and we don't want to offend anyone." She turned to her sister. "The linens are not here. At least, I don't see them."

"I told you they're upstairs," Margaret answered. "I'll go and look."

"I'm coming with you," Judith said. "There are far too many things stored in the earl's bedchamber. You go in there alone, and you might never come out again."

The two laughed as they started for the doorway, one on the heels of the other.

Marion, feeling dazed, looked around the room. This couldn't be real. But it was. It had to be. But maybe it wasn't. She wandered to the window and threw open the shutters. Right below her, two of the Armstrong warriors were talking. They looked up.

Marion smiled weakly and waved at them. They waved back.

"We're at Fleet Tower, are we not?" she called out to them.

"That we are, m'lady," one of them called back, looking at her oddly.

"And this is my family," she announced, not asking, but desperately hoping they would correct her.

"They are your family," the second man called up.

Her family was crazy. She was crazy. And now Iain's men knew it, too.

"Damn." Marion closed the shutters. She realized she was leaning on the blasted window seat. She jumped back and moved toward the arched doorway. "Aunt Margaret. Aunt Judith," she screamed up the stairwell.

The two aunts could not have been too far up the stairs, for they bustled back down the steps in an instant. "What's wrong?"

"What is wrong, dear?" Judith repeated, taking her hand and patting it.

"What are we going to do?" Marion asked with a half sob.

"What are we going to do about what?" Margaret asked, sitting Marion down on a chair. Her aunt put a hand on her forehead.

"Feverish," she whispered to her sister.

Judith gave a knowing nod.

Marion motioned with her head toward the window seat. "What are we going to do with Sir George?"

"That's not your worry, dear," Margaret said calmly. "We'll take care of it."

"Not your worry." Judith continued to pat Marion's hand.

"How could I not worry?" Marion exploded. "There is a dead body in that window seat. The body happens to belong to an emissary of the King of England. The poor man was sent to the Borders to witness my wedding. He is not going to show up because he is dead. Every English soldier north of York will be sent up here to look for him. They won't leave a stone unturned. And where are they going to find Sir George Harington's body? Rotting among the linens in my family's great hall."

"Now, Marion," Margaret said sharply. "You're getting hysterical, and for no reason."

"No reason at all," Judith agreed, shaking her head. "We told you the linens are not in the window seat with him."

Marion suddenly understood Uncle William. She understood why he was crazy. At that moment, she wished she had a sword. She wanted to run up the stairs, away from these two madwomen, and shout, "*Freedom!*" at the top of her lungs.

"You're worrying too much," Margaret said, caressing Marion's hair.

"Too, too much," Judith agreed.

"Sir George's body won't stay in the window seat," Margaret assured her.

"Not at all." Judith nodded.

"What are you going to do with him?" Marion asked.

"I told you before, William is down in the dungeon making room for him, as we speak," Margaret explained.

"Right now." Judith pointed a gnarled finger to the floor, in case Marion didn't know where the dungeons were.

She should have guessed. Sir William was in on it, too. "Is he going to bury him down there?"

"Not exactly bury," Margaret said.

Judith shook her head, agreeing. "Not bury."

"He is going to lay him out in armor."

"With the others," Aunt Judith finished.

It took a moment before her words sank in.

"Did you say 'others'?" Marion asked weakly.

25

IAIN FELT MUCH BETTER about the security of Fleet Tower once he and his three men were done with their inspection of the walls. Built nearly three hundred years ago, the tower house had withstood many skirmishes and attacks by small bands of outlaws and the lairds of the surrounding clans. Iain was certain his own ancestors had laid siege to the place at least a dozen times over the centuries. The greatest point of defense for the house was exactly what his men had referred to. Fleet Tower was almost inaccessible from every direction but from the main road and the front entrance. And the portcullis could be closed, and that entrance could be guarded.

"You should go. Take the men," Iain told Alan once they were back where they had started. "Tom and John will be enough to keep watch for the night."

The seasoned warrior appeared resigned to that, but he still paused. "What concerns me most right now is the whereabouts of the three missing Englishmen," Alan confessed. "If the bloody fools don't show up alive in time for your wedding, we'll have more to worry about from Lord Dorset and his English soldiers than Jack Fitzwilliam and his mangy pack of dogs."

Iain frowned. "I was too outspoken when the Council of Regents sent word that blasted emissaries were being sent to witness the wedding."

He'd been outraged when first told of the demand being made by the English court. Another example of who was really running things in Scotland. Before the loss at Flodden Field, there was no question. No more, though. Now the Tudor king felt perfectly free to demand proof that there would be an end to the problem of a few outlaws in Scotland's Borders area.

Iain's word was not good enough. The Scottish regent's promise meant nothing. King Henry wanted his own men to witness the union of the two clans. Refusal meant that they would send troops to occupy and take charge of the area. Iain had been angry and openly defiant. This was Scotland, and the slight chance of isolated acts of banditry spilling over to the south of the Borders was hardly reason enough for the Tudor court to be rattling its long swords.

The Tudor court had been as stubborn, and the Council of Regents had gone along. The regent himself had traveled to Blackthorn Hall to speak to Iain about what his people and Scotland stood to lose. There was no question that the English troops would overrun them. Only twelve years had passed since the king had died in battle at Flodden Field, and neither Scotland nor the Armstrong clan had recovered enough to stand against England.

Grudgingly, Iain had given in, leaving Lady Elizabeth to become the welcoming hostess.

Iain knew the truth behind her seeming willingness. She was doing her duty. He and his mother had many differences, but they had one common bond—their hatred of the English. In addition to the hundreds of their Armstrong kin who had been cut down by English arrows, halberds, and cannon, she'd lost a husband and Iain a father.

Still, Iain had not been able to accept the situation in silence. Now there was no doubt who would be blamed for the missing Englishmen. That is, unless Iain could find the real culprit, Jack Fitzwilliam.

After all, who stood to gain the most by getting Iain into this kind of trouble?

26

"Indeed, dear. There have been others."

Marion leaped off the bench. "You mean...*others*?"

Margaret and Judith each put a hand on their niece's shoulder and pushed her back down onto her seat.

"You're getting hysterical again, my dear," Margaret warned.

"Not good." Judith shook her head.

Marion glanced up into one concerned face and then into the other. They were looking at her like she was the one who had lost her mind.

"What do you mean by 'others'?" she managed to croak.

"Other gentlemen," Margaret answered.

"Other Englishmen," Judith corrected.

With her elbows planted on her knees, Marion buried her face into her hands. She was dreaming all of this, she told herself. She was dreaming. She had to be dreaming. If she repeated it enough times, she figured it might even be true. That was what the nuns believed about prayer. Repetition was crucial. Say it, chant it, pray it enough times and your sin would be forgiven. *She was dreaming.* This was her prayer.

She opened her eyes. The same faces were looking down at her. "How many...others?" she asked hesitantly.

The two sisters went back and forth with their special look. Then there was some counting on the fingers and the murmuring of names.

"Eighteen?" Margaret finally announced.

"No, this makes nineteen." Judith shook her head.

Marion slithered off the chair to free herself from their hold. Neither of them appeared to mind.

"No, this has to be eighteen," Margaret insisted. "We cannot count the first one."

"We can, too," Judith argued. "He was English."

At the window, Marion opened the shutters and leaned out. She took a chest full of fresh air. The two women continued to argue in the background. Unfortunately, the drop to the courtyard was too short. At best, she might break a bone if she jumped. Marion tried to decide if being lame would do her any good. What if she landed on her head? Perhaps she'd forget everything she heard.

"Marion!"

She focused on one of the men calling her name from the courtyard. It was Iain. He waved at her.

Perhaps if she went to the top of the tower...

"How is the visit going with your aunts?" he asked.

Suddenly panicking, she scrambled back from the window and closed the shutters. She moved back a step into the room.

"Please go away," she whispered at the closed shutter. "You don't want to know any of this."

"We were never sure about the first one. We thought he might have been an outlaw wearing stolen English armor," Margaret argued.

"You thought that. I didn't," Judith said. "And he did speak with an accent."

"I felt sorry for him, so he couldn't have been an Englishman," Margaret insisted.

"It's too late to be changing our minds about him. He's down there with the others. We must count him."

"Very well," Margaret said with a sigh.

"And Sir George makes nineteen," Judith said with an air of finality.

"*Nineteen?*" Marion cried, whirling around to face her aunts.

Margaret shrugged and moved around the platters on the table. "If we must count the first one, then we have nineteen."

It was impossible to think straight. It was hard to recognize that these two murderers were the same sweet old ladies that had nurtured her and braided her hair and fed her. She even remembered how gentle they'd been with the baby black squirrel that she'd found at the base of the oak tree. They were murderers.

Still, she told herself, this was her family. Her trouble.

Another thought struck her. But she was already married to Iain, which meant this was his trouble, too. As her guardian and now as her husband, he was guilty of any crime that she was guilty of. That was the law. Nineteen dead Englishmen in the dungeon of her tower house. He was as good as dead if word of this got out. They'd have his head on a pike.

"No," she said aloud.

"Did you say something, dear?" Margaret asked.

"She said 'no.'"

Were they doing such things when she was just a child? Did her father know about it? She had to know it all.

"How long has this thing been going on?" she asked.

The two women looked at her as if they didn't know what she meant.

"Who was the first one to die?" Marion clarified. "And when did it happen?"

Again, there were some exchanged looks and a short argument on the number of years.

"It was the same year as you left," Margaret said.

"No, it was in the springtime after you left," Judith argued.

"No, dear. It was the same year." Margaret shook her head.

"We didn't get back from Blackthorn Hall until there was snow on the ground that winter," Judith argued. "There was no snow when the Englishman showed up at our door."

Marion forced herself not to yell at them again. "Very well," she said through gritted teeth. "It happened after I was sent to the Isle of Skye."

They both nodded at that.

"Who was he?" she repeated.

"We never learned his name," Margaret started.

"No name," Judith agreed.

Margaret sat down on a bench at the table. "And we really can't take credit for him, as we didn't poison him."

"Nineteen!" Judith crossed her arms stubbornly across her chest.

Marion wondered what the difference in punishment would be between killing eighteen Englishmen versus nineteen. *Your head on a slightly shorter pike?*

Margaret shrugged indifferently. "He showed up in the middle of the night at our door. He'd been stabbed in the chest and had very little life left in him."

Nodding in agreement, Judith made the motion of a dagger going into the heart.

"Despite the fact that he was wearing an English tunic, we brought him in."

"But he died on us during the night," Judith said, looking up.

Marion shook her head in confusion. "You had done a good deed by bringing in a wounded man and caring for him. Why did you have to go from that to poisoning all the others?"

The two sisters looked at each other before nodding simultaneously. "Because of Sir William."

"Definitely William," Judith agreed.

"Our brother has been trying to raise an army to attack England since long before your father died," Margaret explained. "He so missed going to fight with the king."

"He missed it," Judith concurred.

"He was so excited to see the dead Englishman here that we couldn't refuse him."

"We couldn't refuse our brother," Judith said passionately.

Marion looked from one woman to the other. "And what did he want?"

"He wanted to take our special guest to the dungeon. He thought if the Englishman were retrained and treated well, he might soon change sides and agree to fight in his...in the Wallace's army."

Marion forced herself to keep a calm face. Becoming hysterical, as they called it, wouldn't get out the rest of the truth. "So...did he change sides?"

"He did."

"He did." Judith nodded. "He's been a devoted follower of William these past twelve years. He is still down there."

There was a twelve-year-old cadaver in Fleet Tower's dungeons. But there were others, too. Marion felt one of her eyes uncontrollably jerk closed. She put a hand on it but couldn't stop the involuntary twitch. She wondered if her aunts ever had the same twitch, and at what age it had started.

"And when did you decide you needed others to join them?" she managed to ask.

"In all our years, I'd never seen William so happy," Margaret said with a smile.

"Never," Judith agreed.

"So we made up our mind. Between the two of us, we decided then and there to add to our brother's troops."

"It was for an excellent cause," Judith reasoned.

"An excellent cause," Margaret agreed. "We lost our brother—your father—to the English. In doing this, we were helping his surviving brother raise an army to invade England. And he would be leading an army of their own kind."

Judith laughed. "That was the best part. Their own men fighting them."

"English fighting the English!"

"Isn't it wonderful, dear?"

"Brilliant," Marion replied without enthusiasm. She wondered if these two knew that dead people could not raise a sword. She shook her head. Considering everything else, she decided that was a fairly insignificant point to make right now.

"How did you find these men?" she asked.

"It wasn't easy," Margaret said.

"Not easy at all," Judith agreed.

"They *had* to be Englishmen."

"Only Englishmen," Judith said definitively.

Well, her aunts were murderers, but at least they were patriots. She wondered if that would help.

"Fortunately, we're close enough to the Borders that there have been occasional Englishmen who show up at our door," Margaret explained. "It's surprising how many would stop here to get in out of the weather."

"Not a very hardy lot, the English."

"Not hardy at all," Margaret agreed.

"One time, we had *three* of them at once," Judith said excitedly, holding up as many fingers.

"Those three loved the food."

"Loved it." Judith nodded. "Do you recall what they said about your mutton pie?"

"I do indeed, sister," Margaret said with a smile. "The wine didn't agree with them too much."

Judith made a motion with her hand of someone falling on his face. "It surely did not agree with them."

"William was elated, though."

"Quite elated," Judith agreed.

"Are they still down there, too?" Marion asked.

"Yes, they all are." Margaret smiled.

"And they happily switched sides, like the rest of them," Judith said cheerfully. "England must be a horrible place."

Marion scratched her head. The twitch in her eye was getting worse. She felt a corner of her cheek jump, as well.

"This poison," she asked. "How do you get it?"

"I mix it myself," Margaret said proudly. "You remember, I was always good at mixing remedies."

"She is still good at it," Judith agreed.

"What is it that you mix with the wine?" Marion asked.

"Arsenic, of course."

"Arsenic," Judith explained.

Of course, Marion thought. Arsenic. She had heard of it. She knew it was very common. In fact, she remembered one of the nuns saying it was quite good for external wounds. If one took it internally, of course, one was dead.

"Of course," she said aloud.

Margaret folded her hands modestly in her lap and looked at her sister. "Everything didn't always work out for us, though. Things don't always happen the way you like them to. We did have some bad years."

Judith nodded. "A few of them."

"Bad years?" Marion asked, wondering what could be worse than killing visitors who showed up at your door.

"There were months and months when no Englishman dropped by," Margaret said.

"None."

"Sir William at times grew quite impatient."

"Quite," Judith drawled.

"But there was nothing to be done."

"Nothing."

"Some of it was because of bad weather we had during the winters," Margaret explained.

"All of it was because of that," Judith corrected.

Thank the Lord for the bad weather, Marion thought. To think that King Jamie and ten thousand Scots didn't have to die at Flodden Field. All he had to do was to send these two women south to feed the English.

"These past few weeks have been the best," Margaret said excitedly.

"The very best," Judith agreed.

"We've never had an English nobleman stop by before."

"And now we have three." Judith smiled broadly.

Marion started to sit on a chair, but nearly missed it. She caught herself at the last moment.

"Three?" she asked weakly.

They both nodded enthusiastically.

Of course. There were three Englishmen missing, Marion thought. How foolish of her to give anyone else the credit for their disappearance.

"And we know all of their names," Margaret said proudly.

"Sir Francis Hastings, Sir William Eden, and—"

"Sir George Harington," Margaret finished. "Judith entertained him today while I was out at the village across the glen."

"Yes, I know," Marion whispered. "You told me."

Margaret stood up and looked over the table. "It was so nice to have this little chat, but we still haven't set the table. The laird should be coming in any time."

"Any time," Judith repeated excitedly.

"You can nibble on these while Judith and I get everything ready." Margaret looked at Marion with concern. "You look quite pale, my dear."

"No. No. I'm well enough, I suppose." Marion touched her face. Her cheek, her eye—one side of her face—was jumping. "I just have no appetite."

"Nonsense. Your appetite will come back by the time we are ready to celebrate that lovely secret about you and Iain."

Margaret left the room with her sister on her heels. At the arched doorway Judith paused. "I feel so much better that you know everything, dear."

Marion looked up.

"As do I, Aunt Judith," she lied.

27

IAIN GUESSED he might have left his bride a tad too long with her slightly eccentric aunts. He could tell by the bewildered look on her face when she'd been leaning out of the window. As much as Marion had defended her family and accused him of one horrible thing or the other in his treatment of them, he knew she was not actually prepared for the reality. When her uncle hadn't recognized her, she'd obviously been hurt. And the two sweet aunts, chattering on nonsensically and ignoring everyone else but each other, had to be another disappointment. But Iain was hardly one to gloat. He just hoped that she now realized why he felt he had to keep her away from Fleet Tower for all these years.

Iain took the courtyard steps two at a time up to the door to the great hall. As he went in, there was no sound of the aunts' voices. He guessed they might have gone up to the residence floors. There was so much that Marion wanted to see, so many old memories that she wanted back. Selfishly, he hoped to be with her when she went through those moments of remembrance. He wanted to be a part of her life in everything.

He didn't have to go far, though, to find his wife. Marion was sitting on a bench with her head buried in her hands. Before he could say anything, he saw her stand up and whirl around. He watched in silence as she walked to the window. Leaning over the window seat, she peeked out through the shutters and then backed up a step.

Iain leaned a shoulder against the wall, watching her. She was a bundle of worry. He could tell by the way her hands were fisted at her sides.

She was talking to herself. She looked up, still whispering, or perhaps praying. Knowing her, he decided she could just as easily be cursing.

She walked back toward the window and closed the shutters tighter. Iain saw her push aside the pillows and lift the lid of the window seat.

Margaret's and Judith's voices drifted in from the stairwell. Marion jumped back, and the lid came down with a slam.

"Why are you so tense?" he asked.

Marion leaped a foot off the ground. She whirled toward him, holding one fisted hand to her chest. Her face was flushed, and she looked slightly distracted.

"What are you doing here?" she asked.

"I just came in from outside."

"No, you were to go to Blackthorn Hall."

Iain glanced at the arched doorway first, making sure there was no sign of her aunts and her uncle. "No, I wasn't. I'm spending the night here at Fleet Tower...with my bride."

"You cannot," she said in a panic.

"We've had this discussion before, my love," Iain said, walking toward her. "I can and I will."

She shook her head frantically and backed away from him. "You have to go. This instant. You have to get away. Go as far as you can from me, from this place."

"Marion." He reached for her, but she put a chair between them. "What is this all about?"

She shook her head, her lips shut. Iain saw her glance at the door. He looked that way, too. There was no one there. He turned back to her. She was totally different from the woman he had left behind not even an hour earlier.

"What's happened to you?"

"Nothing," she said tensely. "I want you to go, Iain. I mean it."

"And I mean it, too," he said in the same tone. "I thought we were done with all these childish antics."

"Childish?" she asked. "I am making an appeal. A civilized request for you to let me be tonight."

"I'll let you be," Iain said with annoyance. "I won't touch you, if that's what you want. But I am not going anywhere tonight." To prove his point, he walked to the table and sat down on a chair beside it.

She threw her head back, looked up to the ceiling, and then began pacing the floor. There was some more mumbling under her breath. Iain decided that whatever she was so wound up about would soon spill out of her. She was not one to hold anything in for too long. He glanced at the food on the table. Everything looked very appetizing. He was more thirsty than hungry, though. He pushed aside the pitcher of cider on the table. He smelled the contents of another pitcher. Ale. In the open cupboard were several more pitchers. He stood up and walked across the hall. There was wine in the first one. Picking up a cup, he poured himself some.

"You're not upset because I took my time with the men outside, I hope," he said, putting the pitcher back.

"I wish my troubles were so trivial," she told him. Her gaze suddenly focused on the cup in his hands.

"Put that down," she ordered, starting toward him.

"I will not," he replied, stepping away from the cupboard and lifting the cup to his lips. "What's wrong with you?"

"*No!*" she screamed. She hit him like a charging boar, knocking the cup out of his hand as the two of them went sprawling on the floor. Marion landed on his chest.

"What was that for?" he asked, gaping up at her. "Are you mad?"

"Yes! I'm mad. And I didn't want you to drink from that cup."

She tried to get up, but Iain's arms tightened around her. "What was wrong with that cup?"

"Nothing."

She wasn't looking at him. "What was wrong with that cup?" he asked again.

"*Nothing!*" she yelled into his face.

He rolled her on the floor until she was pinned beneath him. "This is the last time I am going to ask this question," he said, glaring at her.

Her dark eyes focused on his face. It wasn't his imagination; he saw tears glistening on the onyx orbs. Her face was flushed, her breathing uneven. She grew in beauty, in passion, with every moment they were together.

"Answer me," he said less harshly.

"I didn't want you to drink out of my cup. That was my cup. *My* cup," she said, trying to push him off.

He pinned her hands at her waist, leaned down, and kissed her. She didn't fight him. In fact, he felt the desperate hunger in her. It was there in the way she kissed him back.

"Get off of me, Iain. Please. They'll be coming back any moment," she told him.

"Let them." He didn't move.

"This is completely improper."

"We're husband and wife. We'll tell them the truth."

The pained look quickly clouded her face again. "No! We're *not* married."

He stared at her for a moment. "We *are* married, Marion."

"No. You have a way out," she said grimly. "Luck is on your side. Brother Luke didn't tell anyone of the truth except your mother. She'll gladly keep our secret. Granted, I made a mistake of mentioning it to my aunts, but they'll keep the secret, too. So accept it. We're not married. And we'll not get married at Blackthorn Hall. The entire marriage is off."

"Are you trying to drive me mad?" he asked, frowning down at her.

"No, just the opposite. Take my word for it. Trust me."

The tears were back again. She was a jumble of raw emotions. Iain got up. She scrambled to her feet, too, and tried to walk away from him. He took her hand and forced her down on a bench.

"We are starting from the beginning."

"We are not. You're going." She tried to stand up. He pushed her down again.

"What happened after I walked out of here?" he asked.

She looked toward the arched doorway again, and Iain followed her eyes. No one was there.

"Marion, my patience is growing thin. Answer me."

"I'm giving you a chance to walk away from this unscathed," she said quietly. "Do it."

"Unscathed by what?"

She opened her mouth, but immediately closed it. She threw her hands up in frustration and looked at him pleadingly. "You have to take my word for it. That's it."

The only scenario running through his mind had to do with Jack Fitzwilliam. He wondered if Marion's aunts had said something or passed on a threatening message from the outlaw. Why else would she be so flustered?

"He can't hurt us," he told her.

"Who can't hurt us?"

"Jack, your cousin."

"This has nothing to do with him," she blurted, looking up at him like he'd lost his mind. "I just don't want to be married to you right now. What is so difficult to understand about that?"

"We are not going through that again." Iain heard the voices of Judith and Margaret coming from the stairwell. He straightened up. "Very well. Don't tell me anything. I'll ask your aunts. I wager they'll be much more agreeable in answering my questions than you have been."

His threat got her attention. She immediately stood up. "You cannot ask them anything," she said frantically.

"You just watch me," he said, turning to the door.

"Very well. I surrender." She tugged on his arm, forcing him to turn around. "I'll explain, but not here. Outside."

"Outside?" he repeated, looking at her suspiciously.

Marion nodded. She immediately pasted on a smile as her aunts entered the Hall, their arms full of linens and candles and knives. Iain tried to go to them to help. Marion, though, held him back.

"Iain and I are going outside for a walk around the Tower," she announced.

Both women looked up cheerfully. If there was anything amiss, Iain couldn't tell from the expressions on their faces.

"Don't stay out too late, dear," Margaret said.

"Not too late," Judith repeated.

"The table will be set, and we can all sit down to eat in no time."

"No time at all," Judith told them.

Iain felt himself being physically pulled toward the door to the courtyard.

"This shouldn't take too long," he called to the ladies.

Marion pushed him ahead of her out the door and onto the landing at the top of the courtyard steps. She turned to her aunts. "Don't do anything while I'm gone."

"What do you mean by that, dear?" Margaret asked.

"What do you mean?" Judith repeated the question.

Marion turned around and saw Iain watching her. "Please wait for me outside."

"No." He shook his head slowly from side to side. "Two can play this game."

"I hate you," she whispered, punching him in the arm. She turned again toward her aunts. "Please don't *move* anything while I'm gone."

"But why, dear?" Margaret asked. "Sir William said he's ready."

"He told us that he's ready," Judith repeated.

Iain wondered what they were moving. What was William ready for?

"Wait!" Marion said sharply. "Please promise me you won't. Don't ask Uncle William to come yet. Not until I get back."

"Oh!" Margaret said, delighted. "You want to help."

"Marion wants to help," Judith announced like she was the one passing on the news.

"Yes, I want to help. Just wait for me," she told the two women.

Iain stood his ground. "What is it that you're going to help them with?"

She shook her head, going around him and out the door. The storm had passed by and the night sky was clearing. There was a half moon rising in the east.

"Marion," he said sharply. "What is it that you want them not to do?"

Looking frustrated, she took him by the hand and pulled him down the stairs. "That would be telling the end of the story. I think it would be best if I first told you the beginning."

28

THE TWO SISTERS stared after the newlyweds as they disappeared through the doorway. Judith put everything she was carrying on one of the benches. Margaret did the same. The two worked together to move the platters of food off the table.

"She is far more contentious than I remember," Margaret commented.

"She is taller now. The size must make a difference," Judith reasoned.

Margaret stared at the doorway for a couple of moments. "Do you get the feeling that Marion has changed in more ways than just her looks over the years, too?"

Judith shook loose a heavy damask cloth. She motioned to her sister to help her spread it over the table. "I think she definitely has."

"I liked the little Marion so much better."

"It's not her fault that she's changed," Judith said in their niece's defense. "What do you expect from a child that was left in the keeping of nuns for twelve years?"

The two women let out a heavy sigh simultaneously, although neither of them had spent any length of time anywhere but at Fleet Tower.

"I don't think I like nuns," Judith murmured.

"Nor I. Nuns wouldn't understand us. Or William, either." Margaret frowned in the direction of the window seat. "And I have a strong sense that they wouldn't approve of what we've been doing here."

"Not even Scottish nuns?" Judith asked, somewhat surprised.

"Judging from Marion's reaction, I should think not." Margaret smoothed out the cloth on the table. "Don't you think Marion seemed a wee bit...well, uncertain?"

Judith aligned the two candlesticks on either end of the table. "I think she was somewhat distracted by our secret. But she wants us to wait for her, so she could help. Don't you think that's a good sign?"

"I believe you're right, Judith. Perhaps she does approve."

"She does." Judith nodded.

"She lost a father to the English," Margaret continued. "It only stands to reason that she would want to raise an army, too."

Judith circled the table, arranging the platters of food in the middle.

"I think there are other things that have her shaken up, too," Margaret added.

"I know. Things like the laird," Judith said with a giggle.

Margaret bit her lip to stop from giggling, as well. "Do you think they've already...?"

Judith covered her mouth with her hand, and then nodded whole-heartedly. "I'd say they have."

"Which means she's not getting much rest," Margaret said with some concern.

"I think that's good."

"It's not good if she is going to be irritable with us."

Judith leaned over the table toward her sister, lowering her voice. "But just think of half a dozen wee Williams running up and down those stairs."

"I don't think they'll look like William. Perhaps a half dozen Iains running about."

"That would be lovely."

Margaret clapped her hands excitedly. "In any event, we can have Sir William teach them everything they need to know about raising and caring for an army."

"And perhaps they'll have a couple of wee lassies for us to look after."

Margaret motioned with her head to the cupboard. "Then I'll have someone to pass on my recipes to."

"It's only fair if you gave them to Marion first."

Margaret put plates at each place. "First, I want to make sure that the nuns haven't ruined her. She'll need to prove herself to us first before I pass on anything so valuable."

Judith followed her sister around the table, putting goblets by the plates. "When are you going to teach *me* the recipes?"

Margaret gave a long disapproving look at her younger sister. "You don't remember, do you?"

"Remember what?"

"I've tried to teach you more than a dozen times, but you always forget the proportions."

"I do?"

The older sister nodded. "You do. And that's not the end of it, either. You cannot even be trusted with pouring it in the right bottles after I've mixed it."

"I cannot be trusted?"

"No, you cannot," Margaret said with authority. "How do you think we lost the little livestock we had left last winter?"

"I poisoned them?" Judith asked.

"You poisoned them," Margaret asserted.

Judith sighed and inspected the table, not remembering any of it. "I didn't particularly like taking care of them anyway. It's much nicer to have the villagers bring in the milk and cheeses. The goats were too much work."

Margaret agreed. She stepped back to stand next to her sister and studied the table, too. "It looks like the old days, when the earl was here."

"I should light the candles."

"You should fetch Marion and the laird. Tell them everything is ready. I'll light the candles," Margaret told her.

"I believe they're already in the house," Judith said, looking toward the arched doorway.

"No, they went outside for a walk. I haven't seen them come in yet."

"But I hear them coming up the stairs."

Margaret cocked her head, perplexed. "William was in his chambers upstairs, and Marion and the laird went outside. They cannot have gone down there without us seeing them."

Judith put a hand to her lips, hushing her sister. "But I hear voices."

"Do you think, as William sometimes says, the men are getting restless?" Margaret asked, paling slightly.

Judith shook her head, taking a couple of tentative steps toward the doorway. "It's only a couple of voices. But who do you suppose it is?"

Margaret crept closer to the doorway, pushing her sister ahead of her. "Are you sure someone is down there? I cannot hear anything."

"You never hear anything. You're practically deaf."

"I am?" Margaret asked, as if this was shocking news.

"Hush." Judith stopped.

Margaret held on to her sister's sleeve. "What do you hear?"

"There was a thud, like something dropping. Or perhaps it was a door closing." Judith inched closer to the doorway. "I think they're coming up here."

"That's not good," Margaret said nervously. Moving together, they backed toward the table they'd just set.

"That's not good at all," Judith agreed, blowing out the candles nearest to them. She looked nervously about the room.

"They can't be friends of ours."

"No, friends announce themselves and come through the door," Judith whispered. Turning, she scampered about the great hall, blowing out the other candles.

"They cannot be English, either," Margaret said.

"No. Englishmen act like our friends, too."

The voices coming up the stairs now clearly belonged to two men. The two sisters looked at each other in the darkened room. Only the embers of the fire lit the great hall.

"What do we do?"

"What *do* we do?"

They both pointed to the table.

"We hide."

Lifting the heavy damask cloth that draped nearly to the floor, they both crawled under.

29

SHE COULD LIE.

That was the first of Marion's two choices. She could drum up an astonishing story to explain her behavior and demands upstairs. Her second choice was to tell the truth, which happened to be more shocking than any story she could possibly invent. The first choice didn't offer any solution. The second choice actually presented the possibility of scaring Iain enough to have him see her reasoning and run.

She decided on the second choice.

"How far do we have to walk?" Iain asked, tugging on her arm.

Marion slowed down and looked around her. They had walked halfway around the tower house. The only people they had seen were the two Armstrong men, Tom and John, who were standing on the wall over the gate. The portcullis beneath them had been lowered.

"No one can hear us," Iain told her.

Marion looked up the sides of the tower. There had been many days when, as a child, she'd sat at the top, watching, and overhearing everything that was going on below.

"Yes, they can if they want." She took her husband by the hand and pulled him away from the tower house. Around the next corner was, she recalled, a walled garden.

"I don't think I have ever seen you so nervous, not even the day that I forced you to wed me."

"So you admit it. You forced me," she told him. "That's good. It's reason enough to annul the marriage."

He looped an arm around her waist and whispered in her ear. "No gaggle of bishops would ever consider annulling our marriage, not after I tell them the things I've done to you." He planted a kiss beneath her ear before straightening up. "Never mind what you've done to me."

Despite the cold air, Marion felt herself blush. "You're trying to distract me, make me lose the little courage I have gathered to tell you the truth."

"No more talk of annulment, then," he said seriously.

Marion didn't respond. She guessed that once she was done explaining everything, Iain would welcome an annulment.

She found her way to the walled garden, but all that was left of it was a weathered bench and an untended mass of weeds. In the darkness, you couldn't even make out the paths that once bordered flower beds and herb gardens.

"This is private enough," she said, turning around. There was a tangle of vines growing right up over the wall.

"And for more things than just talking," he commented.

"You're doing it to me again," she complained, turning to him and planting her hands on his chest.

"I'm glad." Iain pulled her to him and kissed her lips.

Marion leaned into her husband, kissing him back with passion, cherishing this moment. She knew it would be short-lived.

"Now you're doing it to me," he said hoarsely, running his hands over her dress.

Marion wished she could forget about everything she had seen and heard inside. She wanted to stay here, in Iain's arms. She wanted to make love to him on the old battered bench and in the overgrown grass and at the very top of the tower house. She wanted to spend her night in his arms and spend her days daydreaming about it.

That was never to be, though. She would miss him; there was no denying that. She loved everything about him. Emotions clawed their way up in her throat, and she tasted the salt of her own tears.

Marion made Iain sit beside her on the stone bench. The shadows of the night masked her misery. She started from the very beginning, telling him what she'd seen and heard. There was no way to gentle the blow, nor hide the truth.

He needed to know the trouble they were all in.

30

THE TUNNEL WAS cold and damp and pitch-dark. As the two men made their way along the low, narrow passageway, spider-webs clung to Bane's face and hair and shoulders, and he tried to ignore the sound of the rats scurrying past their feet in the dark.

The blanket-wrapped body he and Jack were dragging along seemed to grow heavier with every step. Finally, after what seemed like years, they reached the trapdoor Jack said opened up to a landing on the dungeon stairs. Pushing open the ancient oak portal, they shoved the unwieldy corpse through and climbed in after. Once through the trap door, though, Jack hoisted the body up onto Bane's shoulder and turned away. The wiry little man could only make it up to the next landing. A candle flickered on the curving wall farther up the stairs.

"He's breaking my back," Bane whined to his leader. "There is no way I can carry the filthy bugger another step."

"Drop him here on the landing, then," Jack Fitzwilliam ordered. "The rats will watch him while we visit with my beloved family."

Bane didn't have to be told twice. He dropped the dead body to the floor. The man's head made a cracking noise as it hit the stone wall, but there were no complaints out of him. He'd done the last of his complaining in his rooms at the inn when Jack had cut his throat. Happily, his officers drinking downstairs hadn't heard a thing.

"There's something foul-smelling down there, Jack," Bane said, looking back down the steps.

"I've always believed this tower house guarded the gates of hell, Cardinal."

"I think you may be right in that."

Jack looked down at the body sprawled at their feet. "Move him over. He's taking too much room."

"It's not like anyone is going down there," Bane complained.

"I said he is taking too much room," Jack said more sharply, pointing to the corpse.

David Bane knew better than to rile his leader. Cursing under his breath, he leaned over and propped up the body against the wall.

"Better?" He looked up. Jack was already ascending the stairs. Bane hurried to catch up to him. This house was already terrifying him. Hell's gate or no, there was no way he wanted to get lost here.

Jack halted at a landing. There was an arched doorway, and Bane stopped behind him, peering around his shoulder into the darkened room. It looked to be the Fleet Tower's great hall.

"Do you think they're already asleep?"

Jack reached for the candle burning in a sconce in the stairwell and lit the candles on either side of the doorway. Light stretched into the room, and the two men noticed the food spread on the table.

"We were expected," Bane said, slithering past his leader and going to the table. "And I was so hungry."

Jack paused in the doorway. Like a wolf on a prowl, he swept his gaze over every corner, his nose taking in all the scents.

"What are you waiting for?" Bane asked, tearing open a loaf of bread. Scooping out the soft inside, he stuffed it in his mouth and threw the crust on the floor. "I hate the crusts of these fancy breads."

"They're here," Jack murmured. "I can smell them."

"No one is here. Only you and I." He shook his head at the platter of cheeses and went for the meat pies.

"By 'sblood, what did the cook do to this mutton?" Bane complained, spitting it out at his feet. "I think a filthy Dutchman must have spiced the sauces."

There was a slap on his knee, and Bane leaped off the ground at least a foot. "The devil take me! What was that?"

He stepped back, reaching for his dirk.

Jack had already drawn his knife, too. Bane stepped back beside his leader.

"Come out of there!" Jack barked.

As the men watched, two old women crawled out from under the table and, with some help from each other, stood up.

"Well, I'll be damned," Jack said.

"Probably so," the thinner of the two women said angrily. "But who are you?"

"What are you doing here?" the other one asked.

"And how dare you ridicule our cooking?" the first one asked, pointing a finger at David Bane.

"How dare you?" the other one repeated.

Bane took another step back, thinking it was safer to stand *behind* his leader.

"And you will *pick up* the mess you have made."

"You *will* pick it up," the round-faced one said, shaking her finger at them menacingly.

Jack slid his dirk back into its sheath and laughed, a deep amused laugh that told Bane all was going to be well. The two frowning women, however, didn't change their fierce expressions.

"Aunt Judith! Aunt Margaret! You never change, do you?"

The two women stepped closer to each other, staring at him uneasily.

"Who are you?" they asked at the same time.

"It's Jack. Your nephew."

The thin one shook her head first; then the second one shook her head before the two of them looked at each other and shook their heads.

"No, you're far too ugly to be Jack."

"Far too ugly," the portly sister repeated.

Bane looked up at Jack's face, which grew dark as his anger returned. This was a very dangerous moment for the two old women, but they didn't even know it.

As he looked at his leader, he had to agree that the man was hideously ugly, but Jack didn't think so. In fact, he was rather vain when it came to his looks. The tall man's face, scarred as it was, now showed spatters of blood from their friend in the stairwell and dirt from the passageway they'd traveled through. Bane made a motion of wiping his face with his sleeve, but Jack wasn't paying any attention.

"Speak up," demanded the one he'd addressed as Margaret. "How dare you come in here and spit out our food and then claim to be our nephew?"

"How dare you?" Judith repeated.

"I didn't spit out the food. Cardinal Bane did," Jack said casually.

Margaret's expression immediately softened. "Cardinal?"

"Cardinal?" Judith clasped her hands.

The two women smiled at Bane, acting like they had long forgotten not recognizing their nephew. Bane bowed politely but didn't dare approach.

"Wait just a moment," Judith said. "I know you. Aren't you the lad from the village across the glen?"

"I believe he is," Margaret agreed. "But he's all grown-up."

"He still has the same hooked nose."

"And the same large ears that I recall flapping in the wind," Margaret said, smiling.

Bane looked up at Jack and took a step away. He'd been a member of Fitzwilliam's gang only since the summer, but he knew that he'd never shared this information with the outlaw when he'd joined him.

"What was his name?" Judith asked.

"David," Margaret remembered.

"Everyone used to call him David Bones, if I'm not mistaken."

"That's right, dear."

"The wee troublemaker was all nose, ears, bones, and nothing else," Judith finished cheerfully.

"He obviously still has no taste for fine food," Margaret said scornfully as she pointed to the food on the ground.

As a boy, David had been terrified of these two women. He had never accepted any job that would have brought him inside the gates of Fleet Tower. He'd always had an entirely uncomfortable feeling about them. Happily, Sir William never strayed out of the castle. David had known about Jack Fitzwilliam for years. It was simply good fortune that he'd run into his gang immediately after being dismissed from the abbey at Cracketford for filching from the abbey's wine cellars.

There were many rumors floating about regarding Jack's religious fervor. David had simply been at the right place at the right time, joining the outlaws and offering to save their leader's soul from eternal damnation.

Jack took a threatening step toward David. "You told me you were a priest."

David took a step back. "I was a priest. I *am* a priest. It was you that made me a cardinal."

"He was sent away to become a monk," Margaret corrected.

"He ended up as a drunk monk, from all accounts," Judith explained.

"A drunk monk!" the two women repeated, giggling.

"That has a nice sound to it," Margaret added.

He was not a drunk. Granted, he loved the feeling of floating you sometimes had when you drank just the right amount, but he didn't think there was much sense in explaining any of that right now.

"You never told me you were from one of my own villages."

David saw Jack's hand go to the handle of his dirk.

"Jack, listen to me. I'm a priest. Your priest. In fact, I'm your cardinal." He inched backward, not trusting the temper of a man who he knew would cut out his heart just for a laugh. "And what does it matter what village I was born in? I'm your man. I know you're the rightful heir of the McCall lands. You're the true Earl of Fleet now. You know that. I know that."

Jack continued to approach him. David circled around a chair, now actually backing toward the two troublemaking hags.

"I made you my spiritual adviser, my messenger of God. But you lied to me."

"I didn't lie. I just didn't reveal everything because I didn't think it mattered." He bumped up against the table. He considered crawling under, but Jack's hand was suddenly clamped around his throat.

"Please, Jack," he gasped, trying unsuccessfully to peel away the fingers.

"You lied to me. My priest doesn't lie to me."

David knew he had to think quickly. He had personally witnessed this man cut throats and break necks and choke the life out of a victim. His leader had once boasted of killing nineteen men himself. As Jack slowly drew his dirk, David had a horrible thought that he was about to be gutted like a fish. He was about to become number twenty.

"But Jack, the good Lord wanted it this way," he managed to croak. "It was divine intervention to have a McCall peasant rise in the holy orders to help the rightful heir find his place."

The hold on David's neck didn't loosen. The blade of the giant's dirk glinted red in the light of the dying fire. Jack's eyes were as lifeless as a dead man's.

"Hearken, we beseech thee, O Lord, to our prayers," David cried out as loudly as he could muster. "Bless with the awful hand of Thy Majesty this dirk which thy servant holds, that it may be *righteous* in the defense of your church..."

The hold on his neck eased. The hand released him and dropped away. Jack bowed his head and held up the dirk with both hands to be blessed. David finished the prayer and said another in Latin before making an elaborate sign of the cross in the air over the knife.

Jack turned and walked away from him.

"Well, Jack Fitzwilliam. It's been a very long time," Margaret said in her high-pitched voice.

David stared at her. You wouldn't know that she'd nearly seen a man's insides ripped out in front of her.

"Very long," Judith repeated.

David stretched his neck, turning it from side to side. He just wanted to be sure his head was still connected to his shoulders.

"How long has it been?"

"How long, Jack?"

"Nearly four years," Jack muttered, looking at the food on the table.

Judith looked at her sister. "Is that a long time?"

Margaret nodded before turning to their nephew. "What have you been doing since your last visit?"

"Yes, Jack, what have you been doing?" Judith repeated.

David figured that after Jack's wee show of force, the McCall crones had decided to remember their nephew. Bane reached down and picked up a wedge of cheese and bit off a piece. The cheese was dry, though, and he was about to spit it out when he saw Margaret glowering at him. He forced himself to swallow the bite.

"I've been raising an army," Jack answered.

"Well, that certainly runs in the family," Margaret giggled.

"Definitely," her sister agreed.

"What's that you say?" he snapped.

"Where are your men?" the older sister asked.

"Where?" Judith repeated.

"In hiding, awaiting my orders."

Margaret turned to the table, pulling the platters of food out of David's reach. "That's a good thing that they're in hiding. We definitely don't have enough food left to feed an army."

"Definitely not."

"Unfortunately, we can't even feed you and Bones."

"Definitely not," Judith agreed.

"Cardinal Bane, if you please," David said, stepping back as Jack shot a deadly look at him.

"This is only left over from dinner yesterday. We've had no supper."

"No supper at all," Judith repeated.

Leftover food, David thought. The taste of the dry cheese was in his mouth. He eyed the pitchers of drinks on the table.

Jack looked over the table and the four settings. "Are you expecting guests?"

"Not guests, only family," Margaret answered.

"Only family," Judith repeated.

The twisted smile on Jack's face was too frightening even for David. The defrocked monk moved casually backward until he was standing by the cupboard.

"Tell me my dear cousin, Marion, is here," Jack said, glancing behind him toward the stairwell.

"You know there is going to be a wedding," Margaret said instead of answering.

"A wedding." Judith nodded excitedly.

"But they're already married," Margaret said lowering her voice.

"That is a secret, though," Judith whispered.

A secret that Jack was already well aware of, David thought. A secret that had played right into the outlaw leader's plan of setting up Iain Armstrong. He reached for one of the pitchers in the cupboard and took down a cup, too, quietly pouring himself some wine.

"She is a dear."

"A bonny thing."

Jack's smile became a snarl. "Is she staying here at Fleet Tower?"

"She is really quite tall now, as well," Margaret said, carrying on her own conversation.

"Quite tall." Judith held a hand up above her head, showing how tall Marion was.

"Not as tall as you, Jack."

"Not nearly as tall."

"Her eyes are black."

"The color of onyx," Judith told them.

"The devil take her. I don't care how tall she is or how she looks or if she has one eye or three," Jack snapped. "I want to know if she is staying here or not."

The two sisters moved closer together, linking their arms to support each other. Jack's temper had a way of unnerving people. David found his own hand was trembling as he brought the cup to his lips.

"No wine," Jack snarled at him. "I want you sober."

"Just a sip, Jack, to wet my lips?"

"No wine!" he barked.

With a longing glance at the cup, David put it down.

"I asked you before." Jack turned to his aunts, moving toward them with measured steps. "Where is Marion?"

"You shouldn't really be so against her. You two are cousins, after all," Margaret asserted.

"Cousins," Judith averred.

"She hasn't done anything to wrong you."

"Nothing."

Jack glared menacingly at them. "Marion's every breath has become wrong. Her head sitting prettily on her shoulders has become wrong. The wee bitch should never have been born. She should never have lived this long. She is a thief who has stolen everything that truly belongs to me. Because of her, I have been denied my true place in the world. I should be the laird of Fleet Tower and all that belongs to it. All of this land would be mine. God himself has ordained it so. Is that not correct, Cardinal?"

"That is so, Jack. It's the will of God."

Silence fell over the great hall for a long moment.

"Aren't you happy, Jack?" Margaret asked weakly.

"You do have nice friends," Judith suggested, motioning toward David Bane.

"Friends," Jack snorted derisively, and then his face grew hard, his black eyes glittering with hatred. "Because of Marion, I hide in caves like some wounded animal. But this is the end of that life. This is the end of Marion and her husband. No Armstrong dog will rule what is rightfully mine. Now, where is she?"

The two women huddled together. There was some whispering between them, but David couldn't make out the words.

"The wedding is to be held at Blackthorn Hall," Margaret explained quickly.

"Blackthorn Hall." Judith pointed toward a window.

"You're lying to me, Aunties." Jack nodded toward the table. "You're expecting her."

"In the morning," Margaret said.

"Not before," Judith added.

The outlaw's gaze moved over the platter of food.

"They're just leftovers. Cardinal Bane can attest to that," Margaret quickly explained. "This afternoon, Brother Luke was here for a visit. The dishes have been out since."

"Brother Luke." Judith nodded fervently.

Jack stared at the two quavering women for a few more moments before walking to the window. "Who is bringing Marion over tomorrow?"

"The laird," the McCall sisters said simultaneously.

"*WHO?*" Jack thundered.

"I mean, Iain Armstrong," Margaret amended.

David saw the look of satisfaction on his leader's face before he pushed open the shutters and looked out.

"Why is the portcullis down?"

The two sisters looked at each other before Margaret answered. "The lair--I mean, Iain's men did it. They were worried about our safety."

"Very worried." Judith nodded.

"There are no servants left at Fleet Tower," Margaret said quietly.

"We are all alone," Judith whispered.

Jack backed away from the window and turned to his aunts. "Where is my father?"

"In his chambers," Margaret answered. "Going over his maps, I should think."

Judith nodded. "He likes his maps."

"Anyone else here?"

Both women shook their heads from side to side.

"As you know, we really don't have much room," Margaret replied.

"No room for guests," Judith agreed.

"We never have."

"Barely room for us."

"What are you telling me?" Jack asked sharply. "No room for your own nephew?"

"Since things are really so cramped here, we thought you might want to leave," Margaret said hopefully. "Tonight."

Judith motioned toward the doorway.

"We can wrap some food to take with you on the road, of course."

"But you didn't come on the road, did you?" Judith asked.

"No, Judith. The portcullis is down," Margaret answered, turning to Jack. "How *did* you get in here?"

"They must have come through the tunnels," Judith answered brightly, not giving their nephew a chance to answer.

"Are the passages still open?"

"Obviously." Judith motioned with her brows to the two men.

It was almost amusing to David how these two women could carry on a conversation like this. They asked questions; they answered themselves. They never stopped talking. He eyed the cup of wine on the shelf again.

"So you are going." Margaret said it in a tone like it was already decided. "We'll just go in the kitchen and—"

"No, we're not going, Aunt Margaret. In fact, we're planning to stay here for a while."

"But no room," Judith whispered.

"Have you already forgotten? I am family, and this is my home as much as it's yours."

"Oh," the two aunts said.

"And Cardinal Bane stays with me."

There was some whispering between the two women, some shaking of the heads, a few nods. Again, Margaret was the one who spoke for them. "You can have the earl's old chamber."

"It's certainly big enough for the two of you," Judith added.

"We have stored a few valuables in there."

"Valuables."

"But there is room enough for you."

Judith pointed to her sister to show that she was in agreement with what Margaret said.

"You really should be on your way by the morning, though,"

Margaret added. "The la--I mean Iain won't find it entirely satisfactory if he finds you here."

"Not satisfactory at all." Judith shook her head.

"Well, ladies, one of us will find our meeting satisfactory." Jack's hand went to the handle of his dirk. His gaze was commanding as it snapped back to the sisters' faces. "Up to your bedchambers, now."

"Aren't you coming?" Margaret asked, still clutching her sister's arm and not taking a step. "We'd like to be sure you're comfortably settled into the earl's chambers."

"No need. We shall make ourselves at home."

"But really, Jack—"

"And Cardinal Bane and I have some business to discuss first. Now, GO!" he ordered.

The two sisters scrambled a few steps toward the arched doorway, but they both quickly returned, reaching for the platters of food on the table, stacking one on top of the other on the tray and taking the pitchers.

"You can help yourself with the wine in the cupboard," Judith whispered to David once she had her arms full.

David nodded. He waited until Jack was watching the two women hurrying out before he reached for the cup he had poured before.

"Put it down," the outlaw barked without turning around.

"Really, Jack," David whined. "I'm so thirsty and I—"

"I'll not tell you again," he growled menacingly.

The monk's hand shook as he put the cup back on the shelf. It was so unfair. He looked at the table. The old women had managed to take the other pitchers with them, too. No food, no drinks, nothing.

Jack waited until the sound of footsteps moving down the corridors quieted before he turned to him. "You will go back through the passage the same way as we came. Go to where we left the men on the far side of the glen. Tell them to return to the inn where we found our Englishman tonight. They are to proceed as I planned. The English soldiers are to think it was Iain Armstrong who abducted their commander. If my men are questioned, they're to tell them that they followed Iain and his men. I want the English soldiers here at Fleet Tower right after Iain's arrival tomorrow."

The idea of crawling through that filthy passageway wasn't too pleasant, but David knew better than to refuse. He'd already escaped with his life once tonight.

"What about the body in the stairwell?"

"I need to find a good place for the English to 'discover' him tomorrow."

"Don't you want help moving it before I go?"

"No, he won't go anywhere," Jack answered.

David considered taking the cup of wine with him, but there was no way he could take it without Jack seeing him. On second thought, perhaps he would just ride to the inn with the men and have a drink or two there. Jack hadn't said he couldn't. The thought cheered him up considerably.

"And I want you back here after you deliver the message to the men outside."

"Immediately?"

"Immediately," he ordered.

31

MARION STOPPED TALKING and stood looking at him expectantly.

In the moonlight, in any light, she was so beautiful. Iain wanted her now more than he ever wanted any woman in his life. He thought of how she'd looked kneeling astride him in the bed at the inn on Loch Lomond. The moonbeams had set her hair on fire and made her smooth skin glow. Her body, so perfect, had enticed him then as it was enticing him now.

If she came one step closer, he would take her here and now, and he didn't care if Sir William *and* the two aunts were watching from the parapet.

She was waiting for an answer from him.

He tried to focus. For the life of him, he could not understand why she would made up such stories. For weeks in Skye, she'd tried to put him off with tales of her unbreakable schedules of seclusion and such. And for what purpose? To avoid the unavoidable.

And now what could be motivating such behavior? She simply had to know that their marriage was fixed in stone. No matter what wild tale she invented, he was not going anywhere. Nothing she could say would ever convince him to walk away. And he knew that she had come to want this marriage, too. There were certain things that she could not lie about. There were certain moments when he could look right through her soul. It was during those moments that he was certain she wanted him as much as he wanted her.

And did he ever want her now.

"Marion, when your aunts mentioned entertaining me, I thought we agreed that making love was part of our evening activities. Why don't you come over here and let me entertain *you*?"

"You don't believe me, do you?" she asked, staring at him, hands on her hips.

"I've come to appreciate your many talents. Aside from being a woman of undeniable physical charms, you're also a gifted storyteller."

She threw her head back and ran her hands through her hair. She made a noise that sounded like that of a strangled animal.

"But let's explore the first of those talents. Come over here, my love."

"Iain, this is NOT a story."

Iain stood up and took hold of her shoulders, forcing her to look into his face. "Marion, what are you trying to tell me?"

"I'm trying to tell you the truth, and you're only thinking of sex."

"It's your fault. If you weren't so beautiful, I—"

"Stop. You're behaving like a...a man!

"I am a man. The man you married. The man who would like to take you on his lap and—"

"Stop! I'm trying to make you understand that there is a dead body in that great hall, and that there are more in the dungeon."

"You're trying to tell me that those two sweet old ladies are the murderers of an entire company of English soldiers."

"Not a company. Nineteen," she said.

"Of course," he said good-naturedly. "Two old women have subdued nineteen English soldiers."

"I don't know if they were all soldiers or not." She pushed away from him, start to pace back and forth. "I should have known that you would be too thick-headed to recognize the truth and see reason."

"Especially when it's so believable," he said. He put out a hand and stopped her. "But what should be readily believable is how much I want you now. Those gates are secured. My men are keeping watch. Your aunts and Sir William are doing...whatever they do. Why don't you and I—"

"That's it. This is your last chance." Marion pushed his hand off her arm, and there was definitely a note of sadness in her voice. "I want you to go. If you admit publicly to our marriage, then you become responsible for me and my family."

"I've been responsible for you all for years."

"No, it's different now. You're responsible for my actions, too. For my misdeeds. And for the misdeeds of my family of lunatics."

"I tried to bring up the problem of your uncle, I believe, but someone almost took my head off for mentioning it."

"Sir William is the least of our problems...*my* problems, right now. There is the wee matter of Aunt Judith and Aunt Margaret and the nineteen dead bodies." She grabbed a fistful of his shirt. "Iain, listen to me. You have to walk away."

He took her hands in his. "First, I still don't believe you. Secondly, even if I did, do you really think I could walk away from a situation like this and let you face it alone?"

"This is not about facing anything. It's about having *your* head on a pike above the gates of York."

"And you think your punishment would be any less severe?" Iain asked seriously.

"They might let me rot in some prison somewhere," she said in a quavering tone.

"And that's acceptable to you?"

"It's better than letting anything happen to you," Marion said quietly. "I'm related to them. Their blood flows in my veins. I must be insane like the rest of them. But you're innocent of all this."

Iain pulled her against his chest, his arms wrapping around her. "What am I going to do with you?"

"Believe what I told you?" she asked, looking up.

"About those two sweet old ladies?"

Marion shook her head. She pushed away from him.

"I'll tell you what," he said. "I'll make a bargain with you."

"What bargain?"

"We go and look at these corpses you say may be in the dungeon."

"And in the great hall."

"Wherever you like. But if there are no bodies..." He pulled her close to him. "You and I put all talk of annulment behind us and..."

"Yes?"

"And you make love to me as I know you can."

Marion stared at him for a moment and then took his hand. "I can see I have no other choice."

"I like that kind of talk," he said.

"That's not what I mean. I can see I'm going to have to introduce you. It's time you met my aunts' special guest."

32

All of this was his.

Jack Fitzwilliam walked the length of the great hall. He touched the tapestry on the wall, ran his hand over the damask cloth on the table where the food had been. He looked up at the blackened beams and the ornate paneling along the walls.

How many times, as a lad, had he considered burning it all to the ground?

He moved to the large chair near the hearth. It had been the earl's chair, and no one else was ever allowed to sit in it. He glanced about him, and then sat down. The cushions were comfortable, and the arms suited him perfectly. The carved wood hand rests were smooth beneath his fingers.

When he was young, he had never been allowed to touch this chair or even come into the great hall. Not while the old earl lived. So he'd sneaked in when the laird was not around. His lordship had always considered Jack no more than a mistake. The bastard son of an idiot brother. He did not accept, respect, or tolerate him. Jack was treated with less esteem than if he'd been a servant. He was to be kept at the Tower, but he was never to be acknowledged.

It wasn't right, but Jack was now in a position to change all that.

He slipped his dirk out of its sheath and carefully carved the letter J in the left hand rest. He liked to leave his mark on everything that he meant to keep. He had been the only male McCall heir, but the old fool of an earl had turned to their enemies—to Iain Armstrong—to take control of their land. But John McCall was long dead, and Jack was the one who would now decide the future for his clan.

Across the great hall, a shadow appeared in the arched doorway. Jack saw his father, wearing his old-fashioned armor. The old man moved into the room without a sound. This was the only thing they had in common. They could both move as silently as a shadow when they chose to. Jack stood up.

"Well, if it isn't my son," Sir William said. "Jack Fitzwilliam."

Jack didn't like to admit it, not even to himself, but he was always pleased to have his father recognize him each time he stopped here.

The old man slapped him on the shoulder. "You look well, lad. How is your mother?"

"Dead," Jack answered.

"I'm elated to hear it." William nodded. "What brings you here?"

"I'm in search of my cousin Marion," he said, hoping William could offer more information than his aunts.

"Marion. Marion." William looked up, tapping the side of his nose. "And who is this Marion?"

"Your niece. The late earl's daughter."

"Yes. Yes. She was here just this afternoon."

Jack smiled. He should have guessed that those two wily old women would try to protect their spoiled protégé from him. "Where is she now, Sir William?"

"Up on the parapet. The south bartizan. That's where I stationed her. She is keeping watch for Longshanks, the thieving cur."

Jack remembered the parapet of the tower house had always been Marion's refuge, even as a child. That was where she hid whenever Jack visited. It made sense she'd be hiding there now.

"Is she standing watch alone?" Jack asked.

"Of course," William answered. "I've no men to spare these days. She must carry her weight, you know."

Jack nodded. "And where is Iain Armstrong?"

"Iain Armstrong?" William started tapping his nose again.

"Marion's betrothed," Jack said, hoping to freshen the old man's mind. "He lives in Blackthorn Hall across the—"

"Ah, yes. The laird."

He gritted his teeth. "Yes. Iain."

"Why, he was here this afternoon, too. A good lad."

"And is he still here?" Jack pressed.

"No! No! We couldn't feed him. Not enough to go around. I have my army to feed, you know."

"Where is he now?"

"He left to check on his men. He'll be back tomorrow, I should think."

Jack was satisfied. Everything made sense. Never once, since the Earl of Fleet's death, had he ever seen the portcullis lowered. And yet, tonight it was. Now he understood why. Iain would lock up the castle to protect his wife. And the lie Jack's aunts had told him made sense, too. They wanted the outlaw to assume Marion was not here—at least, not until her husband arrived tomorrow.

Jack's fingers wrapped around the handle of his dirk. He had been waiting for this opportunity for years. Turning the Armstrong laird over to the English tomorrow would not be enough to secure his own position. Marion could always marry again. Jack would always be facing the same situation he was facing now.

He stepped around his father and moved across the great hall toward the stairwell. Marion had to die, but he didn't want the murder to be too obvious. Perhaps just a fall from the tower parapet, he thought. She would break her neck in the fall.

Jack smiled. That definitely had possibilities.

33

Margaret and Judith hovered in the doorway to the kitchens, keeping quiet until they saw the shadow of their nephew going up the stairs.

"What do we do now?" Judith asked, relieved that she could finally speak. "Do we go to bed?"

"We bar the door to the courtyard," Margaret answered.

"The door to the great hall?" Judith asked, perplexed. "But Marion and Iain are outside. How will they get in?"

"We don't want them to come inside," Margaret explained to her sister. "They're safe out there, but I think Jack will kill them if they come in."

"So they're safe outside, but dead inside?"

"Exactly, dear. Safe outside, dead inside."

"Safe outside, dead inside," Judith repeated to remind herself.

"Now, come with me," Margaret said, taking her sister by the arm.

"Where are you taking me?"

"To the great hall, to bar the door."

Judith nodded, remembering. "Safe outside, dead inside."

The two old women moved quietly down the narrow hallway and peeked up the circular stairwell. There was no sign of Jack. Peering into the great hall, they were relieved to see their brother standing in the center of the room, staring up at the shields on the wall.

"Oh, Sir William. We're so glad you're here," Judith said.

Lost in his own world, the old man did nothing to acknowledge them.

Margaret grabbed her sister's sleeve and pulled her to the door. "Help me with this."

It was a struggle, but between the two of them, they were able to lift the heavy oak beam and bar the ancient door.

"What happens if they knock?" Judith asked afterward.

"We have a few things to do in the kitchen. We'll hear them from there."

"Do we let them in, then?"

Margaret shook her head. "No, we talk to them from the window and tell them to go away."

"Tell them to go away," Judith repeated, satisfied. "Safe outside, dead inside."

When they turned around, their brother had not moved from where he had been standing. He continued to stare with rapt attention at the weapons on the wall. Margaret tapped him on the shoulder. He still didn't move.

"Sir William?" she called.

There was no acknowledgment.

"Sir William Wallace?" both women called.

He turned so quickly that the visor of his helmet dropped forward onto his face. He lifted it up and saw the two women.

"What is it, ladies? Can you not see I'm busy?"

"Your recruit, Sir William," Margaret said, pointing to the window seat. "He is impatient to join the rest of your army."

His expression immediately brightened. "Is it time?"

The two sisters looked at each other first before nodding simultaneously.

"I am elated to hear it. Eee-lated." He held his visor up and moved toward the window seat.

Margaret grabbed Judith's sleeve again and dragged her toward the arched doorway. "Come with me to the kitchens. We have much to do tonight."

"Much to do," Judith repeated.

"We'll have a houseful of guests tomorrow."

"A houseful of guests." Judith clapped. "Any 'special' guests?"

"You heard Jack's instructions to Cardinal Bane. We might just have an army of Englishmen at our door," Margaret said with a giggle as the two women disappeared inside the kitchens.

34

WILLIAM MOVED the cushions aside and lifted the top of the window seat. As promised, the recruit was waiting patiently for him.

"Good of you to join us, my man. I'm elated to see you."

He leaned forward to help the man out of the window seat, but his visor slipped down, blocking his vision. He straightened up to adjust it. As he did, his gaze fell on the barred door.

"Didn't that bloody woman say the door was to remain unbarred?"

The recruit said nothing.

"What's worse," William added, "how are my men going to reach me with the door barred?"

He walked to the main entrance and lifted the oak beam from its iron hooks. He walked back to the recruit.

"Well, my man. Are you ready?"

He reached into the window seat and, after some pulling and shifting of the deadweight, took the man by the arms and hauled him up onto his shoulder. William staggered momentarily, taking a few steps in different directions before finding his balance.

"The men are elated to have you joining us," he huffed at the new soldier. "I must warn you, though, that you will be losing some of this weight. We maintain strict schedules down there. You will be training eight to ten hours a day. Then there will be other duties that you need to attend to, as well."

William had to shift the weight on his shoulder again. At the arched doorway, the body bumped against the side of the opening, staggering William slightly. He backed up and moved through the doorway more carefully.

"Another thing I should tell you is that food is sometimes scarce. I try to bring you down whatever I can." William lowered his voice as he glanced down the narrow hallway that led to the kitchens. "Watch what you eat and drink. Those witches in there have been known to poison our drinks."

The stairwell going down to the dungeon was dark, and William took the candle from the sconce on the wall. Even in the dark, he knew these passages better than the palm of his hand, but his new recruit wouldn't know his way without some light.

"Any questions?"

There was no response.

"I am elated. You'll fit in just fine."

William's foot hooked on a soft item blocking the stair. He tripped, and he and his recruit tumbled forward a couple of steps before they crashed against the wall. Somehow, he kept his hold on both the candle and the new man.

"Bloody hell!" he growled.

William regained his balance and turned to look at the obstacle.

"Not trying to desert, I hope," he snapped, lowering the candle. He smiled. "Why, not a deserter at all."

William stood looking at the man. Why, the good fellow even brought his own blanket along.

"Another recruit, I believe." He paused as a suspicion suddenly entered his head. "Hold, there. Why was I not told about you?"

There was no response.

He shifted the recruit on his shoulder and studied the red-soaked blanket and tunic. "You're here in disguise. You were sent by the English to spy on us. Admit it, man."

The man appeared speechless. He wasn't even trying to fight him after being discovered.

"Answer me," William shouted. "We don't go easy on spies here in Scotland."

The spy's head remained bowed. His chin never lifted from his chest. The man was no recruit for the Wallace's army. He was an imposter and a coward.

"You will remain where you are, dog. I will return in a moment to take care of you." He turned and continued to assist his new recruit down the steps to the dungeon.

"Bloody imposter," William shouted back up the stairwell. "We don't take kindly to your type around here."

35

MARION DIDN'T GIVE Iain a chance to check on his two men at the gate. She didn't even allow him to exchange a few words with them. As far as she was concerned, the most urgent business right now was showing him the dead body of Sir George Harington.

"You might not believe this," Iain said in a low voice, "but I'm very much looking forward to getting *inside.*"

Even with all she had on her mind, she couldn't help feeling the double meaning in his words. There was a smoldering fire deep inside of her that only Iain knew how to stoke.

No, she told herself. *Don't let him distract you.*

"You will be sorry that you didn't believe me," she whispered under her breath as they climbed the stairs to the door of the great hall.

"We don't have to go through with this, Marion. No matter what you saw, no matter what you show me, I still intend to take you upstairs immediately afterward and ravish you. And that's the truth."

She swallowed hard. She wished he wouldn't say things like that.

"The truth?" she asked. "You wouldn't know the truth if you fell over it."

"Perhaps I won't even wait to take you upstairs."

Entering the great hall, she stopped dead at the sight of her uncle standing in the middle of the darkened room, staring at the shields and weapons on the wall. All the candles had been extinguished and the food had been cleared away.

"It appears your aunts have retired for the night...leaving us to our own devices."

She didn't say anything. She knew what he was thinking. It was definitely warmer in the hall than it had been.

"So where is our friend?" Iain whispered into her ear.

Marion didn't think it would be wise to show him the body with Sir William around. She gestured with her eyes toward her uncle.

He nodded. "Then perhaps you'd care to show me your bedchamber first," he whispered, "since the great hall is occupied."

She glowered at him. He was taking all of this far too lightly.

"Uncle William?" she called.

He continued to look up at the shields. Marion walked over and stood beside him. She couldn't understand what was so interesting about the ancient shields and lances.

"Sir William," she said softly, touching him on the shoulder.

He could as well have been a statue. There was no answer. Marion looked pleadingly at Iain.

"Sir William," he called. "Sir William Wallace."

The old man awoke out of his reveries.

"Ah, here you are, lad. Back already. Elated to see you." He stepped around Marion like she was a piece of furniture and directed his words to Iain. "Tell me, what news do you have for me?"

"Your presence is requested on the tower, m'lord. There are troops approaching from the south. We don't know if they are friends or foe, but the rumor is that Edward Longshanks himself may be leading them."

"Just like the cowardly dog to try a sneak attack. I'll go and see to that immediately."

Sir William moved to the arched doorway, drew his sword, and ran up the stairs, shouting, "*Freedom!*"

"Thank you," Marion said grudgingly. She waited until her uncle's shout died away up the stairs before she took Iain by the hand and pulled him toward the window seat.

"He's in there." She pointed. "Sir George Harington."

The shutters of the window were open, and the moon was shining on the window seat.

He looked at the pillows and back at Marion. "Very well. Let's have a look."

She shook her head. "I have seen enough of him. You open it." She took a few steps back.

He shook his head in disbelief, walked to the window seat, moved aside the pillows, and opened it.

Marion waited, holding her breath, expecting some kind of reaction. But there was none.

"Well?" she asked.

He looked at her and then put his head into the opening.

"Ah, Sir George," he said. "Nice of you to come to the wedding. Hope your journey was uneventful."

"What are you doing?" she cried.

Iain straightened up and turned to her. "I never realized how deep the storage space beneath this window seat was. You could certainly hide a body, or maybe even two, in there. But is there a false bottom to it or do the corpses climb out on their own?"

Marion charged past him and looked into the window seat.

"Empty," she blurted. "It's empty."

"So it is," he said softly.

Marion stared wildly around the great hall. "They've moved him. I told them they should wait for me. But they moved him anyway."

"I love the way you look with the moon in your hair."

He'd slipped his hands around her waist. She turned in his arms.

"I'm telling you, Iain. He was in there."

"I believe you, but he isn't there now. And a bargain is a bargain."

"You can't be serious."

He certainly was, for in the next instant, his mouth descended upon hers.

"Iain, there is a time and place for everything. Right now, I cannot settle my mind until I know what my aunts have done with Sir George."

"Sir George be damned," Iain said, kissing her again. His hands were all over her, touching her, setting her on fire.

"Iain," she said softly. She was frustrated and confused, but hopeful at the same time. Perhaps, she thought with increasing vagueness, what she thought she'd seen , what she thought she'd heard, was all just a dream. Just a touch of the family madness.

But that was too much to ask for. It couldn't be possible.

"I don't know what kind of a game it is you're playing with me," he told her between kisses. "But you're driving me mad with desire. I want you, Marion. I need to have you."

She found herself suddenly swept off her feet. Iain carried her toward the deeper shadows at the far end of the hall. He set her down on the other window seat. The shutters were closed over it, and it was dark here.

"We should go look in the dungeon," she whispered. "He was probably taken down there."

He kissed her again, deeply.

"We will," he told her, pulling up her skirts. "Right after we're done here."

She glanced around her in panic. "We cannot make love here. Anyone might come in."

"Your uncle will be on the parapet for some time, I believe. And I can't hear your aunts."

"But they could show up anytime."

"It's dark, my love," Iain told her, pushing her back gently. She was protected by the darkness, by the corner of the paneling, by Iain's body.

"I cannot believe I'm letting you do this to me," Marion said in disbelief. A moment later, though, she gasped with pleasure as his fingers found the source of her womanhood.

"You have been doing it to me, Marion. I'm only returning the favor."

She slipped her arms around his neck as he lifted the front of his kilt. He lifted her off the ground, and she wrapped her legs around his hips. Marion's breath caught in her throat as he entered her. Her moan of pleasure was swallowed by his mouth as he sealed her lips with a kiss.

Considering everything else that Marion had been through tonight, the strangeness, shock, and confusion of making love to her husband in Fleet Tower's great hall suddenly seemed perfectly normal.

"What do we tell them we're doing," she asked breathlessly, "if someone were to come in now?"

"We tell them, my love, that in uniting our families, we've found it a perfect fit." He moved inside of her, withdrawing slightly before burying himself to the hilt. "Absolutely...perfect."

36

STANDING in a hallway on an upper floor, Jack heard his father's shout as he charged up the steps. He moved to block his path. It took Sir William only an instant to recognize him and lower his sword. He sheathed the weapon.

"If it isn't my son," William said cheerfully. "Jack Fitzwilliam."

"I have searched the parapet and every room on this floor, but I cannot find Marion. Where is she?" Jack asked shortly.

The old man slapped him on the shoulder. "You look well, lad. How is your mother?"

"Dead," Jack answered impatiently.

"I am elated to hear it." William nodded. "What brings you here?"

"I'm looking for Marion. You told me she was up on the parapet. But she's not there."

"And who is this Marion?"

Jack took a couple of deep breaths. He stopped his hand from inching toward the dirk at his belt. He could already feel his fingers around the old man's throat.

"Marion is your niece," he said through clenched teeth. "The earl's daughter."

"Ah, yes. Indeed. She is on the parapet, keeping watch."

"I just came from there," Jack said thinly. "She is *not* on the parapet."

"But she is," William insisted. "The wee sprite has an excellent hiding place, I believe."

"Hiding place?" Jack asked suspiciously.

"You sound like Judith, the old witch." He slapped Jack on the arm. "Come with me, and I'll show you her hiding place."

Shaking his head, Jack followed his demented father back up the stairs to the roof of the tower house. He was beginning to think that his aunts had spoken the truth. Marion was not here, after all.

37

HIDING in the narrow hallway just outside the door to the kitchens, Judith heard every word that passed between her brother and his brute of a son.

"Old witch, am I?" she murmured indignantly.

Jack was clearly not giving up in his search for Marion. That was not a good thing. She looked over her shoulder at her sister to ask what to do. Margaret was busily measuring and mixing.

Judith didn't want to distract her. She would just take charge of this herself.

She tiptoed to the bottom of the stairwell and listened. The two men were almost at the top. She heard the door that led out onto the tower roof squeak open. Making up her mind, she hurried up the stairs.

She'd never had anything against Jack Fitzwilliam before. She and Margaret both thought his visits did a great deal of good for their brother. The two sisters had even done their fair share of defending their nephew with Iain. Jack was their family, and good or bad, they needed to care for and stand up for one another.

Today all that had changed, though. Jack's violent talk in referring to Marion had scared the two sisters. They always knew Jack was jealous of everything that Marion had as a wee one and of all the other things that were left to her after the earl's death. Before tonight, though, the two women never knew Jack planned to harm her.

Their late brother, the Earl of Fleet, no doubt had his reasons for arranging things as he did. Margaret and Judith knew better than to question those decisions. The same thing could be said about Sir William. He was perfectly happy to be the Wallace. It had never crossed their minds that Jack Fitzwilliam would not wish to honor the memory of his uncle and just let things happen as he'd arranged them.

"I guess we were wrong," Judith whispered as she reached the door to the tower roof.

The night wasn't too cold, and the fresh autumn air wafted in around her. There was nothing like fresh air to clear unpleasant thoughts, Judith decided. She took a deep breath and then hesitated, suddenly trying to remember why she'd come all the way up here.

Then she heard the two men's voices drifting in from the parapet, and she remembered. She struggled with the door, but the rusty hinges didn't want to cooperate. She moved behind the door and, putting her shoulder to it, pushed hard until the door creaked and groaned and then closed with a loud bang. Judith quickly dropped the bar in place and hurried down the stairs to the kitchens.

"Where were you?" Margaret asked, looking up from her bowls.

"Oh, here and there," Judith said, smiling. "Tell me what to do. You know I like to help."

Margaret had a list of safe chores that her sister could do, and Judith went happily to work.

38

EVERYTHING ELSE HAD BEEN BLOTTED from Marion's mind; only a warm, soft-edged feeling of bliss remained.

Wrapped in Iain's arms, their bodies still joined, she felt her limbs throbbing from the moment they had just shared. She didn't want to think of anything but him right now. She didn't want to be anywhere but in his arms.

He kissed her softly and ever so gently withdrew from her, pulling her clothing back in place.

"I'm sorry, Marion. I lost control. I had to have you," he told her, his large hands cupping her face. He gazed into her eyes. "I'm afraid there could have been a dozen people sitting around this great hall and I still would have wanted you."

"I am glad." She smiled, leaning against the side of the window seat. For some reason, her legs were not strong enough to carry her weight at the moment. "I needed you, too."

He touched the tip of her nose, ran his thumb across her bottom lip. "This is going to be the story of our lives. When it comes to you, I have absolutely no self-control. I love you, Marion."

"And I love you, Iain," she said, speaking her heart, not thinking what the consequences of voicing the truth might be.

He kissed her softly, his mouth making love to her the way his body had done a few short moments before. She was helpless when it came to her husband. He knew how to bring to life all her senses, how to make her burn, how to make her want him again. She clutched at his shirt, kissing him back with the same ardor.

"You keep this up," he told her, "and I'll be tearing your clothes off and making love to you on that table next."

Marion wrapped her arms around him, pulling his body against her. "I love these threats of yours."

"I don't call that a threat, my love. Consider it planning for your future. I intend to make love to you at all hours of the day and night, at every opportunity." He placed kisses on her neck and laid his hand flat on her belly. "Until you are round here with our bairn."

"Our bairn," Marion whispered. Iain's mouth, hands, and words were distracting her from something that she had to remember. They were back at Fleet Tower. Something important, she thought.

"Our child," he continued, "will have your bonny face and eyes, but he'll have my patience and temperament."

"I think we just saw something of your patience," she said with a smile.

"Our child will be a mixture of the best of our families, the perfect mingling of Armstrong and McCall blood."

"Our child will have McCall blood," Marion blurted out, realizing in horror what was being said. The warm cloud that surrounded her dissipated in an instant and she pressed her palm against Iain's chest. She stared into his face. "Do you realize that any child of ours will have the same blood running in his veins as Sir William and my aunts?"

He smiled. "This child will have your charms. That's all that I care about."

She shook her head. "You don't understand. We cannot have a child, Iain. Not ever. In fact, we shouldn't be married."

She tried to move around him with no success.

"Marion," he said sharply, putting a hand next to her head and trapping her. "I thought we were done with all that nonsense."

"It was no nonsense. Sir George Harington is waiting in the dungeon," Marion blurted hysterically. The bubble having burst, everything rushed back. "You told me you would go down there with me."

"I will, if that's the only way we can put an end to this madness."

He stepped back, and Marion nodded, satisfied.

"You don't have anything to fear in being married to me," Iain said.

"It's not I that should be worrying," she told him, adding, "You'll be sorry that you didn't trust me."

Feeling damp from their lovemaking, Marion remembered where she had seen folded pieces of cloth. Pulling open the window seat they'd just made love on, she reached inside to get one.

"This is not something I've invented. I know I may have, in the past, made up a few--"

She paused. Her hand brushed against something. It was cold and felt like skin. Marion leaped back. The top of the window seat fell in place with a bang.

"A few things? You have a lifelong reputation of telling stories and playing tricks and--" Iain looked at her and stopped.

Marion's hands flailed in the air. She couldn't find her voice. Finally, wiping one hand frantically on her dress, she pointed with the other at the window seat.

"Here we go again. What are you saying now?"

She pointed again. "The...the..."

"Are you hurt?" he asked with concern, coming to her.

She pushed him toward the window. "In there. Look in there."

Iain grabbed her wrist, forced her to stand still so he could inspect the hand she kept wiping on her skirt. With her free hand, Marion kept pointing.

"There's someone in there." She pushed him in the direction of the window.

He didn't seem totally convinced, but he turned to the window seat and pushed aside the pillows. It was too dark in this corner. As he pulled open the shutters above it, Marion ran to the table, grabbed a candle, and lit it from the embers of the fire. By the time she got back, Iain had the lid of the window seat up. He was staring inside.

Marion peeked around him and gasped. There was blood on the man's tunic and on a blanket that he'd been wrapped in. His throat had been cut, nearly severing the head from the body. She wiped her hand ferociously on her skirt.

"Oh, my God," she cried. "Who is he?"

Iain took the candle out of her shaking hands and placed it on the windowsill. "This isn't the body you saw before?"

"No." Marion shook her head. "The other man wasn't wrapped in a blanket, and his throat hadn't been cut."

She forced herself to look into the man's face. She shook her head adamantly.

"That's definitely not Sir George Harington. I never saw this man before."

Iain was not joking now. His face was grim.

"What have they done, Iain? Who is he?"

Marion found herself shaking uncontrollably. She remained at Iain's side as he lowered the candle into the window seat. Pulling the blanket from around the body, he inspected the man's bloody clothes.

"An English nobleman, from the look of his clothes." He lifted the man's hand and looked at the signet ring.

"Bloody hell," he muttered under his breath.

"You know him?"

"Let's say that the abyss has just opened up beneath us."

"Who is he?" she asked shakily.

"The Marquis of Dorset. The English king's military leader in the north," he said grimly. "I've corresponded with him enough times over the course of this past year to recognize his bloody seal. But it doesn't make sense!"

Marion had to take a step to the side and lean against the wall. The loud pounding in her head was deafening. "What is he doing here? How could my aunts have done this?"

"This is not the work of two old ladies," Iain told her. "Maybe Sir William. But I doubt that, too. There is no way that he could have gone to York or anywhere else. And this man could only have been killed in the last day or two."

"So you see, I was not telling you any tales before," Marion said. "There *is* something ghastly happening here."

He shook his head. "I still find it hard to believe what I see."

"It doesn't matter. Please, Iain, go while you still have time. We cannot let them hold you responsible for this and for all the others."

"I am *not* going anywhere," he replied firmly. He straightened from the window seat and looked toward the other window. "And you're certain you saw a body in there, too?"

She nodded. "Sir George was in that one, but there was nothing in this one. I looked in this window seat when I was searching for a table-cloth and linens. There was no dead body here."

"That means, then, that someone placed him in it during the short time that we were outside."

"It must have been Sir William," Marion asserted. "He was standing here when we came in. He must have carried the body up from the dungeon."

"But what would Dorset be doing at Fleet Tower?" Iain asked, carrying the candle to the other window seat and inspecting the inside of that one again. "Brother Luke said that Dorset would be coming to the wedding, but that he wasn't expected to arrive in the Borders until a day or two before the event."

"He must have come early," she suggested.

"Without an armed entourage?" He shook his head.

Marion pushed away from the wall. "I'll go and get Aunt Margaret and Aunt Judith. There must be something that they have not told me. They have a great deal more explaining to do."

"No need to go and get them," Iain said.

He was right. Marion heard the back and forth chatter of the two women as they approached the arched doorway into the great hall. Iain walked over and began to close the window seat containing Dorset. Marion stopped him.

"Don't," she said. "Let them see it or we'll never know the answer."

"This is too gruesome a sight for two gentle old ladies."

Marion shook her head. His loyalty to her aunts was more stubborn than hers. "Iain, they have murdered nineteen men prior to this. I think they should be able to handle it."

Iain gazed at her for a moment, and then left the window seat open. Perhaps, she thought, he was finally trusting her.

Margaret and Judith were carrying on a conversation and not paying any attention to them.

"I last saw the broach in the earl's chamber," Margaret was saying.

"It's not there any longer," Judith countered. "I think William has it."

"Then he must have taken it from the earl's chamber," Margaret responded. She was carrying a ceramic bottle with a stopper in the top, and she placed it in the cupboard. "He should give it back."

Judith returned to the arched doorway. She peered up and down the dark stairwell. "I think he is wearing it under his armor," she called over her shoulder. "He won't give it back."

"But he must. That is a wedding gift to Iain." Margaret looked at the door to the courtyard. "Didn't we bar that door before?"

"Oh, did we? The wind must have blown it open."

"We barred it," Margaret repeated, sounding exasperated. "To keep Marion and the laird out."

"Oh, yes," Judith said brightly, coming back in.

"Now, why would you want to do that?" Marion asked from the corner by the window seat.

"Safe outside, dead inside," Judith answered cheerfully.

Margaret turned around and saw them. "Oh, you're back from your walk."

Marion tried to think through what Judith might have meant, but the two women were already coming toward them, and there were more pressing questions that needed to be asked.

"We had to take the dishes back to the kitchens. I hope you're not hungry anymore," Margaret asked, going directly to Iain.

"Hungry?" Judith questioned.

He shook his head.

The dead body was only a step away, but neither woman appeared to see it, as they each took one of Iain's hands.

"Judith and I talked," the older sister said.

"We talked." Judith nodded.

"And we don't think you and Marion should stay here for the night."

Judith shook her head from side to side. "You shouldn't."

"You should take her and go now, in fact," Margaret suggested.

"Right now," her sister agreed.

"And don't come back tomorrow morning, either."

"Not tomorrow," Judith agreed.

"Or even the day after, perhaps."

"Definitely not the day after," the younger sister asserted.

Although Marion was ready to scream, Iain's voice was gentle.

"Is it possible that your desire for us to leave tonight might have something to do with him?" Iain motioned toward the window seat behind him.

Marion was glad Iain asked the question. The sisters always seemed to hear him when he spoke. They both looked that way.

"Oh, my heavens," Judith said with surprise. "That isn't very nice."

"No, indeed," Margaret exclaimed. "He is soiling my mending."

They let go of Iain's hands and walked toward the window seat for a closer inspection.

"Who can this be?" Margaret asked, poking him.

"We've had no introduction, I'm certain," Judith answered.

"An Englishman, wouldn't you say?"

"Definitely."

Marion stepped between them.

"Are you saying that you've never seen this man before?" Marion asked skeptically, looking at the dead body again.

"Never," Judith said, obviously surprised at the question.

"He has never joined us for pastries," Margaret said, sounding insulted.

"Or shared a cup of wine, either," the younger sister added.

"Who does he think he is, coming in here without an invitation?" Margaret huffed.

"With no invitation," Judith said indignantly.

"Perhaps Sir William invited him in," Marion suggested.

The two sisters didn't respond. Marion wondered if they'd heard her.

"Perhaps Sir William invited him in," Iain said, repeating Marion's words.

"Oh, no." Margaret shook her head adamantly.

"Never," Judith concurred.

"Sir William doesn't like company."

"No guests."

"How does he raise his army, then?" Iain asked.

"We recruit them," Margaret said proudly.

Judith nodded. "We do it all."

"And we know who it is that we bring in."

"Absolutely."

"The last one was Sir George Harington," Margaret told him.

"I invited him in," Judith said with a giggle.

"He is down training with the men as we speak."

Judith pointed to the floor. "In the dungeon."

Marion appreciated the look her husband sent her over the two women's heads. There was no doubt that he was finally starting to believe what she had been telling him.

"If this young man thinks he can simply go around us and join William's army by just showing up here, he is very wrong," Margaret stated.

"Dead wrong," Judith affirmed.

"If neither of you two nor William is responsible for inviting this man in here, then who is?" Marion asked.

The sisters continued to look at the body.

"Would one of you answer Marion's question?" Iain asked them.

They looked at him and smiled.

"Of course, dear."

"Let me see," Margaret began thoughtfully. "There are others who might have brought him in."

"Other people." Judith nodded.

"Who else has been here tonight?" Iain asked.

"Cardinal Bane could have done it," Margaret suggested.

"Definitely," Judith agreed. "Cardinal Bane."

"And who is Cardinal Bane?" Marion asked before realizing her mistake. She motioned to her husband, and Iain repeated the question.

"Why, Cardinal Bane is Jack's spiritual adviser," Margaret answered.

"Jack Fitzwilliam?" Iain asked.

"Of course, dear," Margaret replied.

"We think he may be a bit of a fraud, though," Judith added.

"But the two of them travel together."

"Always together, it appears."

Iain's hand was on his dirk. "Is Jack here?"

"Oh, yes. Of course, dear. That is why we want you to take Marion and go."

39

PRESSED against the curved wall of the stairwell, David Bane listened to the voices coming from the great hall. He heard his name mentioned and strained to hear more.

The Armstrong laird was here. By the devil, he wished he'd taken that drink now, in spite of Jack's order.

He listened to the voices. The young woman speaking must be Marion, he supposed. He could hear the old McCall crones. He wondered if Jack knew the two people he was after were already here.

Inching up to the landing, David knew he had to find his leader right away, as there was so much he needed to tell him.

He peered out into the darkened hall. The four of them were standing on the far side of the room, near one of the window seats. He scurried across the opening, letting out a sigh of relief once he was past the doorway. Taking the stairs two at a time, he was breathless by the time he reached the upper landing. Looking around him, he realized he knew nothing of the layout of the ancient house. There were doorways, hallways, and more stairs, and he didn't know if it was safe to just poke his head into the rooms searching for Jack. The old madman, Jack's father, could be anywhere.

Nonetheless, he approached the first door he saw. As David put his hand on the latch, though, he heard the sound of banging in the distance. Going back to the stairwell, he realized it was coming from farther up.

As David climbed the stairs, the banging became louder. He passed another floor and continued to the next. It was nearly pitch black up here, but above him was another landing. He could just make out an oak door. The pounding coming from the other side of the door was fierce now, and as he reached the landing, he recognized Jack's voice as the outlaw leader cursed and beat on the stout oak.

He quickly unbarred it, and Jack charged through it like a wounded boar.

"I'll kill those two old women with my bare hands," he bellowed. "They locked me out on the bloody ramparts."

"You might want to keep your voice down," David said quickly, plucking at his sleeve and trying to get him to slow down. "Jack, wait. Please. You don't want to go down there."

At the floor below, Jack whirled on him. "What are you saying?"

"You don't want the people down there hearing you."

"What people? Who is down there?" he asked, moving toward him.

The torchlight filtering down from the parapet made Jack's face look almost diabolical, and David shuddered, in spite of himself.

"Iain Armstrong and your cousin, Marion," David told him in a hushed voice.

Jack drew out his dirk with one swift motion and turned toward the steps. "This is all too perfect."

David knew it was a foolish thing to do, but still he moved into his master's path. "Wait. You'll want to hear what I have to say first. I have so much to tell you."

Jack glared at him menacingly. "Very well. Tell me quick. And it had better be good."

"About time we heard something." The voice came out of nowhere and suddenly an armed phantom was standing beside Jack, glaring at David. "Out with it, man. What do you have to report?"

David shrank back against the wall, pressing his fist to his chest and staring at the strange old man.

"Sir William McCall, my father," Jack told David before turning to the old man and barking, "Go keep watch for the English."

"No shirking of duties here, lad," Sir William retorted. "This is *your* watch."

"No, it's *yours*," he drawled threateningly.

"Who do you think you are to order me about?" the old man asked fiercely.

"I'm your son."

David watched Jack turn slightly. The blade of his dagger flickered as it caught the light of the torch.

Sir William put a hand on Jack's shoulder and looked carefully into his face. "If it isn't my son. Jack Fitzwilliam. You look well, lad. Tell me, how is your mother?"

"She is coming at the head of a company of Englishmen," Jack said impatiently. "Go keep watch for her."

"I'm elated to hear it." Sir William nodded and turned to David. "Carry on, my good man."

As they watched the old man climb the steps and disappear out onto the parapet, it occurred to David that this explained a great deal about why Jack was the way he was.

"Is your mother really coming with the Englishmen?"

Jack cuffed him hard on the side of the head. "She's *dead*, you idiot."

David rubbed the spot on his head. "That's right. I forgot."

Jack pointed down the stairs with his dirk. "How many men are down there with him?"

"None. It's only Iain Armstrong, your cousin, and your two aunts." David put a hand on Jack's shoulder again to stop him. "But you should hear the rest of it."

"Make it quick."

"Dorset is missing."

"What?" He grabbed David by the collar, lifting him off the ground. "What did you do with him?"

"Nothing. I don't know what happened to him," he whined, struggling to get hold of the giant's hand. "But I have more to tell you."

Jack let him back down. "What is it?"

David stretched his neck from side to side. "I found the men where we left them at the far side of the glen. The two that we left at the inn had just arrived when I reached them."

"They left the inn?" The muscles in Jack's jaw clenched and unclenched.

"It's all right," he said soothingly. "They brought word that Dorset's troops had already left the inn. They're heading this way. They discovered he was missing and questioned the innkeeper. The serving wench you paid was worth the coins you gave her. She told them it was an Armstrong plaid on the men she'd seen talking to Dorset."

Jack nodded, then slashed at the air with his blade. "None of that is any good to me with Dorset's body missing."

"There's more," David said quickly. "When I came back through the passageway, I started up the stairs. That's when I saw the Englishman was missing. Just then, I could hear voices upstairs. They weren't yours, so I backed down toward the dungeon. There was a torch lit down there, so I thought I might be able to find another way. Have you been down there?"

Jack reached for David's throat again, but the defrocked cleric stepped back. "What about the dungeon?" he snarled.

"Bodies," David whimpered. "Lots of dead bodies. Nineteen of them I counted. All dressed up in armor. Some of them in English armor. Lined up in rows. Most of them are only bones. Some are rotting and...well, the stench is horrible. There are some fresh bodies down there, too."

"What did I tell you about drinking?" Jack growled, grabbing him by the cowl.

"I haven't had a drop!" David said quickly. He crossed himself. "I swear, Jack. Not a drop touched my lips from the time I left you."

"Do you expect me to believe there are nineteen bodies—some of them Englishmen—lying on the floor of that dungeon?"

"It's the truth. All dressed in armor, swords in hand."

Jack released him and slowly climbed the stairs, with David on his heels. Outside on the parapet, the old man was standing by the edge, staring out into the darkness.

"Sir William, where do you keep your army?"

"In the dungeon, of course," the old man said without looking back at them.

"Of course," Jack repeated, turning back to the cleric. "Was Dorset among them?"

"No. There was no sign of him. I don't know what happened to him."

Jack started back down the stairs.

"There is no point in facing him, Jack," David said reasonably, following him down. "What does it matter if the marquis is missing?

There are enough bodies down there to condemn Iain Armstrong. Why take the chance of getting wounded in a fight with him? Let your scheme work as you planned it. The English troops will be here any time."

Jack stopped at the landing and stared down the dark steps for a while. "True, but that will not take care of my dear cousin, Marion. She must die, too."

"Does it need to be now?" David asked, choosing his words carefully. "With Iain Armstrong gone, she is at your mercy."

David watched closely to see if his words would have any effect on his leader. For the cleric, the only bad thing in traveling with a gang of outlaws was the fighting. He was no good at it, not even with a short sword. It was all too messy. Give him a good hanging or witch-burning, anytime.

Jack was obviously thinking about it. From David's perspective, if Jack and the Armstrong laird started fighting, then David would be obligated to draw a weapon, too. That meant he might get hurt. No, that wouldn't really do at all.

Suddenly, Jack put his dagger back in its sheath and started down the hallway. "Follow me."

The outlaw moved quickly in the dark, turning down a narrow passage and climbing three steps to a tiny room. The moon was shining in a small slit of a window, and David could see a straw pallet on the floor and a large wooden chest against one wall. Jack knelt by the side of the chest, feeling for something near the bottom. The cleric heard a small click, and his leader straightened up and pulled the chest away from one wall with surprising ease, revealing a narrow opening behind it.

"Another secret passage?" David asked with mixed feelings. "Let me guess. This passage connects with the one we used to come in. We go down, join the men outside the castle, and watch from a distance as the English take Iain Armstrong."

Jack took the monk by the back of the cloak and pushed him into the narrow space ahead of him. There was no light, and David nearly fell through an opening between two walls. He panicked for a moment, but then realized that he was standing on the rung of a ladder. There was no floor to speak of, or any stairs, either, only the rickety old ladder leading downward.

He opened his mouth to say something more, but Jack's hand immediately clamped over it.

"This leads down to a door in the paneled wall of the great hall. No more talking, or they will hear us."

The cleric nodded, and Jack took away his hand.

"What are you planning to do down there?" David asked in a whisper.

"Fetch my cousin," Jack rasped in his ear. "She's lived too long as heir to Fleet Tower."

40

"I'M certain that they must have left the way they came in," Margaret was saying. "Through the passage on the way to the dungeons."

"Did they?" Judith asked her sister. "I don't remember."

"I know Cardinal Bane left," Margaret reminded her.

"Oh, yes. He went to get more men or something."

"But if Jack didn't go with him, I suppose he might be upstairs," Margaret told them.

"He might be," Judith said vaguely. She was obviously trying to remember something.

"We told him he could stay the night in the earl's chambers."

"I was upstairs, but I didn't see him in the earl's chambers," Judith said.

"You and I were up there *before* he went up."

"Oh yes, dear. You're quite right. That was *before*."

What a fool Iain was, thinking he could keep Jack out just by closing the gate. He'd never even considered the possibility of a secret passage.

If Jack and his band of outlaws were really in the tower house, first and foremost he had to protect these women. While the two women chatted away, Iain barred the doorway to the courtyard and then closed and barred the double doors beneath the arched doorway. Now, at least, Marion and her aunts would be reasonably secure in the great hall while he tried to understand what was going on.

He stood by the arched doorway for a moment, listening for any sound. He couldn't very well go in search of Jack. He was not willing to risk leaving Marion behind. Crossing the hall, he opened the shutters and asked Marion to keep watch for his two men outside. If he could get their attention, then at least he could send one of them off to Blackthorn Hall for help.

He surveyed the great hall for weapons. On the wall there were a number of shields and long lances. Reaching up, he pulled one of the shields down and leaned it against the window seat. Fourteen feet in length each, the lances were too long to be of use in close fighting, and the shafts proved to be too thick to break.

"My aunts just said that Jack brought the dead body of Dorset here," Marion told him as he laid the lances aside. "Does this mean that the English troops are nearby, as well?"

Iain looked at his bride. Her biggest fears were coming true. He went to the window again and closed the window seat on Dorset's pale face.

"Iain, I know I can explain my way out of this if you leave right now," she said, clutching at his arm. "I'll tell them that my cousin, Jack, is the one responsible for the murder of Lord Dorset and Sir George. They never have to know about the others in the dungeon."

"I'm not going anywhere, Marion," he told her, caressing her face. "We'll find a way."

Iain turned his attention back out the window. John and Tom had been making their way along the top of the curtain wall the last time he'd seen them. They were due back here any time.

Margaret was at the cupboard, rearranging cups and pitchers and moving them to the table. Judith was on her sister's heels, whispering endlessly. Iain turned to Marion.

"Do you know anything about that secret passage leading into the castle?"

She shook her head. "I was too young to know anything about it. But I'm not surprised that it exists."

"I'm thinking that if we could block that entrance, we can at least stop any more of them from coming in."

Marion nodded. "Let me ask my aunts."

She took a couple of steps in their direction and then turned around, shaking her head.

"There's no point in me asking them. I'll keep an eye out for your two men, and *you* ask them."

Iain had no doubt that Marion was right in what she was thinking. If Jack murdered Dorset—and it certainly appeared that he did—then by bringing the body here, he intended to lead Dorset's men here and incriminate Iain and Marion both. But that scheme would only work if Iain couldn't catch Jack before the English troops got here.

He laid his hand on Margaret's arm. She was the more likely one to remember. "Lady Margaret, do you know how your nephew got into the castle?"

"Why, of course, dear," Margaret said immediately. "They came in through the underground passageway."

"And do you know where that passageway enters the tower house?"

"Certainly. There is a trapdoor on the stairwell leading to the dungeon."

"On the stairwell," Judith repeated, nodding with certainty.

"And is that the only way they might have come in from outside the walls?" he asked.

"Polite guests always come in through the courtyard," Judith answered.

"But is that the only *secret* way?" he repeated.

Judith and Margaret exchanged a few whispers before the older sister answered. "We believe so. The men always knew so much more about those things. Our brother the earl knew every panel and every door and where each one led. William knows, too, for I'm certain that there have been times when he's gone rambling through the country-side without a by-your-leave."

Iain turned to Marion. She had moved from the window seat that contained Dorset to the other one. Too many dead people for one day, he guessed. "No sign of John or Tom yet?"

She shook her head.

Time was of the essence. Iain had to somehow block that passageway or Jack and his men would break down the door and cut all of their throats. Why, they could then tell Dorset's men they were heroes, even though they couldn't quite manage to save the English commander's life.

"I need to go down there and block that entry," Iain told Marion. "I want you to come with me."

"But we could miss your men on the wall."

Iain looked at the two sisters. They were discussing the table setting, lost in a world of their own. There was no way he could trust them to give his men a message. He had to take a chance. He walked to the window and handed Marion his dirk.

"Don't be afraid to use it. Yell, scream, do whatever must be done if you hear or see anything."

She nodded hesitantly, taking the weapon from him.

41

MARION FELT a yawning chasm open in her chest as she watched Iain go. In her entire life, she had never felt as helpless as she was feeling now.

Her cousin, Jack, was not what worried her most. It was the thought of English troops arriving at Fleet Tower and taking her husband that was tearing her apart. She didn't know what Iain could do. With everything happening at once, she couldn't think straight. There seemed to be no way out of their dilemma.

With obvious reluctance, Iain had wanted the door left unbarred while he hurried down to the dungeons. She was glad of it, for she didn't dare leave from the window to bar the door and unbar it when he returned. She wished his two men would soon finish their rounds of the castle walls. It would be good to alert them and also to get their help.

A sound from the other window seat drew Marion's attention. Stunned, she gaped at the sight of her aunts leaning into the window seat. They were tugging and pulling on something.

"What are you doing?" she cried out.

"He's lying on top of a tapestry our mother began," Margaret said. "It's a record of the family history."

"Our history," Judith repeated, leaning in again and tugging on the dead man's arm.

Marion took a quick look outside before turning to her aunts again.

"I looked in there before he was placed there. There were only scraps of cloth folded in the bottom."

"No, dear. Mother's tapestry is in there," Judith said adamantly, not giving up.

"And we need it for the wedding," Margaret explained, helping her sister.

"For your wedding."

Marion couldn't believe her eyes, but the two women had the dead man by the shoulders and were struggling to drag him out of the window seat. The late Marquis of Dorset might as well have been a piece of furniture.

"Please leave him where he is," she begged. "I don't need the tapestry."

"No, dear. You must have it," Margaret said.

"You must," Judith agreed. "Mother said so."

Oh, no, Marion thought. *Now they're communicating with their long dead mother!*

The upper body of the dead marquis was already halfway out of the box.

"With all the blood, the tapestry is probably already ruined," she said hopefully. "There is no point in dragging him out here."

The two women weren't listening to her. Each had an arm now, and they were pulling with all their strength.

How foolish of her to think things could not get any worse. She had visions of Dorset's body lying on the floor of the great hall, and the English soldiers discovering them all there. Of course, her aunts would simply offer them all a cup of wine and a meat pie!

The marquis's corpse was now stretched out straight, suspended horizontally in the air with the two women holding his arms, and his feet still caught on the edge of the window seat.

"Aunt Margaret, Aunt Judith," she called authoritatively.

Her aunts both turned to her. "Yes, dear?"

They had heard her. It was a miracle.

"We must put him back," she told them.

"We need to get the tapestry first," Margaret said, panting a little from the exertion.

"The tapestry," Judith said, pointing with her chin.

Marion tucked the dagger into her belt and moved quickly to the open window seat. Dorset's blood had indeed stained the topmost cloths. "There are only scraps of cloth here, I tell you."

"Look underneath them," Margaret said in a strained tone. Dorset's weight was obviously getting to be too much for her.

"Underneath," Judith echoed, mimicking her sister's tone.

Marion couldn't believe she was going along with this madness. She leaned into the large space and tried to push aside the soiled pieces without getting the blood all over her.

"I'll be," she whispered a moment later as an old tapestry appeared at the bottom.

With her prize in hand, Marion straightened up just as Dorset's feet came free. Turning, she saw her aunts—still holding on to the corpse—falling backward onto their buttocks. The body of the dead nobleman landed on their outstretched legs, pinning them to the floor.

"By all the..."

She dropped the tapestry and started to go to their rescue, but the sharp edge of a blade at her throat caused her to reconsider.

42

IT DIDN'T TAKE Iain long to find the trapdoor. Carrying a candle from the great hall, he'd simply followed the stairs down until he found the bloodstains on the floor in the dark corner of a landing. After a short search, he found heavy blocks of stone that he quickly hauled up and piled on the trapdoor.

Hurrying back up the steps, he charged into the great hall and came face to face with his greatest fears.

Judith and Margaret sat sprawled on the floor with Dorset's body across their legs. Beyond them, Marion stood in front of Jack Fitzwilliam, his dagger at her throat. On the wall in the corner, a panel was open, revealing yet another secret passage.

Bloody hell. Iain's world tilted, and everything fell out of focus for a moment. He couldn't lose her. Marion mattered more to him than land or title

or his own life.

"Let her go, Jack. Your fight is with me." Iain crossed the hall.

"Stay there," Jack said, raising the dirk higher. "You're wrong. *Our* fight is finished, and you've lost."

Marion moved onto her tiptoes, her eyes flashing with anger.

"I have already taken care of you by bringing to Fleet Tower the dead body of his lordship the honorable Marquis of Dorset. There are servants at the inn where he was staying who have already reported they saw the Armstrong plaid, and heard your name called by the people who kidnapped the English leader," Jack told him. "All that remains now is to do away with my wee cousin here."

"Would someone be kind enough to help us down here?" Margaret called from the floor impatiently.

"Down here," Judith repeated.

Iain ignored the two women's pleas and took another step toward the villain. "If you so much as nick her with that dirk, I will skin you alive."

Jack laughed. "Do you really think you can frighten me with empty threats?"

"That is no threat, Jack," Iain said, his voice cold and hard. "That is my vow."

The outlaw hesitated a moment, then laughed again. "You forget that I'm the one with the upper hand here. In a short time, the English troops will be here, and your life will be worth nothing."

"I would expect nothing more than such a cowardly scheme from a bastard cur like you. Since you cannot strike me down yourself, it only stands to reason that you would try to find a way to have others do it. What you fail to realize is that before the English get here, I will cut every ounce of flesh from your bones and feed your heart to the—"

"Halloo!" Margaret said in a high-pitched singsong voice. "We cannot move down here!"

"I cannot breathe, you three," Judith added. "He is too heavy."

"In heaven's name," Margaret wailed. "Can't *any* of you give two old women a hand?"

"*Anyone?*" Judith shouted.

The ruckus the McCall sisters were making was increasing in volume, and Iain saw Jack's eyes flicker toward them. Iain took another step closer and glanced at his own dirk at Marion's belt. Her eyes followed the direction of his glance. A moment later, her hand started inching toward it, but she paused when Jack's dagger pressed against her throat as he turned her slightly.

"*Cardinal Bane!*" he shouted.

Iain heard mumbling coming through the open panel in the wall behind them.

"Cardinal Bane, come out here."

"But I can see you have everything under control, Jack," the whining voice called out.

"*Now!*" Jack bellowed.

A small wiry man wearing the robes of a cleric crept out of the passage opening, his dirk drawn. Iain could see the little man was shaking badly.

"One of you come over right now and lift this uninvited guest off of us," Margaret ordered. "The rudeness of some people."

"Some people," Judith repeated indignantly.

"This is certainly no way for a gentleman to act."

"No way," Judith agreed.

"And the English are always puffing themselves up about their fine manners," Margaret complained.

"Always puffing themselves up," Judith told her sister.

"Quiet my aunts down," Jack shouted to his man over the unending chatter. "Shut their mouths, I tell you."

"But Jack," the wiry man started helplessly. "But how? I can't."

"This is no way to treat your own kin, Jack Fitzwilliam," Margaret wailed.

"*Jack* Fitzwilliam." Judith spit out the name like a curse.

Iain moved even closer to Jack. He saw Marion's hand was once again edging toward the dagger.

"I cannot kill old ladies," the little cleric blurted out.

"I didn't say kill them, you fool," Jack yelled. "I said shut them up. Lift the bloody corpse off them. Do anything, but make them stop talking."

As the outlaw's frightened henchman moved in a wide arc around Iain, there was suddenly a shout from the courtyard. Iain realized his man John was calling up to the open window. At Jack's surprised look in the direction of the window, Iain took another step toward him, but the outlaw stepped back toward the open panel in the wall, dragging Marion with him.

"You come closer to me and you'll find her head lying at your feet," he threatened.

"There is no getting out of this, Jack. My men are here before yours, before the English." There was no reason for the outlaw to know that there were only two Armstrong men outside and not a hundred. "I will make a bargain with you, though. I'll let you run for it if you let Marion go."

Out of the corner of his eye, Iain could see the cleric bending over the sisters. Grunts and muttered curses from the little man told him that the McCall sisters were being rescued from the weight of the dead Dorset.

"One thing you can be certain of," Jack threatened. "She'll not walk out of this castle alive."

"Nor will you," Iain told him.

"You think that matters? You think that frightens me?" He snorted. "What is life to me? Nothing! And it's because of her."

"She's done nothing to you," Iain snapped.

"She's been my life's curse from the day she was born. She took everything that was mine and everything that was intended for me. I will not let her live no matter what fate awaits me."

There were more shouts from the courtyard. From the outside, there was a shove on the door to the great hall. Iain heard John's voice, calling to him.

"Don't answer him," Jack ordered.

There was no reasoning with him. The only solution lay in killing him; Iain could see that. Still, he had to figure out how to get to the madman before he cut Marion's throat.

"Don't you walk away from us now," Margaret called out.

"Stay right here, David Bones," Judith ordered.

"We cannot leave him on the floor," Margaret said.

"Definitely not on the floor."

The sisters were obviously talking about the dead body of Dorset.

"Leave him there," Jack ordered. "And the two of you will shut your mouths."

"That's no way to talk, Jack," Margaret scolded.

"Just shut up and go sit at the table."

"At the table," Margaret repeated. "That is an excellent idea."

"We'll sit him at the table," Judith agreed.

"Lend us a hand, Cardinal Bane," Margaret ordered.

"I said leave the body there," Jack said, fuming.

"Right now, Cardinal Bane," Margaret said in an authoritative tone.

"Do what you're told, David Bones," Judith snapped. "Now!"

The cleric appeared to be more frightened by the McCall sisters than by his leader, for Iain watched the man jump to assist them.

"I don't want him at the table with the food," Margaret ordered.

"Definitely not near the food," Judith added.

"Put Sir William's chair next to the earl's chair...yes...yes...right there," the older sister ordered.

"Right there," Judith confirmed.

Jack's frustrated gaze shifted in the direction of his aunts for the briefest of moments. There was not enough time for Iain to do anything. He saw his wife had used the opportunity, though, and had her hand at her waist, inches away from the dagger.

"I told you to leave him," Jack shouted.

Bane appeared to be deaf to anything but the women's commands.

"Lift him. Hold him by the shoulders. That's it. Slowly. I don't want any of his mess on the chair," Margaret was saying.

"No mess," Judith agreed.

The banging on the door started again, louder now. Iain realized both of his men were on the other side.

"Are you in there, m'lord?" Tom shouted.

"A large group of men are approaching along the village road," John added. "They're carrying torches, but we cannot tell if they're our own men or the outlaws."

"Shall we raise the portcullis?"

"Answer them," Jack said to Iain in a low tone. "Tell them yes."

The outlaw was assuming they were the English troops. Iain didn't answer his men. A closed gate bought them some time. Marion's fingers were wrapped around the dagger's hilt now, but the weapon was still tucked in her belt.

"That's much better," Margaret said from behind him.

"Much," Judith agreed.

"But don't expect us to entertain him, Jack Fitzwilliam," Margaret announced.

"Not us. You brought him here."

"You take care of him," Margaret finished.

Iain glanced back and saw Bane crossing the great hall. He looked back at Marion and Jack. The outlaw was looking across the hall at the cleric.

"Come away from there," Jack ordered his man. "Come away from the...NO drinking, I said. I need you sober, you fool."

Iain looked around. Bane was pouring out a cup of wine.

"Put that down!"

"But I need this, Jack, to calm my nerves. Just one."

"Pray, Cardinal. Pray."

Surprised by the sincerity in the villain's tone, Iain stared at Jack.

"I'm sorry, Jack. Prayer won't work for me right now. I'll just have a sip of this and then I'll pray," the cleric said.

Iain turned and watched Bane drink down the cup of wine. He sat at the table and poured himself another cup.

"Get up, Bane!" Jack shouted. "By God, you come here or I'll—"

Suddenly, from the passageway behind Jack, Sir William sprang out into the hall shrieking like a banshee, sword drawn.

"The English are coming!" he shouted.

As Jack's head jerked around in surprise, Marion drew the dagger out of her belt and drove it deep into her cousin's thigh.

The outlaw's knife hand dropped from her throat as he roared in pain and reached his wounded leg.

Iain charged, pulling Marion behind him and smashing Jack backward along the wall. The dirk, still in her hand, went clattering to the floor as Jack raised his dagger and lunged at Iain. Although Jack Fitzwilliam was the bigger man, Iain was much faster. Fending off the blow with his arm, he scooped up his dirk and faced the outlaw.

They circled, each looking for his advantage. Jack slashed out with the dagger, and Iain eluded the blade, staggering his foe with a fist to the face. With each passing moment, with each lunge and return blow, Iain was gaining the advantage. The blood was spurting from Jack's thigh. The little cleric was still sitting at the table, unwilling to help his leader.

Iain knew he could finish the villain here and now, but the ugly reality of killing Jack Fitzwilliam in front of these people presented a grim picture. Marion was his wife and the others were his responsibility, but they were also Jack's kin. Despite the outlaw's evil intentions, Iain decided that he would have the dog rot in some dungeon rather than have this family think of him forever as the one who killed Sir William's son.

Iain backed up a step. "Throw down your weapon, Jack. This is finished."

"Never," he snarled. "The English are coming, and you'll be the one they're after."

Limping badly now, he started toward Iain.

As he came toward him, Iain saw Sir William lean his sword

against the wall and snatch up the ancient shield leaning next to it. As Jack lunged at Iain again, the old man swung the shield at his son's head.

Jack's face showed momentary surprise, and his hand dropped at his side, the weapon falling to the floor. His black eyes, so full of venom a moment ago, crossed and then rolled upward in his head as he sank to his knees and then fell over.

"I told you, lad," Sir William bellowed at the body at his feet. "The English are coming. Arm yourself!"

Margaret rushed to her nephew's side. "In heaven's name, William, what did you do?"

Judith was immediately beside her sister, fussing over the fallen giant, as well.

Iain's instinct was confirmed. He was relieved that he hadn't been forced to kill the man with these people watching.

"Well, he is still alive," Margaret announced, touching the man's brow.

"Still alive," Judith echoed, looking up and smiling at Marion.

Iain quickly kicked Jack's weapon to the other side of the room. He looked again at Bane, who still hadn't moved. As he turned to look at Marion, she rushed into his arms.

"You saved my life again," she whispered.

"And you showed once again what a fighter you are," he told her.

"But the English are coming. What are we going to do?" she asked fretfully.

"One thing at a time. I need to bind Jack first, so he doesn't get any fresh ideas when he comes around."

"That was a very accurate blow, Sir William," Margaret told her brother proudly, looking up at him from beside Jack, who was starting to moan. She turned her gaze toward Marion. "And that was such a senseless quarrel between you and your cousin."

"Totally senseless." Judith waved a hand in the air.

"There is no reason for him to carry such a grudge against someone who is not even his kin."

"Not even his kin," Judith agreed.

Iain felt Marion stiffen at his side. "What did you say?" she asked.

As always, the McCall sisters were not hearing her. They continued to carry on their own conversation.

"It was our good brother's wishes. As the earl, it was his right. And Jack should have let it go at that," Margaret advised.

"The Earl of Fleet was our brother," Judith explained, as if none of them knew that small but important fact.

Sir William was leaning out the window and shouting to the two men in the courtyard. "Tom Halliday, John Blair. Keep the gates closed, lad. The English are coming."

Marion grabbed Iain's hand. "Please, ask them what they mean about me not being Jack's kin."

He repeated her question.

The two sisters exchanged some whispers, and then Margaret explained. "Our brother the Earl of Fleet married Marion's mother when she was already with child."

Judith held out four fingers and nodded. "Four months."

Iain and Marion stood in stunned silence for a moment until she found her voice. "Who was my father?"

There was silence from the two sisters.

"Who was her father?" Iain repeated.

"We never knew his name," Margaret said.

"Never." Judith shook her head.

"We think he was a noble friend who died in a fight with the English, though," Margaret continued.

"A noble friend," Judith sighed.

Jack still hadn't moved, and neither did his partner at the table. Sir William continued to busy himself, giving orders to Iain's men through the window. The two sisters were again whispering to each other. Marion clung tightly to Iain's arm.

"Who was told this? Who, other than you two, knew this?" she asked her aunts.

They continued with their own talk. Iain repeated the question. Margaret looked up and smiled at both of them.

"Only us and, of course, Marion's mother. But the poor dear died at childbirth."

Judith sighed. "She died."

"Sir William was too busy preparing for his battles, so there was no point in telling him," Margaret added.

"We didn't tell him." Judith nodded.

"So Jack didn't know, either!" Marion said.

For once, they decided to hear her. They answered together. "He certainly did not."

Marion turned to Iain. "How ironic. He is the true McCall, not I. He really *is* the true heir to Fleet Tower."

Iain had Marion at his side. She was alive and well. There was nothing else that mattered.

"But that's not the way the earl wanted it to be," Margaret countered, shaking her head adamantly.

"Not the way," Judith echoed, mimicking her sister.

"Our brother said the family wanted new blood."

"New blood."

"That's why he didn't want any of us to marry and have children," Margaret said in a matter-of-fact manner.

"No marrying, no children." Judith shook a finger.

"Jack Fitzwilliam was a mistake."

"A mistake, to be sure."

"The earl was very upset about that."

"*Very* upset," Judith said, making an angry face.

Marion's hold on Iain's arm had tightened even more. Iain wondered if the same thoughts were running through her head. The Earl of Fleet knew that madness was running rampant in his family. That was why he wanted an end to their line. By making Marion his heir and then arranging the marriage with Iain, the earl was taking care of the future of his clan.

How consistent with his thinking, Iain realized, to insist that Marion would not be raised by his own sisters.

Perhaps the old earl thought madness of this magnitude could be contagious.

43

DEAD AND UNCONSCIOUS bodies lay around her, blood covered the floor, but all Marion wanted to do was to dance across the great hall.

She was not related to them. She was not a McCall. Any child of hers and Iain's would not inherit their lunacy.

Reality returned quickly enough, though. Her cousin, Jack, began to move his head. There were more calls from outside. Sir William kept shouting, "The English are coming!" at the top of his lungs.

"How are we going to explain all of this?" she said in a loud voice to Iain.

"Stay away from Jack. I need something to tie him with."

Marion let him go. She was certain that Jack had been about to kill her. She watched her husband pull pieces of cloth from the window seat and tear them into strips. Jack was beginning to mumble something under his breath.

"Get him a drink, Judith," Margaret ordered, holding her nephew's head in her hands. "I think he wants to say something."

"Definitely a drink," Judith repeated, pushing to her feet and scurrying to the table.

As Judith came back with a cup in her hand, Marion saw Sir William turn quickly from the window and look directly at Iain.

"The enemy is at our gates," he shouted. He spun back to the window after his announcement, paying no attention to his son lying at his feet.

Jack was quickly regaining consciousness now, and Iain tied Jack's hands before leaving him in the care of the aunts. Then, as her husband stood up, Marion saw from the corner of her eye a sudden movement by the table.

"Iain!" she cried.

Even as she called out, though, Marion saw that the outlaw called Bane had simply fallen off his chair and was lying flat on his face. He seemed strangely quiet.

She took a couple of steps toward him, but Iain was at the man's side first. He put a hand on Bane's chest and looked up at Marion.

"He's dead," he said incredulously.

"Dead?" she repeated. Bane's unseeing eyes were open.

"He's not breathing," Iain told her. He rolled the little cleric over. "Though he doesn't appear to be wounded anywhere."

"The wine," she whispered. "He took a cup off the shelf. It must have been Aunt Margaret's wine."

They both looked up to the table and where he'd put the cup down before. It wasn't there. Marion turned to her aunts. Margaret had Jack's head in her hands, and Aunt Judith was holding a cup to the man's lips as he drank.

"Stop," Marion blurted. "Don't give him the wine."

She ran to them. Jack had been ready to kill her tonight, but Marion didn't wish the same fate on him.

"Aunt Margaret, Aunt Judith," she cried, kneeling next to them and forcing the cup out of Judith's hand. She was too late. It was empty.

"Give it back," Jack sneered, still groggy. "Must you take *everything* that is mine? I'll kill you. Before the sun comes up, I'll kill you. I swear I will."

"What was in this cup?" Marion asked, ignoring the brute's threats and smelling the cup.

"You be quiet, Jack," Margaret told her nephew. "That is far too much talking."

"Far too much," Judith agreed.

"It's time you had a nice rest."

"A nice long rest." Judith caressed the outlaw's head.

"What did you give him?" Iain asked quietly, crouching beside Marion.

William turned from the window again. "They're raising the

portcullis. The Bruce and the Highlanders have arrived ahead of the English. *Freedom!*" he shouted, raising his sword and turning to the window again.

Marion didn't know if she should believe Sir William or not.

"We gave him some wine," Margaret answered as soon as her brother had quieted down.

"Just wine," Judith said innocently.

"What kind of wine?" Iain asked.

"Why, elderberry wine, of course," the older sister answered. "All of our visitors are quite fond of it."

"She makes it like no one else," Judith added.

"Is this the same wine that you used to recruit the Englishmen in the dungeon?" Marion asked.

"Englishmen?" Jack croaked, trying to spit. He struggled to sit up, but the sisters held on to his shoulders. He didn't seem to have the strength to fight them.

"Now, just stay calm, dear," Margaret assured him.

"Calm and quiet," Judith whispered.

"It will all be over very soon," Margaret said in a motherly fashion.

"Very soon," Judith cooed.

Marion looked desperately at her husband. "Is there anything we can do?"

He shook his head. He seemed as baffled as she was. The McCall sisters were whispering gently to their nephew, who seemed to be getting calmer by the second. He tried to say something back to them.

Marion stared at them. If she didn't know better, it looked like a touching family moment.

"They're in the courtyard," Sir William shouted. "Form your ranks, men. Prepare to attack!"

Marion realized that perhaps there was some truth to Sir William's exclamations. She could hear the sound of horses arriving in the courtyard. Iain stood up and pulled Marion to her feet. It was obvious that Jack was no longer a threat, but Iain wasn't letting her get too far away.

Together, they went to the window and looked out. Marion was relieved to see Armstrong men, carrying torches, pouring into the courtyard. Alan and Brother Luke were just climbing down from their horses, and Iain called to them to come into the great hall.

Marion glanced in the direction of her aunts as Iain went to unbar the door. Jack was quiet, his eyes closed. Margaret and Judith were smiling and stroking his hair.

The door to the great hall swung open, and Marion saw Brother Luke and Alan rush in, swords drawn. Both men stood speechless for a moment, and Marion looked around her. It was definitely a startling scene.

Brother Luke, still holding his sword, began to make the sign of the cross and murmur prayers in Latin.

Alan found his tongue quickly. "M'lord, the English troops are not far behind. They arrived at Blackthorn Hall in the middle of night looking for Sir George Harington."

Brother Luke stopped praying and added, "They didn't know he was missing."

"They're the troops that were accompanying the Marquis of Dorset, but now he is missing, too. Kidnapped from an inn on the south road."

Both men's gazes fell on the Englishman with the nasty cut at his throat.

"Meet the Marquis of Dorset," Iain told them.

Brother Luke wiped away the sweat forming on his forehead. Alan's face was grim.

"Iain," Luke said. "They were claiming that it was Armstrong men —and perhaps even you—who took Dorset from his rooms."

"All Jack Fitzwilliam's work." Iain motioned to him next. The McCall sisters had laid his head down and were rising to their feet.

Brother Luke pointed to Bane. "Who is that?"

"He called him David Bane. He was Jack's personal cardinal," Marion told them.

"David Bones, from the village across the glen," Luke said. "Oh, yes, I knew him. A ne'er-do-well who never should have joined the abbey. He was tossed out not long ago, I believe."

"We're going to have a reasonable explanation for all this before Dorset's men arrive," Iain said. "How far are they behind you, would you say?"

"Your mother was trying to detain them for as long as she could," Brother Luke told them. "But they can't be far behind."

"How are we going to explain the bodies in the dungeon?" Marion broke in.

"What bodies?" Alan asked.

"There are more bodies than these three?" Brother Luke asked, shocked.

Some of the Armstrong men had come into the great hall, and Margaret and Judith were greeting them and giving them directions. Marion turned back to Iain.

"I will explain everything only once," Iain told his uncle. "You can listen when I tell my tale to Dorset's commanders."

"Do you know what you're going to say?" Marion asked hopefully, turning as her uncle shouted out the window at the newly arrived men. They appeared to be cheering him on.

Margaret and Judith hurried over to speak to Brother Luke.

"You've come back for supper, Brother Luke," Margaret said excitedly.

"But we have no supper left," Judith reminded her sister.

"I'm not here for your hospitality tonight, my dear friends," the portly monk explained.

"Very well," Margaret said, looking behind her before taking his arm. "Then perhaps you'd like to pay your respects to the new earl."

"The new earl?" Marion asked.

"He'll just be the earl for a wee bit," Aunt Margaret whispered to her.

"We promised him," Aunt Judith added, pointing.

Marion and Iain turned and looked at Jack Fitzwilliam, sitting in the earl's armchair. David Bane was in a chair to his left and Dorset in a chair to his right. It was a macabre sight, and the Armstrong warriors who had followed the aunts' directions in putting them there stood by with sheepish looks on their faces.

"Lady Margaret, why is David Bane there?" Iain asked.

"Well," Margaret explained, "even though he was a drunk and a fraud, our nephew appeared to take great comfort in his presence."

"Great comfort," Judith echoed.

The two women went over to the three corpses and began arranging them carefully.

"I have my explanation," Iain told Marion. "I know exactly what I'm going to say."

"What will you say?"

"It's all Jack's work. All of it."

"Because he wanted to become the McCall laird?"

"That, and because he hated the English. He wanted to stir up trouble and leave us to take the blame."

"But what about the bodies in the dungeons?" Marion asked.

"I'll tell them that ever since the old earl died, Jack has been storing his murder victims here. He was a madman who believed that Edward Longshanks is still alive and invading Scotland. Somehow in his twisted mind, he came to believe he was the son of William Wallace, and he was building an army of dead turncoats."

She looked over at Jack and his cardinal. "And how did these two die?"

"Jack bled to death of his wounds and Bane died of a weak heart."

"What about the witnesses at the inn?" she asked.

"Those witnesses were bought. That will be the easiest part. But it was still Jack's doing."

Marion wanted to feel comfortable with these answers, but she wouldn't know until the English troops came and went. She looked at her uncle as he waved his sword out the window at the men and shouted, "Freedom!"

"What are we going to do with him when they get here?" she asked. "He can ruin all of it."

Iain paused. "We can take him to the abbey at Cracketford. Now, before the English arrive. He won't be too far away, and he'll be well cared for. And I can have Tom and John, his two trusted men, accompany him there."

Marion's immediate response was relief. He would be close, and she could make sure he was well cared for.

"We have to try," she told Iain.

He seemed relieved, too. "I don't think we'll have any difficulty convincing Sir William, but those two may be a different story." He was looking at her aunts.

"Perhaps I can help with that," Brother Luke said.

44

PULLING Margaret and Judith away from their corpse arranging and into a corner of the great hall where they could talk was a huge challenge. Somehow, though, Iain managed it.

With Marion and Brother Luke beside him, it made three of them versus two old ladies. He might have a chance, he thought.

"Lady Margaret, Lady Judith, the time has come for Sir William to be moved to Cracketford Abbey," Brother Luke started without any fanfare.

"No, we are not dead yet," Margaret replied, shaking a finger at the clergyman.

"Jack is dead, but we are not," Judith said cheerfully.

They didn't have much time. Dawn was breaking over the eastern sky. Iain decided to intervene. "Sir William must go to the abbey today, before daybreak. We are not waiting for anyone else to die."

Both women turned to Marion. For the first time, he realized, they seemed to think she was the only one who could help them.

"He is our baby brother, Marion. We cannot be separated from him. Tell them they can't take him away," Margaret urged.

"Tell them. Tell them," Judith encouraged.

Marion put a hand on each woman's arm. "You saw what happened here tonight. There were uninvited guests, dead bodies, weapons used. There will be English troops swarming into our courtyard in a matter of an hour. Iain wants to move Sir William from Fleet Tower because he is concerned for the Wallace's safety. They're after him."

"After William?" Margaret asked, concerned.

"He is not safe here?" Judith asked.

Marion shook her head. "The word is out. The English know about him, so they're coming after him. As his kin, it's our responsibility to protect him. Don't you agree?"

Both women nodded. She had their attention.

"We have to move him *now*, before the armies arrive," Marion repeated. "We cannot do that without your help. Sir William won't go anywhere without your blessing. So will you help us?"

Margaret and Judith looked at each other. There was some whispering between them. As always, the older sister offered their decision. "We'll help. But he'll not be going alone."

"Not alone," Judith agreed.

"His two men, Tom and John, will be accompanying him," Iain repeated. "We don't expect Sir William to find his way to Cracketford Abbey alone."

Both women shook their heads. Margaret explained. "If he goes, then we are going, too."

"They have to take us, too," Judith insisted.

Iain saw Marion light up at her aunts' words. She looked at Brother Luke. "Is there a convent attached to Cracketford Abbey where my aunts could stay?"

"Of course," Luke replied. "I know the Mother Superior very well. They will be extremely pleased to have your aunts. And just think how close you all will be. You can visit them anytime. I can visit them, too."

"That would be delightful," Margaret said cheerfully. "We can see Sir William and Brother Luke every day."

"Every day," Judith said happily.

A stray thought darkened Margaret's expression. "But what would William do with his army? He has invested a great deal of time in training them."

"A great deal of time."

"I will take over their training," Iain quickly offered. "I will make sure they remain in excellent fighting condition."

The two sisters looked at each other and again there was some whispering back and forth. Margaret looked up. "Then it's all settled."

"Settled," Judith echoed brightly.

Iain reached over and took his wife's hand. He heard Marion let out a sigh of relief.

"When are we leaving?" Margaret asked.

"When?"

"Right now," Iain told them. "You all need to go now, before the English arrive."

"I will bring your things over tomorrow," Marion offered.

"And I will travel with you now to make sure all the arrangements are to your liking," Brother Luke offered.

Margaret and Judith reached over and took each other's hands. "We'll have a new kitchen."

"There will be a new hall to dine in."

"Lots of visitors."

"Lots of Englishmen," Judith said excitedly.

"No more Englishmen," Marion interrupted, looking seriously in each woman's eyes. "No more making wine. No helping William recruit for his army. Do you understand?"

Margaret and Judith smiled at the laird. They could no longer hear Marion's words. "We are ready to go as soon as your men are."

EPILOGUE

BECAUSE OF THE time it took to resolve the problems resulting from the deaths of the English emissaries, the date of the ceremony was pushed back another fortnight.

The news of what happened spread on the wings of birds throughout Scotland. As a result, the wedding at Blackthorn Hall between the McCall and Armstrong heirs became a much larger event than originally planned. More guests, including clan chiefs from as far away as the Western Isles and Fife, started arriving. Legends about a graveyard of English soldiers in the dungeons of Fleet Tower began to spread, and Scotsmen far and wide came to see the place and hear the story again.

Iain always made Jack out to be a hero and a son of Scotland who, in his last days, unfortunately lost his way, blinded by his own ambition. In the end, he would say, Jack Fitzwilliam simply could not tell friend from foe.

To Marion, Scotland was all about heroes and legends, and it set well with her for Jack to take his place among them.

The wedding was to be a Scottish affair. To Iain's and Marion's delight, the unwanted English guests carried their fallen heroes southward. As Iain had foretold, the English had their villain, and with Jack Fitzwilliam's death and the scattering of his band of outlaws, the English king would have to be satisfied.

Now, however, with Marion's aunts and uncle settled at Cracketford

Abbey, the young woman's greatest worry was her mother-in-law.

From the first moment of her arrival at Blackthorn Hall, though, Marion had been pleasantly shocked to discover Lady Elizabeth nothing but affectionate and likable. At first, Marion could not understand the matriarch's change of heart, but Iain later confessed that he'd told his mother about Marion not being true blood kin of the mad McCalls. As Marion could much better understand now, the information had been a great relief to the older woman.

The night before the ceremony, Marion was surprised even more when her mother-in-law came into her bedchamber with a dress the color of ivory over her arm.

"Your wedding dress," the older woman told Marion, spreading the beautiful gown on the bed and showing her the intricate handiwork of gold thread.

Marion was struck speechless with the gesture. There had been seamstresses in and out of her room for the past few days, but she had expected a simple gown that would fit her body. *Nothing* so elegant.

"This is far too beautiful."

"And you're far too dear to me for anything less elegant," Lady Elizabeth told her, drawing Marion in a warm embrace.

The young woman was touched by the gesture and kindness. "You are doing so much for me."

"It's nothing." Lady Elizabeth shook her head. "In the morning, there will be three of my women at your door to give you a bath and do your hair and help you dress for the church."

"I don't believe I have ever had this much attention," Marion smiled, pleased with it all.

"Your aunts arrived from the abbey convent for the wedding ceremony tonight and your aunt Judith wanted to know if you still wished her to mend a gown for you for tomorrow. I thought if you had other help, it might make everything more enjoyable for you."

Marion nodded, wholeheartedly agreeing. "What are they doing now?"

"I don't know. They insisted on going down to the kitchen. Something about a special recipe that your aunt Margaret wanted to have on hand for the celebration."

Marion was immediately alarmed. "What kind of a special recipe?"

Lady Elizabeth shook her head in confusion. "I didn't ask. I didn't want to offend them."

"Oh, they will not be offended," Marion said in a rush. "Now, if you'll forgive me, I think I'll just run down to the kitchens to find out about this recipe."

Marion raced out of the chamber and down the hallway only to come face to face with Iain.

"What's wrong?" he asked, taking her hands.

"My aunts are in the kitchens."

He nodded with understanding. "Brother Luke just came into my room, telling me that Lady Margaret and Lady Judith were here. He mentioned something about them wanting to check on the wines."

Hand in hand, they ran downstairs.

With all that was happening, Blackthorn Hall's extensive kitchens were a very busy place, but Marion and Iain had no trouble finding the McCall sisters, chattering away and busily measuring out wines into pitchers in a bright corner.

They rushed to the old women's side. The sisters were very excited to see them, and Marion took hold of the hands of both of them.

"Aunt Margaret," Marion said when she'd heard all the news of the abbey and Sir William. "There is no reason for you to be working in the kitchen tonight."

"But there is, my dear."

"There is," Judith said.

Marion was relieved that they were deciding to hear her tonight. "The cooks and their helpers are seeing to everything for tomorrow."

"You're guests," Iain added. "You shouldn't be working."

Margaret giggled. So did Judith.

"But we're family, dear." She patted Iain's hand. "And what we're going to make, no one else has a recipe for."

"No one," Judith agreed.

Marion and Iain sent a desperate glance at each other.

"What is it that you're making?" Marion asked hesitantly.

"A special wine," Margaret answered.

"Wine, of course." Judith smiled.

Marion put both hands on Margaret's shoulder. She lowered her voice. "There are no Englishmen attending our wedding. Everyone here will be a loyal Scotsman. All friends. We cannot poison friends."

Both sisters giggled and shook their heads.

"This is a different recipe, dear," Margaret said.

"Completely different," Judith agreed.

"What is it that you have in the wee bottle?" Iain asked, pointing.

The two sisters shared another conspiratorial laugh.

"The juice of the mistletoe," Margaret whispered.

"Mistletoe," Judith whispered.

Marion looked at them, confused. "And what does that do?"

"It's for fertility," Margaret answered, patting Marion's cheek.

"That means it helps you have babies." Judith made a rounding gesture over her stomach.

"Oh!" Marion said, blushing slightly as she looked at Iain. "Well, I suppose that's all right."

"Wait a moment." Iain looked at them suspiciously. "Tell me *more* about mistletoe."

Thank you for taking time to read *Love and Mayhem*. If you enjoyed it, please consider telling your friends or posting a short review. Word of mouth is an author's best friend and much appreciated.

Be sure to check out the preview of *Ghost of the Thames* at the end of this book.

GHOST OF THE THAMES

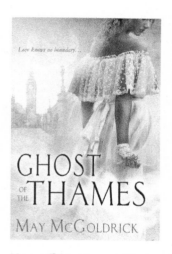

In Victorian England, a stranger, led back from the shadowy edges of death by a ghost, finds herself cold and bloody on the filthy banks of a river in a city she does not know...

From the opium dens and rat-infested warehouses of Limehouse to the glistening facades of West End mansions, a woman known only as Sophy searches for her identity. But the mist-shrouded alleys of Victorian England hold grave dangers for the friendless.

Captain Edward Seymour, the last of a long line of distinguished Royal Navy officers, is searching, as well. Returning from sea to find that his niece has disappeared, he begins combing every inn and hellhole of the city's darkest corners, desperately hoping to find some trace of the girl.

No one knows the streets of London like Charles Dickens, a young novelist with a reformer's soul, and Sophy and Edward turn to him for help. Flush with his early literary successes, he is working hard to use his knowledge of the city and his newfound fame to right some of the social ills that plague Victorian England. But with each step they take toward the truth, Death draws ever closer...

Get GHOST OF THE THAMES from your favorite retailer

AUTHOR'S NOTE

We hope you have enjoyed our medieval send-up of Joseph Kesserling's American theatrical standard, *Arsenic and Old Lace*. This book is for those fans who have been after us to go back to the medieval period. To our loyal readers, you may remember the priory on the Isle of Skye. That was where Fiona Drummond got her start in *Angel of Skye*.

For readers who are new to our work, we have been busy building a vast interconnected series for you. Here's the list detailing our tales of the Scottish Highlands. Enjoy!

A Midsummer Wedding — the prequel to all the Macpherson series tales. Alexander Macpherson, the patriarch of the family, meets his match in Elizabeth Hay.

The Thistle and the Rose— while the smoke still lingers from the battle of Flodden Field, Colin Campbell and Celia Muir, a woman-warrior who holds the fate of Scotland in her hands, are introduced. This story is on the list of "Best Historical Romances of All Time." *Thistle* introduces Alec Macpherson, Ambrose's older brother.

Angel of Skye—Alec Macpherson, the oldest son of Alexander and Elizabet, has served King James with his sword. Now he would give his very soul to protect Fiona Drummond from the past that haunts her and the intrigue that could change the future of Scotland.

Heart of Gold—Alec's younger brother Ambrose, second son of the Macpherson family, feels a burning desire for Elizabeth Boleyn, the exquisite natural daughter of an English diplomat. But the hated English king wants her, as well, and will stop at nothing to have her. Ambrose was introduced in *Angel of Skye*.

Beauty of the Mist— John, the youngest Macpherson brother, has been tasked with bringing home his young king's intended bride, but en route rescues mysterious Maria, adrift at sea.

The Intended— Malcolm MacLeod, Alec Macpherson's ward in *Angel of Skye,* and Jaime Macpherson, daughter of Mary Boleyn (*Heart of Gold*), have to find their way back to Scotland from the dungeons of the Tudor king.

Flame—Gavin Kerr, introduced in *Heart of Gold*, finds that the castle he has been awarded holds more than he expects, the "ghost" of the previous owner, Joanna MacInnes, who haunts the burnt towers and the secret passages.

Tess and the Highlander (RITA© Award Finalist)— Colin Macpherson, the youngest son of Alec and Fiona (*Angel of Skye*), washes up on a remote island off the coast of Scotland, only to find a solitary young woman, Tess Lindsay.

The Highland Treasure Trilogy:

The Dreamer (Book 1)—When her late father was branded a traitor to the king, Catherine Percy finds sanctuary in Scotland. But a case of mistaken identity puts her in a compromising position with John Stewart, the Earl of Athol (*Flame*).

The Enchantress (Book 2)—Level-headed Laura Percy (the second Percy sister) takes shelter in the Highland, but when she is abducted by William Ross, the fearsome Laird of Blackfearn, all her well-made plans are torn asunder.

The Firebrand (Book 3)—Adrianne Percy (the youngest Percy sister) is hidden in the Western Isles, safe from her family's enemies, until her sisters send Wyntoun MacLean to return her to the Highlands. Colin Campbell and Celia Muir (*The Thistle and the Rose*) make an appearance in this exciting trilogy finale.

The Scottish Relic Trilogy:

Much Ado About Highlanders (Book 1)—Alexander and James Macpherson, the two older sons of Alec and Fiona (*Angel of Skye*) find more trouble than they counted on. Alexander wants his runaway bride back, but a deadly secret from Kenna Mackay's past has surfaced, and a heartless villain is closing in.

Taming the Highlander (Book 2) (RITA© Award Finalist)—Innes Munro has the ability to read a person's past simply by touching them. Conall Sinclair, the Earl of Caithness, carries scars courtesy of English captors. Both of them are reluctant to let the other close, but neither can deny their growing attraction.

Tempest in the Highlands (Book 3)—Miranda MacDonnell is shipwrecked on the mythical Isle of the Dead with the notorious privateer Black Hawk. Alexander Macpherson and Kenna Mackay (*Much Ado About Highlanders*) play an important role, and Gillie the Fairie-Borne (*The Firebrand*) appears in the novel as he searches for his lost family.

In addition, we've been building a world of stories set in Georgian, Regency, and Victorian England and Scotland. Go to our website for information on more than a dozen more novels.

As authors, we love feedback. We write our stories for you, and we want to write stories that you will cherish and recommend to your friends. Please sign up for news and updates and follow us on BookBub.

Finally, if you liked *Love and Mayhem,* be sure to leave a review online.

WHAT TO READ NEXT...

Ghost of the Thames

In Victorian England, a stranger, led back from the shadowy edges of death by a ghost, finds herself cold and bloody on the filthy banks of a river in a city she does not know...

From opium-drenched hovels and rat-infested warehouses of Limehouse to the glistening facades of West End mansions, a woman known only as Sophy searches for her identity. But the mist-shrouded alleys of Victorian England hold grave dangers for the friendless.

Captain Edward Seymour, the last of a long line of distinguished Royal Navy officers, is searching, as well. Returning from sea to find that his niece has disappeared, he begins combing every inn and hellhole of the city's darkest corners, desperately hoping to find some trace of the girl.

No one knows the streets of London like Charles Dickens, a young novelist with a reformer's soul, and Sophy and Edward turn to him for help. Flush with his early literary successes, he is working hard to use his knowledge of the city and his newfound fame to right some of the social ills that plague Victorian England. But with each step they take toward the truth, Death draws ever closer...

Get GHOST OF THE THAMES from your favorite retailer!

ABOUT THE AUTHOR

USA Today Bestselling Authors Nikoo and Jim McGoldrick have crafted over fifty fast-paced, conflict-filled novels, along with two works of nonfiction, under the pseudonyms May McGoldrick, Jan Coffey, and Nik James.

 These popular and prolific authors write historical romance, suspense, mystery, historical Westerns, and young adult novels. They are four-time Rita Award Finalists and the winners of numerous awards for their writing, including the Daphne DeMaurier Award for Excellence, the *Romantic Times Magazine* Reviewers' Choice Award, three NJRW Golden Leaf Awards, two Holt Medallions, and the Connecticut Press Club Award for Best Fiction. Their work is included in the Popular Culture Library collection of the National Museum of Scotland.

facebook.com/MayMcGoldrick

twitter.com/MayMcGoldrick

instagram.com/maymcgoldrick

bookbub.com/authors/may-mcgoldrick

Made in the USA
Monee, IL
18 April 2022

94946401R00163